THE
LAST
LAUGH

THE
LAST
LAUGH

MINDY McGINNIS

KATHERINE TEGEN BOOKS
An Imprint of HarperCollins Publishers

Katherine Tegen Books is an imprint of HarperCollins Publishers.

The Last Laugh

Library of Congress Control Number: 2021944119
ISBN 978-0-06-298245-2

Typography by Erin Fitzsimmons
22 23 24 25 26   PC/LSCH   10 9 8 7 6 5 4 3 2 1

First Edition

For Kate & Demitria
We are the Luckiest of the 13s.

Chapter 1

Ribbit

Saturday

Life isn't fair.

This is a statement of fact, not an application to participate in the suffering Olympics. Some of us are born with good looks, some with money. The lucky few get both, or use one to attain the other. I was born with legs that were too long, snagging inside of my mother, refusing to unfold and let me out into the world. They probably had the right idea.

Because I don't belong here.

This is another misleading phrase that usually comes before a long list of woes, damages that have been done to a person—and yes, I have those. And yes, there is an actual list. But I'm not saying I don't belong in Amontillado, because I do. I'm an Usher. The heavy legacy of our name hangs around our necks like the stones that make up the walls of our house. The sagging, moss-covered, collapsing family home. Proud, like us. Once regal, like us. Rotting from the inside out, like us.

I don't belong here because I don't belong anywhere, and it's reflected back at me every time I speak to someone. They answer too slowly, don't say the right words. Their mouths are tight, the smile thin. No one is ever actually glad to see me. And once I learned that, I learned how to navigate in this world. Because you can't make people like you, but you can make them think they need you. And that's almost the same thing.

My mother needs me to carry on the family name, the name she forced upon my father, who meekly followed her lead. Boys need me to be the butt of the joke, the reliable punching bag, the one who will shake it off and stand up again, smiling through bloodied teeth. But you can only swallow so much of your own blood before it turns your gut black, tinting everything inside you darkly. Girls need me to do the right thing, be the good guy, hold open the door, find the lost dog, make the beer run, and grab some tampons, too, if somebody needs them.

And that's okay, because that's who I am. I *am* the good guy.

You can see it on the video, the one that literally

everyone has seen, the livestream from the Allan house. #HonestUsher and #TrueLoser are still trending. I am internet famous and furiously hungover, watching the replay of last night's video, because I can't remember anything that happened. But I can recognize an old story in a new setting, the one I've been living since kindergarten.

The story is called "Make a Fool of Kermit Usher," and I know all the steps. First, change his name to Ribbit. Then, make jokes about his frog legs. Next, don't invite him to birthday parties. Or, maybe invite him because his mom is on the village council and it will be clear that you can't have that bouncy house in the park unless he gets to jump on it, too. But make sure he knows why he gets to be there.

Wait for him to get older, let the jokes get dirtier. Make them about his dick, not his legs. Talk about him behind his back, quiet enough so adults don't hear but loud enough that he does. He still gets to come to the parties, and he still knows why. It's not because he's wanted; it's because he's useful. He will do the things, all the favors, get what's needed, go the extra mile, ask how high to jump and if it's off that cliff, okay, just say nice things about him once he's gone. Even if you don't mean them.

Because I know you don't mean them.

I know because I just watched myself be eviscerated in real time for the entire world to see. I know because Hugh "Huge" Broward held court, asking deeply personal and increasingly penetrative questions while I nearly drank myself to death, answering with complete honesty because I was too drunk to come up with a lie. I know because the entire school would rather vomit all over themselves and pass out lying in their own mess than miss a single second of "Make a Fool of Kermit Usher."

It's an old game. It's a good game. It's a game I know how to win.

Because life isn't fair, and you can't make people like you.

But you can get revenge.

Chapter 2

Tress

Saturday

I killed my best friend yesterday.

Technically, it was today. Felicity Turnado took her last breath after midnight. I can't say for sure what killed her, whether it was the blow to the head with a brick, general blood loss, or dehydration. It could possibly be asphyxiation, because she was hanging pretty low in her manacles, bent over double, crushing her own lungs. I guess she could have OD'd, as well. I don't know how many beers she had before she followed me to the basement of the Allan house, or if she'd popped any Oxy, either. If she did, she didn't buy them from me. She had definitely contracted the nasty-ass flu that was going around, too, so it could be a combination of all these things that killed her.

At least the panther didn't eat her.

That's the one thing I can definitively rule out, and, ironically, the one thing that the general populace of Amontillado, Ohio, has identified as the culprit.

The texts started this morning.

Anybody seen Felicity?

She was there, right?

Pretty sure I saw her . . .

IDK watch the stream.

Did you guys see the cat on the vid?

Yeah, my mom thinks it ate her.

Her friends were concerned enough to fall to the level of including me in a group text, which says a lot. Gretchen Astor, Maddie Anho, Brynn Whitaker, David Evans, and Hugh Broward are recovered enough from their twenty-four-hour flu bug to give a shit about their friend who didn't have the chance to learn that the life expectancy of the virus wasn't that long. Unfortunately, Felicity Turnado's was much shorter.

I'm not contributing to the conversation. I know how to commit murder. I don't know how to get away with it. But I'm pretty sure that the less said, the better.

Except Hugh isn't going to let that fly.

A separate text pops up, just between him and me.

You saw her, right?

Yep, right before she died. For a few hours before that, too. Also, I broke her ankle with a trowel. I don't text any of that. I don't answer Hugh at all, and it's not because I can't think of anything to say that isn't incriminating.

It's because I'm pretty sure I'm bleeding out.

"Shit," I mutter, watching as another stream of ruby-red blood seeps out from under the duct-tape bandage I made for myself after the panther took a swipe at my arm. I can't exactly seek medical help because the town has enough issues with Amontillado Animal Attractions without the owner's granddaughter wandering into the ER after being mauled. For one thing, they'd kill the cat. For another, they can't, because he's running free and wild right now.

Which is a big fucking problem.

"TRESS!"

Cecil's voice barrels through the trailer, and I jump, dropping my phone. It bounces off my arm and sends a jolt of pain straight up to my collarbone. I grit my teeth to bite back a scream, to stop myself from swearing at Cecil, and to just feel something. To hear my teeth grinding together inside my own head. To feel the pressure on my upper and lower jawbone. To taste the little bit of blood that rises when I take it too far.

Because that's what Tress Montor does. She takes shit too far.

"TRESS!"

I get up off my bed, pulling down my sweatshirt

sleeve. I don't think Cecil would care much that I'm hurt, but he will be curious about why I'm currently held together by duct tape and he won't like the answer. If he knows that I let the cat go, I might as well tear off this bandage and drip-dry in the hallway until there's no blood left in me.

Except, I don't think this bandage is coming off. Like, ever.

Duct tape is one of the few things in this world that you can actually count on to work, and it is working so well at holding this wound together that I'm pretty sure the two of them can't be separated. At least, not without tearing me open some more. I can feel my pulse beating in the tips of my blue-tinged fingers, the pressure pushing out and up, against the silvery tape. I remember all the little particles of glue that flew through the air as I wrapped and wrapped the cuts, the fine dust that I trapped inside the slashes of my arm.

"TRESS!"

I find Cecil in the living room, his pile of empty beer bottles stacked precariously on the end table. He's as hungover as half the teenagers in Amontillado right now, but he's got more practice at how to handle it. It usually involves yelling at me and then drinking another beer. Sure enough, he's on step two already, a light foam around his lips.

"What?" I ask, and he glances up at me with his

one good eye, the other milky and dead in the socket. Instinctively, my hand goes to my pulsing wound. The cat has had a piece of both of us.

"You find that cat?"

"Nope," I lie.

"Well . . ." He glances around the room, as if the thin walls and cigarette-stained ceiling might have an answer. They don't.

"Well . . . shit," he concludes.

"Yep," I agree.

I don't tell him that the cat already ate Gretchen Astor's dog, that it made a guest appearance on a worldwide internet sensation livestream last night, that it's the prime suspect in the death of Felicity Turnado, that the entire town is about to come down on our heads. I don't have to tell him, because shit gets blamed on us even when it's not actually our fault.

Except this one is totally on us. Me, specifically.

Cecil spits on the floor, adding to a growing stain between his feet. "Guess we're going to have to do something about that."

"Yep," I say again, scratching absently at my arm, which has started to itch. In my hoodie pocket, my phone vibrates once. Twice.

There's a lot of things I'm going to have to do something about.

Chapter 3

Rue

BlackSmoothShine is gone,
LiquidEyes blinked at me as he left.
Noble and precarious.
Goodbye, CatWalker.
(HELLO, TWENTY DOLLARS, STAY
BEHIND THE YELLOW LINE.)
My handwords for the DarkHair, SilentCrier, FoundChild.
Always three, I know them by these.
Her mouthwords for me, Rue, PrettyGirl, SweetHeart.
His mouthwords for me, tight, growled, teeth show—
Dumbass, ShitEater, Fucker.
Hands say—one finger, longest, pointed up.
(THAT ORANG-O-TANGY CAN SIGN!)
Their mouthwords, loud in my ears, near my cage.

Can't be escaped.
I hear and keep, stuck in my chest,
Can't rise up, can't speak,
The story of LostChild. Never told.
No mouthwords for Rue, PrettyGirl, SweetHeart.
Only move hands, and say,
Please. Please. Please.

Chapter 4

Ribbit

Saturday

I always know where Mother is in the house.

When I was small, it was because I was scared to be alone. I would wander through the third-floor hallways, tattered rugs beneath my feet, wallpaper like skin falling away from plaster. Mesmerized, I pulled at old pieces, destroying what an older, nobler Usher had built, looking at the bones they'd left behind. This house, with us inside. I would realize, with sudden terror, that I was alone, and race through the house calling, pleading. *Mother! Mother! Mother!* Whether she answered depended on her mood.

All things depend upon her mood.

I learned not to stand too close—*you're on my heels, Usher!* Or too far away—*Usher? Where are you? I need you!*

Always *Usher*, never *Kermit*, the name she'd given me not rolling off her tongue the way our ancestral surname did. She said it loudly, and often. *Usher. Usher. Usher.* It echoed through the empty halls of our home. It weighed on my father like a too-large sweater, his Troyer shoulders not filling it.

Right now, Mother is downstairs in the kitchen. I know this, not because it's a Saturday, and not because she is making pancakes or doing something otherwise domestic down there. I know this because her phone just rang, the sound traveling up through the radiator to my bedroom.

I also know who is calling. It's Principal Anho.

I know this because of an email that arrived in my in-box roughly ten minutes ago, rerouted from my mother's email account that she keeps as head of the school board. I set it up to forward everything to me shortly after showing her how to log in.

To the Faculty & Board—
Many of you may already be aware of an off-campus gathering of students this past evening. As rumors swirl, it's important that we keep the health and safety of our children as the highest priority.

The first threat—to their health—appears to have passed. The flu that affected the neighboring school district of Prospero has jumped to our population. However, the Prospero superintendent assures me that their students recovered within twenty-four hours of their initial symptoms, and we can expect ours to, as well. With that in mind, I will personally oversee the deep-cleaning and disinfecting of our buildings so that we may return to school Monday morning.

The second issue I'd like to address is the reported disappearance of a student. The school is working closely with the local police department and the family of the student in question in order to locate her as quickly as possible. It is important to note that, at this time, there is no reason to believe any harm has come to her.

The third reason for me reaching out to you over the weekend is regarding social media. I have received numerous phone calls and messages regarding the existence of a video that was taken during the nonschool-associated gathering that details the bullying of a student. Steps are being taken to ensure that the student is in a safe mental space, and the perpetrators and participants will be punished accordingly.

Last, as the student body comes together this week to celebrate homecoming, let us do all we can to ensure that this week is a positive, spirit-filled celebration of our town, our community, and our students.

Go Ravens!

"Fly high!" I say back to my phone, the familiar school chant falling from my lips. My eyes flick back over Anho's email, making note of her phrasing. She's done a great job of distancing the school from any responsibility (*off-campus, nonschool-associated*), but also making it clear that she'll still be involved with the cleanup (*perpetrators and participants*), then she ended on a high note, reminding everyone that it's homecoming week. It's a nice piece of political writing, small-town minds being handled carefully with comfort and the promise of justice being served.

"Well played, Anho," I mutter, smiling to myself.

Downstairs I hear Mother's voice rise, the higher notes of annoyance slipping through the radiator near my bed. I wonder what Anho just said, and if she admitted that her own daughter—Maddie Anho—was a *participant*. I pull the livestream up on my phone, sliding my thumb until I find the clip I want. Maddie, drunk and teetering in a princess costume, asks me how hot she is on a scale of one to five.

This was early in the night, and I vaguely remember my answer.

On-screen, I hold up my hand palm up and give her a medium to less-than-interesting rating with a wobble. She visibly deflates.

Alone in my room, I laugh. On the screen, I scramble to reassure her.

"I mean, I'd bang you," I say.

I nod, agreeing. I would.

"But you're not really my type. Your mom, however . . . I would *totally* do your mom."

From downstairs, an outraged shriek. Whoops. That will make any future parent-principal meetings slightly awkward. As usual, my drunk self is an honest self, and I seem to have declared to the world that I would bang Principal Anho.

But whatever. I would.

Bored, I flick through the video further.

"Okay, okay, okay," Hugh says. We're about forty minutes into the debacle, and he's pretty green around the gills, having to focus hard on his phone to ask the next question. "Did you know that Ribbit autocorrects to *rub it*? Do you rub it, Ribbit?"

"Hell yeah," I say, both in my bed and there, on-screen.

I mean, duh. I sort of recall making a jerking-off movement to Brynn Whitaker at some point last night, and a small blush rises at the thought. Brynn has never been anything but nice to me. That was uncool.

I hear footsteps coming up the stairs. Mother's, measured and regular. I imagine her spine, straight and stiff, propelled upward. Her face rising above the banister, her mouth set in a hard line, her hair pulled back tightly, the thin skin of her temples stretched to the splitting point.

"Usher?"

She knocks and says my name at the same time, the old, heavy door rattling under her knuckles, bony and insistent.

"Yes?"

"Can I come in?"

She asks it like it's a question, not a foregone conclusion that all bends to her will. Another practiced move, well played. I have watched her for years. I don't answer, because I don't have to. The door cracks open, and Mother peers in.

"The school called," I say, beating her to the punch. "I'm fine."

She steps into my room, closing the door behind her. This is a conversation for Ushers, not for her husband.

"Did they do something to you?" Her face is more pinched than usual. I don't know if she's holding back anger that her only child must be defended (again), or that she's exhausted to have been called upon to make things right (again).

"It's okay, Mom," I say, sitting up in bed. "I'm fine. I drank too much. Nothing new."

She crosses her arms over her chest, staring down at me. "You know what drink does to you. It's in the blood."

"I know," I agree, raising my shoulders in a shrug. It hurts. My body aches, last night's memories still in my muscles, if not in my mind.

Mother's brow creases as she considers this. "She—"

"Felicity," I say quickly, the name filling my mouth, as it always has. Too big. Too heavy. Too much for a little boy to carry. "Felicity Turnado."

Mother stares back at me, studying every flicker in my face. "Actually, I was going to say *Tress*. Don't finish my sentences for me, Usher."

"Sorry," I say, dropping my eyes, the vertebrae of my neck bowing, defeated, deflated, following the accustomed path.

"Where was Tress? Why did she let that happen to you?"

I shake my head, baffled. It's a fair question. My cousin and I have an agreement: my errand boy status to the top tier of the student body gains her admission to their parties, where she can sell her skunk weed or pills to the slightly more upscale clientele. In return, she keeps an eye on me to make sure I don't get drunk and do anything stupid. Last night's video begs the question—where was she?

But there's a bigger question, more pressing. The one on the lips of everyone in Amontillado today, my mother included.

"Where is Felicity Turnado?"

I shake my head again, honest confusion clouding my slowly churning brain. If I knew where Felicity was, believe me, I would be with her.

Mother's eyebrows come together, a fine line forming in between them. "Did you do something?"

"No!" It comes out more explosive than necessary, rattling off the back of my teeth to fill the bedroom, bouncing into the radiator and down to the kitchen. I take a deep breath, filling my lungs to the bottom. I do this, sometimes, to calm myself. I do this, sometimes, to confirm to myself that there is no river water there.

"No," I repeat, more calmly this time. "No, I did not *do something*."

Mother seems to accept this, which is not surprising. The truth is, I never *do something*. Unless it's to please someone else. She makes more noises, asks more questions. I answer them smoothly, easily. There is no need to lie. I remember very little. On the surface, I answer her, all my focus on my mother. Inside, a greater question burrows, echoing through my bones.

Does Felicity need me to save her? (Again?)

Mother leaves, but I barely notice. I'm in fifth grade, wet and tired, shaking, carrying an unconscious Felicity Turnado in my arms. She's heavy, and I stumble, the blood running from her temple smearing across my chin as we collapse together onto the ground. I remember her nightgown pushing up, her thighs visible.

My brain latches on to that—Felicity's thighs—and my thoughts follow a different story. One that I've told myself at least a thousand times. In that one, we're both older and nobody is bleeding, but we are definitely tangled up with each other. I'm following that path to its inevitable conclusion when my phone goes off. I barely glance at it, concentrating on what I'm doing. But the name on the screen is distracting enough for me to let that particular daydream go . . . for now.

It's Gretchen Astor.

Hey Ribbit . . . I need you to do something for me.

Oh . . . do you? Just like with Mother, it's not a question, simply an assumption that her will and need is enough to propel me into whatever action she'd like.

She's not wrong.

I stare at the words for a moment, remembering Mother's drawn face, the clear disappointment that once again, she would have to *do something* to protect her son.

Do. Something.

I believe I will.

Chapter 5

Tress

Saturday

I have been sent into town, the last place I want to be.

I'm standing in the paint aisle of the hardware store, the list Cecil made for me quaking in my hand. I can't settle my shakes long enough to read it, which will earn me a smack upside the head if I get back to the trailer and forgot something. I can feel my heartbeat in my arm, and I rest my good hand there, applying pressure.

It's an old trick, something I did as a child. Nasty cuts, blistering burns, deep scrapes. I've had all of them, living with Cecil, and very few ever warranted true medical attention, in his eyes. Well . . . eye. We took care of ourselves, and if that didn't work, I developed my own method of treatment. In my child brain I concluded that the wound was hurting me, and therefore, I should hurt it back. I dug into my skin, pried past scabs, and drew my own blood, all in an effort to teach my body a lesson—no one is going to help you.

No one is going to help me now, either. The clerk gave me the side-eye the second I walked in the door, and the familiar question—*How can I help you?*—has not been asked. Not that I expected it. I come in here every Saturday and buy the same thing—a can of yellow spray paint to redo the safety perimeter around the animal cages. A bright, blistering ring that warns people to keep their distance, for their own good.

I must have one around me, too. People certainly keep their distance, and the ones who don't . . . I think of Felicity, swinging in her chains, staring at me, begging me to believe her. To believe that she didn't know what happened to my parents on the night they disappeared. Maybe she didn't . . . but now she's gone, too. Along with any hope of discovering the truth.

I push harder on my arm, the swollen skin beneath the duct tape giving way, shooting pain into my shoulder and past that. A shocking jolt to my brain. It's not the smart thing to do, but it's the right one. My head clears, and I welcome the reprieve, checking Cecil's list.

Yellow spray paint. One can.

Black spray paint. Six cans. High gloss.

What?

I stare at it for a second before I start shaking again. The list falls from my hand, and I let it lie there while I gather the cans in my one good arm. I dump them unceremoniously on the counter, and the guy behind the register gives me a once-over. I know him, the way everyone knows everyone in Amontillado. He's a Hodges, with the same flat features and slightly pop-eyed look of that whole family.

"What?" I ask, glaring back.

"You hear about the Turnado girl?" Hodges asks.

It's a question, but it comes out as an accusation. I'm not surprised. Three disappearances in this town and they're all connected to me. My mom and dad, and now Felicity, who was in the car with them that night. Yet somehow she turned up on the riverbank, wet and crying, while my parents . . .

I squeeze my arm again, my lip curling with the pain.

"Yeah, I heard," I say.

"Weird," Hodges says, eyes still on my face. "It happening now, and all."

"Yeah, weird," I agree, not fully understanding.

"It's seven years, on the nose," Hodges goes on.

I bark out a harsh laugh. "Check your calendar," I say, pointing at the nearly nude woman in a string bikini hanging on the wall behind him, a pushpin keeping her neatly in place. "It's next month. Seven years is next month."

His eyebrows come together, like I've said something offensive. "You sure about that?"

"I think I would know," I say grimly. "My birthday is Thursday, and my parents disappeared one month after that. Both things kind of stick in my mind. Sorry if that's disappointing for you."

He swipes my card, and I fumble with my bag, trying hard not to use my left hand for anything, not wanting the blue tips of my fingers to be seen. I climb into the truck and wind my way through the switchback up the ridge, every pothole—and there are a lot—sending a fresh wave of agony through my arm. Beside me on the seat, seven cans of spray paint rattle against each other.

Seven cans. Seven years since my mom and dad disappeared.

It's official at that point. They are declared dead and everyone moves on. Not that everyone hasn't already. Nobody else will feel that palpable bump when the day comes and goes. Nobody else will even know. The demarcation between day and night will pass, and my parents will be dead, in the true and legal sense. All official inquiries into their disappearance will cease. I did my own rather unofficial and illegal inquiring last night, and Felicity is dead because of it.

Shit. Shit. Shit.

A wave of panic grabs me, pure and primal. Heat rises

from my whole body, a sheen of sweat following the rush of blood. Black spots fill my vision, and I pull over, killing the engine as an enormous sob wells up from deep inside of me, scratching and kicking its way to my mouth, where it tears through my teeth and lips, a high, keening wail that leaves my throat only to echo from the confines of the cab, flowing back in through my ears.

It's my pain, my grief, my guilt. Something that will never leave me. I can fight it and push and yell and stick my chin out and deny, deny, deny. But inside, the truth crouches, dark and restless. And it will never let me forget that I killed Felicity. She didn't know what happened to my parents, but I kept pushing, kept disbelieving, kept insisting, kept being Tress Montor, right up until she died.

I'll be eighteen on Thursday. Eighteen as in—I'll be an adult. And a murderer. In Ohio that means if Felicity's body is ever found and I'm tied to it, the next thing I'll be tied to is a gurney while I wait to be lethally injected.

I rest my head against the steering wheel, sweat dripping, the pulse of my heart beating thickly in my arm. Okay. Okay. Okay. I did it. Now what?

Now I go home. Now I paint the lines around animal cages. Now I go about my day as if it were no different than the one before. And how different is it, really? My parents are gone and Felicity Turnado isn't speaking to me. Same as yesterday.

I start the truck again, easing out onto the gravel road and cruising past the Usher house. Ribbit's rusted little S-10 is in the drive, the crumbling tombstone of a house reflected in the pond out front. I need to text Ribbit, need to check in on him after last night. There's a flicker of guilt about that, too. I was supposed to make sure he didn't get drunk, didn't follow his pattern of being everyone's jester. Instead, I let it happen because it was the perfect distraction to keep anyone from wondering where Felicity went.

They're certainly wondering now.

I go over the bridge, the steep drop-off behind the Usher house leading down to the river. I try not to look, try not to let my eyes wander the bank, searching for the spot where Felicity was found.

She's lost again.

But this time, she won't be resurfacing.

Chapter 6

Tress

Saturday

"You've got to be shitting me."

I dig deep, looking for the surprise somewhere inside of me. But it's not there. Cecil has finally ceased to shock me.

When I got back home there was a familiar truck pulling out of the driveway. Odell's vehicle has a cage in the back and permanent grease stains on the driver's seat. He'd given me a mock salute as we passed each other, and I'd given him the finger in return. Odell brought the panther to us, years ago, and Lord knows what the new delivery could be. Turns out, it's a tired old lioness without a tooth in her head.

And Cecil wants me to paint it.

"You've got to be shitting me," I say again, but Cecil only shakes his head.

"I've had five calls already today, people wanting to know if our cat got out."

"It did," I inform him, and he jerks a finger into my face.

"Don't go 'round saying that. Don't you dare. You know what happens, people find that out?"

Probably a lot of things. PETA will show up (Cecil calls them the PETA Pity Party People), followed right behind by the ASPCA (Cecil calls them Ass Stupid People Can't Accept Shit. I tried to explain acronyms to him once, but it didn't take). I imagine the cops won't be too far behind the animal-rights people, with questions of their own. Questions that it's extremely important no one ever knows the answers to.

"If they do, we're fucked," Cecil says, his own problems rolling through his head, not knowing what's true for him is true for me, too. The activists will shut down our business. The cops will find an acre of marijuana out back. And that's where things get really interesting . . . because I might be able to plead ignorance of the weed, or maybe even agree to testify against my own grandfather. But my mauled arm lands me at the scene of a crime, and if someone draws conclusions about the few frames from the livestream that caught the cat lurking in the upper corner, I might as well take the court-appointed lawyer and a plea deal.

I don't know what murder one pleas down to, but I

bet I won't get far. The prepared manacles in the coal chute of the old Allan house; the shiny lock I put on the basement door; the smooth wall where I practiced bricklaying. These all stand as evidence that I didn't just kill Felicity; I plotted her murder.

Which means that I've got to do everything I can to keep the authorities from sniffing around our pot-infested lot. I've got to do whatever Cecil says, up to and including painting a lioness black.

"Get at it," Cecil says, pulling open the cage door for me. "She's still got some tranquilizers in her, shouldn't put up much of a fight."

If the lioness even puts up a slight difference of opinion with me, I'm dead. But I realize, as I slip into the cage, hardware bag in hand, that I don't really care. My future has always been a question; the best I can hope for is becoming the Tiger Queen of Amontillado. If this cat decides to take me down, I doubt I stand my ground long. In fact, I bet I tilt my head back, giving her full access to my jugular.

Unfortunately, she's not interested.

I approach, shaking a can of black spray paint in one hand, the little ball inside rattling loudly. She lifts her head, struggles to locate me, then drops it again with a thud.

"Hey, girl," I say, kneeling down beside her. She's an old woman, her teats stretched and sagging, probably from birthing litter after litter to stock someone's pet-ting zoo. One eye opens, the golden-brown iris finds me, then rolls away. I rest my hand on her head, and the giant skull vibrates as she musters up a growl, deep from within her chest. In the other cage, Rue's hands flash. She tells me, *Danger, danger, danger,* an old sign someone else had taught her before she came here. I'd had to look it up online to figure out what she meant. I don't know where she was before us, but judging by her physical state when we got her, knowing what *danger* meant prob-ably came in handy.

I sign back at her that I am okay, but she shakes her head, informing me that there is *danger, danger, danger.* A deep sigh escapes the cat, and I shake the can again, aware of Cecil's eye on me.

"I'm really, really sorry about this," I say to the lion, and spray a thick line of black down the middle of her belly. The skin goose bumps, every hair standing on end. I don't know if the paint is cold, or if she's try-ing to puff up her ruff, unconsciously make herself as big as she can to intimidate me. Unfortunately for her, I've spent a lifetime weighing one scary thing against another, and strangers coming onto our property is way worse than anything she can do to me right now.

So, I paint the cat.

* * *

I'm cleaning myself up as best I can in the tiny bathroom of our trailer. I have only one good hand, and it's the one covered in paint, so I'm holding a soapy rag in my teeth while scrubbing my hand back and forth across it. I'm getting more soap down my throat than onto my skin, and I give up, spitting out the rag and leaning over the sink.

I'm pretty sure I'm going to puke.

I'm also pretty sure that has nothing to do with the soap I swallowed.

There's another panic attack coming, welling up deep inside my belly so that I don't know if I'm going to shit myself or lose it all out the top. Sweat pops on my skin along with goose bumps, and I gag, spitting up a mass of bubbles and bile. I fall to the ground, banging my arm against the sink. A cry of pain escapes me, and I huddle into a ball, curling my injured arm against my chest. I feel my pulse there, tighter than before, pushing against the duct tape. I pull my sweatshirt over my head, not surprised to see the red streaks of infection marching out from under the silver of my bandage.

"I'm sorry," I say again. And I am sorry. I'm sorry about painting the lion, and I'm sorry that the panther is loose, and I'm sorry that I killed Felicity. I've said those words so often, every time I did something wrong, that Cecil's practiced response is etched in my memory.

"Yeah, you are pretty sorry. A sorry sack of shit."

It's not funny, but I start laughing, the peals rising and falling with the beat of my heart, the soft, swollen skin around the tape pulsing along with it.

And faintly, near my breastbone, I hear an answering thump.

With my good hand I grasp the chain and pull the necklace over my head. Half of a heart pendant rests in my palm. Mine reads *Friends*. The other half reads *Best* and it is in the cellar of an abandoned house, resting against the rotting skin of Felicity Turnado.

"I'm sorry, Felicity," I say to it.

And in my hand, it beats.

Chapter 7

Rue

FoundChild is with me always,
Hair in my hand, wound together
Her strands I have saved, gathered, shaped.
Touch to feel, something other than,
LostChild, gone always.
(WHAT ARE WE WAITING FOR? LOOK
AT IT, DADDY!)
In my hand, FoundChild, thought feelings,
DarkHair speaking, when she goes,
But still here, between my fingers
Spike of fear, shock of pain, depth of misery.
FoundChild, feel it with you.
LostChild, feel it for you.
(CHRIST, SHE'S BIG.)

Alone, make handwords, LostChild
Can't see, won't know.
Say anyway.
I love you, I miss you.
FoundChild, see me. Understand.
Danger, danger, danger

Chapter 8

Ribbit

Saturday

"Lunch is on the table," Mother says when I venture downstairs. In the dining room, the table is set for two. It's a monstrous piece of furniture stretching the length of the room, chairs lining each side, a lord's seat at the head, a slightly smaller, less decorative seat for the lady of the house at the foot. Each chair sits cold and empty, expectant for little Ushers yet to come. My duty yawns before me, eight seats to be filled.

Eight.

Beers from last night still churn in my stomach, but it's not just the food on the plates that's making me sick. Those chairs face me down, demanding that I do something, a thing that absolutely requires another person. It was supposed to be Felicity. Always Felicity.

But she's gone.

I will find you, Felicity. I want this with you, Felicity. That is your place, Felicity.

Two full plates welcome me; one at the lord's seat, the other to the right. I go to my accustomed spot, leaving the lord's seat for Lenore, as usual.

The sound of footsteps echo upstairs, Dad moving around the house. Mother's eyes cut to mine and then back to the table, where only two plates of food await. There's a stutter step upstairs, a solid *thunk* as Dad mis-judges a doorframe, whatever he's had to drink so far today already impeding small judgment calls. He makes it to the stairs, and there's a creaking noise as he leans unnecessarily hard against the banister, counting on it to keep him upright.

Mother doesn't move to make a third plate, instead takes her seat. I follow, as expected, forcing a mouthful of egg sandwich, ordering my teeth to chew, my throat to swallow, my stomach to accept food. Under Mother's watchful eye, I will eat. I keep my focus on her as Dad's shuffling steps move closer, the sickly-sweet perfume of alcohol moving in front of him, a shadow he's always cast. I sniff the collar of my shirt, suddenly aware that my pores still leak the same scent. Dad stops at the foot of the stairs, hand on the newel post for support. Mother eats, and I follow her example, eyes cast down.

"You know in some families when the wife says that lunch is on the table, her husband is included in that."

"What families would those be?" Mother asks, not bothering to look up.

It should be a tense moment, one that—in a lot of homes—would be the prelude to a smack, a bruised cheek, a rushed explanation in the ER that involved a weak tale of falling down the steps, or walking into a door.

But in this house, Dad's words carry no weight, and his hands remain balled at his sides. Because other families are not Usher families, other houses are not Usher houses, and other wives are not Ushers. Lenore didn't make a plate for her husband because she had no intention of involving him in this conversation.

Dad has made his contribution to this family. First, he fathered me. I remember when she was younger and his rewards were measured in affection and coy glances, each touch of hers doled out to strengthen not their bond but her hold on him. Every movement—her palm sliding up his back, a tug on his earlobe, a swift caress of his hair—was a string in a web that she kept him strongly centered in.

Dad's second—and last—contribution to this family came seven years ago. After that, Lenore clearly found him to be spent, the mummified catch at the center of her web, juiceless. The touches stopped. The words stopped. He was a dead thing, held still by her strongly wrapped coils, made immobile by the weight of his guilt. He'd thrown his lot in with an Usher and paid the price. Now he'll rot here in the Usher house, embalming himself from the inside out with every drink.

Last week he'd balked at one of Mother's requests, and she'd gripped her knife like a weapon, not a utensil. A baked potato had flown across the room at some point, a concerning break from our usual setting of controlled anger. The simmer of our house hardly ever reached a boil, but when Lenore lost her temper it was best not to be anywhere nearby. When Lenore's rage flowed, anyone within reaching distance was a viable target, and I'd learned early to escape whenever possible. I'd retreated to the river, to the smooth flat rock that has provided some peace in the past . . . and once, something much, much more.

There is still a grease smudge on the wall behind Dad's head from last week's hurled potato. He glances at it, then back to the table where we sit—an incomplete family of two.

"Fuck it," he says, and walks past us and into the kitchen, where I hear the fridge open, the hiss of a beer being opened, and the back door slam shut behind him as he makes his own retreat. Dad doesn't go down to the river like I do. He has his own place, one I came across accidentally as a child. I found him there, huddled in the old dairy barn, crying as he emptied a bottle of whiskey. I'd backed away, not wanting him to know that I'd seen, or the conclusion that I'd come to.

My father was weak.

My mother was not.

It had already been decided by Mother that I was an Usher. Her Usher. The last Usher. But that day, I made the decision for myself, as well. I became an Usher by choice, backing away from Dad's weakness and his tears, going to find my mother standing at the sink, peeling potatoes, her mouth a familiar thin line. She'd handed me a knife, and I'd wordlessly joined her.

We wait for the cloud of Dad's scent to pass. Until it is truly just us again, here in this room.

"It will be handled?" Mother finally asks, as if we'd never been interrupted. Her communications with me are often like this, picking up a dropped thread from before, asking me to follow the jump. In public she is patient and explanatory, walking others down the path her words have paved for them. I am an Usher and expected to keep up.

"I've already had some texts about the party, mostly apologetic," I answer, wiping my lip with a cloth napkin, an embroidered *U* on the edge, large and demanding to be seen. To be respected. "I've been invited to help plan the homecoming bonfire. Kind of a mea culpa."

"Is this the best use of your time?" Lenore asks, her eyes on her food as if it were a casual question. It's not. A life is embedded in those words. A task assigned to me, unfinished.

"I want to," I tell her. "It's—"

"Recognition. Status," Mother says, her fork resting against her plate, tines down. Perfect table manners in a house where the ceiling may crash onto the table at any second.

"I understand your need for these people to acknowledge you, after what they did," she continues. "But inclusion doesn't equal acceptance. This is an overture from them, not an apology."

What they did. My body stripped naked. My mind on display.

"They don't need to accept me. They just need to be where I tell them to be, when I want them there," I say, placing my own fork across my plate. "You're familiar with the tactic, I think?"

Lenore's eyes narrow, her brow creasing, forming wrinkles Aunt Annabelle never got the chance to develop.

She'll always be more beautiful than you. She never aged. She never will.

"Have your bonfire," Mother says. "But remember what you owe me."

The inescapable phrase that follows is one I've heard since fifth grade, a heavy mantra. I speak it in my sleep, lips forming nightmare patterns. I say it now, in unison with Lenore, aware of my duties.

"A life for a life."

Mother studies me for a second, checking the foundations of my resolve, questioning if I have the fortitude to go through with it. I've tried, so many times. I've tried.

A tumble down the ridge.

A fall down the well.

An electric fence with damaging voltage.

A playful push away from the bank as she swam in from the deep end of the pond, in the shadow of the Usher house. And again. And again. Her strength flagging. Her face as she questioned, worried, wondered . . . *Why would you do this to me?* Then she'd gained a foothold, pulled herself onto the bank, and socked me on the chin, sending me over backward. Tress, a whip-thin pillar of anger, always prepared to fight and never resigned to losing.

I'd taken the beating, laid down like a dog, and let her get a kick in my ribs, all the while thinking, *If you want to know where your parents are, you should have let me drown you.*

I cover my face with my hands, resting my elbows against the table. We were kids when I tried in the past, kids who made mistakes, took jokes too far. Kids who might wander into an accidental death as we ran through our wild lives, unfettered animals in a dangerous wilderness. A bloodline extinguished, a tragedy unfolded, things falling into place.

"A life for a life," Lenore repeats, clearing my plate from the table.

I have denied my mother exactly once, stood defiant and unbending, ready to kill to protect what was mine. We were children, Felicity's drenched, unconscious form on the rock behind me, her hair fanned like silver across the water as it flowed, the river taking whatever it could get of her and thankful for the taste.

Just like me.

Red lights on the bridge, the Montors' car, unmoving. Aunt Annabelle's scream still echoing in the trees, a gunshot chasing it, a concussive ring in my ears. Felicity wet in my arms as I pulled her from the water, hoping the fall from the bridge hadn't killed her. Annabelle had saved her from my father by throwing her over the side, but it fell to me to save her from Mother, when she came to claim the body.

Came to claim what she thought was her niece.

I had bartered for her life and made a deal with the devil.

I could have Felicity, but Tress had to die before she

was old enough to learn, old enough to know, and most important, old enough to inherit.

I have to kill my cousin before she turns eighteen.

I have to kill Tress before Thursday.

Because Mother says so.

Chapter 9

Ribbit

Saturday

In most families, when the police want to speak to you they come to your house. In the Usher family, my mother informs the police when and where and how much they can speak to me.

"We're going to the state park," Mother informs me after lunch. As I climb into the passenger seat, she adds, "I didn't want anyone seeing cruisers in our driveway."

That's valid. Even though we don't have neighbors to actually spot the cruisers themselves, a shiny black car threading its way up the ridge would draw attention. Out here, it's us and Cecil, and I'm sure people in town could flip a coin as to who the police were paying a call to. Or just turn up the volume on their police scanners.

"People will know," I tell Mom, snapping my seat belt against my chest.

"People will *guess*," she corrects me. "That's not knowing."

She's got me there, so I hold my peace as we pull in at the park, and follow Mother—sure-footed as a goat, spine straight, exuding no effort—as we climb to the designated meeting place. When I spot the officers waiting on a bench at the convergence of three trails, I bite the inside of my cheek. I'm assuming Mother doesn't know that this is where Tress does a lot of her drug dealing, and I seriously doubt the cops know that, either. It's funny, but I don't dare look amused.

I'm a victim. I've been bullied. I should not be laughing. On the outside, I am beaten, lost, broken. On the inside, I am blooming into something new and fresh; a dark flower, the seed planted long ago, fertilized over a lifetime, germinated last night.

"Mrs. Usher," one of the cops says, coming to his feet, nodding to my mother.

She stiffens further at the *Mrs.* but technically can't correct him. She is married, and she is an Usher. She's the one who chose to confuse everyone by keeping her maiden name and slapping it onto me as well.

The officers look to me, and I glance at their name tags. One is a Boyd, the other a Johnson. Their family tombstones aren't as big as the ones that display *Usher*. I feel another flicker of laughter and stamp down on it.

"Kermit," Boyd begins. "We understand that over the weekend—"

"There was a party," Mother finishes for him. "A large group of teens became drunk and bullied my son into drinking as well."

"He seems willing enough on the—"

"The video?" Mother intervenes again, turning on Johnson this time. "Kermit was already drinking before that recording began. You saw what they did to him. What do you think happened prior to that? Slaps on the back and goodwill for all?"

Actually, there was a lot of puking and William Wilson, Gretchen Astor's dog, disappeared, just like Felicity. A wave of anxiety rips through my gut, and for the first time, I wonder if I'm being questioned about one thing and one thing only. My eyes flick from Boyd to Johnson, but both of them wear the trademark blank looks of police. In Boyd's case, he can also claim he came by it genetically.

"Mrs. Usher," Johnson begins again, but Mother is done being reminded that she is married.

"Lenore," she says, her mouth curling around the word. I know she bites back the *Usher*, wants to let it slip out, to remind them, to buoy herself.

"Lenore," Boyd interjects, "we're not interested in pressing any charges against your son." He waits for this to fall like manna from heaven around my mother's feet, for her to sink joyfully to her knees and thank him for it.

It doesn't happen.

"Clearly," she says. "He did nothing wrong."

"Technically, he was drinking underage," Johnson says.

Mother shrugs, the barest of movements, her shoulder blades flickering. "As were thirty to forty other young people. Are you going to arrest them all? Surely the police don't have a cruiser big enough to haul them all in."

They don't. They have two cruisers. Both of which were bought new last year after Lenore Usher's vote broke the tie from the village council in favor of the purchase. She smiles now, her flashing teeth undoubtedly reminding them that there's another vote coming up—the one that impacts their yearly bonuses.

"No," Johnson says quickly. "Of course we aren't going to arrest everyone—"

"Of course not," Lenore echoes immediately, as if he'd made the statement first, and she approves. "Everyone knows you have much bigger issues to contend with."

She keeps the smile on, bright and fake. Her eyes,

unblinking—like a shark's—move between them. "Or
have you found Felicity Turnado?"

The officers glance at one another. Boyd has a rash
from shaving around his collar, and a blush is rising
under it. Johnson clears his throat and directs his words
at the ground.

"We can't talk about an open—"

"Case, obviously," Mother says. "But she's not offi-
cially been reported as missing."

I bite the inside of my cheeks, wishing I could sever
the muscles that control smiling. Mother has her own
police scanner, and it's never turned off.

"And really," Lenore continues. "I can't say I blame
her parents. The Amontillado police don't have a gleaming track record when it comes to disappearances."

They're both looking at the ground now, not able
to meet the eyes of the woman who controls their pay-
checks, the woman whose sister they never found.

"Now," Mother says, "let's move on to something
more concrete. Charges that *will* be filed. Against the
Broward boy, for starters."

My head jerks up. "No!"

It's loud and insistent, demanding and direct. It's my
voice, and I hardly recognize it. Mother turns to me,
her smile stitched on, the look in her eyes reminding me
that I'm supposed to keep my mouth shut.

I've had my mouth shut for a very long time.

"No," I say again, the simple word scratching past the sand in my throat. "I don't want to press charges."

Lenore's mouth opens, shuts again, her teeth clicking together. "Perhaps we should—"

"Concentrate on finding Felicity," I say, easing my words onto the end of her sentence, clipping them together. Her eyes snap at me, but she won't take it further than that. Not in public.

"What is being done?" I ask, turning to the police. Boyd and Johnson look up from the ground, still cowed by my mother. Johnson glances at Lenore but seems to decide it's better to answer the Usher who's talking than bait the one who isn't.

"The family is organizing a search party," Johnson says. "They're going to focus the search on the area surrounding the old Allan house."

"Or, what's left of it," Boyd adds.

Mother reenters the conversation, the weight of her gaze sliding off me and onto them. "What do you mean?"

"It's been torn down . . . ma'am," Johnson tells her, hesitating before adding the *ma'am*. He's been told to call her *Lenore* but doesn't want to invite that sort of intimacy. And *Mrs.* already misfired. Poor Johnson, she's got him dancing.

"Torn down?" Mother repeats. "The village owns that property, and they wouldn't move so quickly without—"

Without asking me, is what she's about to say. Nobody does anything without asking Lenore. My father's bladder would probably burst inside of him if she forgot to check in with him a few times a day.

"With the—" Johnson's eyes cut to me, apologetic. "The video that's circulating, they wanted it torn down right away. They worried it could become a magnet, and not just for Amontillado kids."

Lenore's face softens, a calculated move. But I can tell she doesn't disagree with the decision, either. We don't want people drawn here. We don't want outsiders crawling over the bones, looking for meat. Especially when I have a date to make more bones by Thursday.

"Perhaps my son is right," she says, making sure the win in this conversation goes to an Usher, even if it isn't her. "Perhaps it would be best not to draw more attention to ourselves."

I was trending on Twitter last night. Amontillado would be hard-pressed to draw more attention than that. But I guess a missing homecoming queen and a loose panther make good headlines.

"The larger world isn't interested in us," Lenore goes on, eyes bouncing from cop to cop, judging how her words land. "I'd prefer to keep it that way."

I'm sure she would. I've seen the village ledgers, and you don't have to be good at math to know that things don't add up. And that's far from the only thing my mother doesn't want outside forces poking around in. She might be able to use her name like a wrecking ball in Amontillado, but the larger world will bulldoze her as fast as the council did the Allan house.

"That's out of our hands," Johnson says, shaking his head. "Your son was on the landing page of CNN this morning."

I was? I immediately pull out my phone to discover that this is true. The clip of choice is of me swinging my junk in time with the grandfather clock behind me. Because I'm a minor, they've smudged my face. Because someone forgot, they didn't smudge the rest.

That's okay. I've got nothing to be ashamed of.

My phone is pulled from my hands, and Mother's mouth goes into a thin, flat line when she glances at it. She closes her eyes, takes a deep breath, clenches her fists.

"Listen to me," Lenore says, and Boyd and Johnson do.

They do because she owns them.

They do because she's an Usher.

They do because, like me, they are powerless to do anything else.

Chapter 10

Rue

OldCat, SadThing, NearlyDead,
Watches me. Not interested.
I make handwords,
Hello, I love you, I am me.
She rolls, leaving an outline of herself,
darker, on the ground.
Back to me, knobby spine cannot see
My handwords for DarkHair, SilentCrier, FoundChild
Danger, danger, danger.
**(AN ACCIDENT. MAKE IT LOOK GOOD.
SOON.)**
Heat leaves, light goes, silence comes.
Mouthwords from the human cage:
**(TRESS! I'M SORRY. GET ME A BEER
WOULD'YA?)**

BlackSmoothShine comes, slinking in the dark.

LiquidEyes touches noses with AlmostDead.

Throatnoises, only for each other.

They can speak and hear. Blood to blood.

I tell CatWalker, Danger, danger, danger,

Our blood cannot. Handwords, mouthwords, throatwords.

No words.

The human cage, mouth is open.

BlackSmoothShine walks, through and into.

Chapter 11

Tress

Sunday

"The damn thing was here! It was in our fucking living room!"

I open my eyes Sunday morning to Cecil standing at the foot of my bed holding a beer bottle in one hand and a dead chicken in the other. I blink my eyes, but the vision remains the same.

"Why aren't you up yet?" he rails at me, shaking both arms. Warm beer and cold blood spatter across my sheets.

"Why are you holding a dead chicken?" I counter, and he elevates it, as if to explain himself better.

"The damn cat brought it!" he shouts. "Came right in the front door!"

I have no idea what to say to that. My head is foggy,

and my arm feels like it's being squeezed through a sausage grinder. I throw my covers back, still wearing my clothes from yesterday. They're slick with sweat, and for the first time since I came to live here, I think Cecil smells better than I do.

"Look," Cecil insists, ushering me into the hallway and to the front of the trailer. There's a ringing in my ears and spots in my vision, but I make it to the couch. Cecil's right. The door is banging on its hinges, the large, padded prints of a big cat standing out clearly in the dirt on the floor. Nearby, loose feathers stick in a puddle of congealing blood.

"Why would it go and do a thing like that?" Cecil asks.

It's a Sunday morning. I'm pretty sure my half of the heart pendant moved in my hand last night. I'm in urgent need of medical attention, and I'm being asked to interpret the motives of a wild animal. I stare at the print and the blood, wondering if it's the same paw that tore my arm open.

"Cats bring their kill home," I remind Cecil. "They think we're inexpert hunters and they need to teach us."

"Teach us?" Cecil shrieks, dropping the beer bottle. "I'll teach it to hunt, by God."

"That is literally the stupidest thing you could say right now," I tell him, not caring if I get smacked. I point to the floor, where a small part of the linoleum has been swept clean. "It sat there, watching you while you slept. It was swishing its tail."

"Damn," Cecil says, a hand wandering to his milky-white eye. "What do you think it wants?"

To set the record straight. Even the score. Get the last laugh.

There's a half-smoked joint on the coffee table, an ember glowing in the tip. I pick it up and take a deep drag.

Cecil watches me, eyebrows drawn together. "You been burning through our product?"

"Nope," I assure him, holding the smoke in my lungs. And it's true. I usually don't, but if recent events don't exactly call for celebration, they do beg for a distraction. I wouldn't mind if it took the edge off my pain, either.

There's a sudden, insistent blaring of a car horn from the road. Cecil and I both freeze, each looking to the other as if to confirm that we hear it.

"Shit," we say at the same time. The very last thing we need is customers for Amontillado Animal Attractions. We hustle outside only to find Lenore and Ribbit sitting in their car, my aunt pressing wildly on the horn. Neither one of them has ever ventured close to the house, not trusting the cages that hold our animals.

"Dad," Lenore yells, rolling down her window. "I need to talk to you!"

Cecil heaves a great sigh, then looks at me with a shrug. "Why don't you get the kid out of the car, give him a break from his mother."

I nod, following along, the heat from the midmorning sun baking me in my hoodie. Ribbit spots me, and cracks the passenger door, eager for the escape. And for something else, it seems.

"You hear about Felicity?" he asks.

"Yeah," I say, ignoring the leap of my heart at her name. "Crazy."

"She was at the party, right?" He goes on, looking to me for confirmation. "I remember seeing her."

"I think so," I mutter, not willing to give much else. "C'mon." I coax him to move along, and we head down the gravel road, walking the familiar mile back to the Usher house. Behind us, I hear Lenore's voice.

"I'm getting pressured by the council," she says. "A henhouse was raided last night, and the owner claims there's the shadow of a very large cat on his porch cam."

"Not mine," Cecil says. "See for yourself."

There's a low whine as Lenore's window goes all the way down, and I hold my breath while she ponders the painted lion from a distance. "I might not be the only person you need to reassure," she says.

My breath comes out in a whoosh. "High-gloss must have worked," I say.

Beside me, Ribbit kicks at a pebble. "What?"

"Nothing." I shake my head. "You okay?"

"Yeah," he says brightly. "I'm fine. Was a little hung-over yesterday. Did you see Felicity at all after—"

"I'm sorry," I say, cutting him off. "I shouldn't have let you get drunk."

We're quiet for a second, my apology hanging in the air between us. It's not often that we need to say those words to each other. In the past, we've always had each other's backs. In the past, I protected him from the wolves. Friday night, I threw him to them, and now the world knows his name.

"I know who to blame," he says quietly, his voice suddenly somber.

A shaky laugh escapes me as I think of Felicity's body, rotting in the dark, half a heart pendant around her neck. "Blame," I repeat Ribbit's word. As if in response, the charm around my neck shudders. My good hand goes to it, clutching it, forcing it to be still—or for my fevered mind to stop making me think it's beating.

"Mother's pissed," Ribbit says, kicking at a glass bottle that is resting in the road. It rolls in front of us, making hollow music.

"What for?"

We reach the bottle and he kicks it again, sending it end over end through the gravel. "Everybody's coming down on her. You know the animals have always been a problem, and her phone's been blowing up."

"Our cat is in his cage," I say, loyal to Cecil for reasons I can't explain. Ribbit takes another kick at the bottle, and I watch it go, the sun flashing off it. The pot snakes through my brain, causing tiny details to stand out, assigning weight to the wrong things. I'm fixated on the litter, barely hearing Ribbit's voice.

"The council pulled down the Allan house," he says, and it matters, somewhere inside of me. It matters because that means the manacles, the lock on the basement door, the mortar pail and trowel covered in my fingerprints, are all buried beneath rubble. Proof of my guilt, tidily covered up by adults who don't want news crews descending on Amontillado.

Felicity's body is under there, too.

In my hand, the heart jumps.

I let go, as if it were a hot coal, my mind searching frantically for something else, something different to focus on. Ribbit pulls back, ready to kick the bottle again. I stop him, a hand on his shoulder.

"Wait."

Chapter 12

Ribbit

Sunday

Tress is high as shit.

I pretended not to notice when I got out of the car, but soon it isn't just the skunk weed in my nose. Tress smells . . . bad. There's a remnant of old sweat, for sure, overlaid with a fresh batch starting to form on her skin. But underneath there's something worse. Something wrong. Something rotting. I'm about to ask her if she's okay when she grabs my arm.

"Wait." She bends down, tottering a little as she picks up the bottle I've been kicking.

"Does this seem weird to you?" she asks.

"Um . . . no?"

Somebody littering where we live is not news. The only reason people come out here is to sneak a peek at Cecil's animals or to throw out something they don't want. Kittens. Trash. Mattresses. There's a washer and dryer set that's been rusting at the edge of the ridge for the past five years.

"Look at it," Tress insists, turning the bottle in her hand, her bloodshot eyes intently focused on it. "This isn't normal."

Okay. I'll play along. It's what I'm good at, after all.

"Why's that?"

Tress taps the bottle against her chin, the beat of it matching my pulse for a moment. "This is organic, certified vegan, non-GMO, responsibly sourced black tea."

"Uh-huh? And . . . ?"

She stops hitting herself with the bottle and instead taps my forehead with it. "Kind of different from our usual recycling haul, right?"

When we were younger Tress and I would wander the ridge with trash bags, hoping to gather enough cans to pay for a pool pass that day. I still remember hauling them into town, our hands sticky with old pop, decayed sugar, somebody's spit cup, remnants of beer. It all came off in the pool, though, the chlorine slicking us clean.

And Tress might be high, but she's not wrong. Those bags were full of cheap beer cans and energy drinks. It takes a certain kind of person to mindlessly litter, and most of them don't have refined palates.

"So whose is this?" Tress asks, her red-rimmed eyes moving from mine to the bottle. "Who is sitting outside my trailer drinking this shit?"

"Don't know," I say, shrugging. "Either a hippie or a millennial."

Tress's eyes narrow, still focused on the label. "A hippie . . . ," she ponders. "Tree hugger, nature lover. That would fit. Somebody from PETA? The ASPCA?"

Either Tress has been hitting the weed hard and paranoia is setting in, or she's right. It wouldn't be the first time Amontillado Animal Attractions has dealt with activists. There was a whole month where one diehard stood at the edge of the road with a sign that read, "Wild But Not Free."

Cecil had *accidentally* let Dee—the ostrich—out of her cage while she was in heat, and the guy figured out real quick that the ostrich was certainly wild, and definitely free with herself.

"But Cecil has permits for all the animals, right?" I ask.

"Yes," she says slowly, lowering the bottle. "And they can't come onto the property, anyway. Legally, they can only investigate during business hours, and Cecil had me paint *closed* across our sign yesterday. If they want to check up on us now, they'll need a warrant."

"And if they get one?"

Tress shrugs, tucks the bottle into her hoodie pocket. "If they get one, we're fucked."

We walk in silence awhile longer, hugging the side

of the hill when we go around the curve. The bridge comes into view. Below it, the river. Above that, my house, darkly skeletal in the morning sun. Rays of light bounce off some windows, others are broken, reflecting nothing. We watch as a bird alights on the roof, adding a stick to the nest she's building on the second-floor balcony. I'll probably be sent up there soon to knock it down. She's incorporating my home into hers, and Lenore Usher won't allow that. Unless the bird is also an Usher. Then that would be okay.

Shit, do I have a contact high from Tress?

"Allan, Astor, Montor, Usher," Tress says, her eyes still on the house. She's reciting the names from the pillar in the center of Amontillado. The founding families.

"The Allan house is gone," she says, her mind stuck on some kind of loop.

"But not the Allans themselves," I say. "I don't think Cecil will ever die."

"Oh, he'll die," Tress says. "That cat isn't just whistling Dixie."

"What?" I ask, but she's not really listening. Her hand is at her neck fumbling with something under her sweatshirt.

"You know, I forget sometimes," she says. "I forget that Cecil is an Allan."

"That's what Grandma Usher wanted," I say, moving forward again. The Allan fortune had been used up by the time Cecil had any chance to inherit. He'd traded on an ancestral name to marry into what the Ushers still had, accepting Grandma's restrictions—she'd be an Usher until she died, and so would any of their children.

She died a little earlier than expected, and horribly, by all accounts. Cancer ate away at her while she refused to go, daring it to take her down before she had a chance to change her will. In it, she repudiated her husband—Cecil—entirely, giving the ancestral Usher home to the older daughter—my mother—and the land split between her and Annabelle—Tress's mother.

"Do you know where you'll be buried?" Tress asks suddenly.

In truth, I'd never really thought about it. There is a family plot on our land, but I'm not sure if it's still legal to inter there. Grandma is there, and I'm sure Lenore will *make* it legal before her own time comes. There are plenty of Usher tombstones—big ones—in the village cemetery, but we don't have a mausoleum, like the Montors do. The Astors—those assholes—have an actual crypt with a sundial on top, like maybe they have appointments to keep in the afterlife. But none of this answers Tress's question—*Do you know where you'll be buried?*

"Wherever Lenore says, I guess," I tell her, and she makes a face.

"What, you're going to die before your mom?"

"No, I mean, like, I'm sure she has it all planned out

and written down somewhere. It's probably notarized and legally binding, and all that shit."

Tress considers that for a moment. "Yeah, probably."

I pick up a stone from the road, throw it toward the river. From this distance, we can see the splash but don't hear it. We're quiet for a second, watching the flow of the water.

"Why are you even asking me about getting buried?"

"The Allan house," she says. At her throat, her hand clenches. "The Montor house collapsed in 'eighty-four; the Astors knocked theirs down and rebuilt in the twenties." She recites the history, our families and their counterparts burned into our minds at a young age so that we could never forget. Then she lifts a finger, pointing to me. "Usher."

She points to herself. "Montor."

Her finger goes back and forth between the two of us. "Allan."

Three of the founding families, powerful names dwindled to nothing. The trailblazers and pathfinders have been distilled down to a drug dealer and a loser, one high and the other a national joke, standing by as the last ancestral home crumbles.

And soon, there will only be one.

Chapter 13

Tress

Monday

I wake to a weight on my chest and teeth in my face.

The cat is back, his liquid eyes staring into mine, velvety paws resting on my chest. My ribs strain against the pressure, the skin across my clavicle drawn taut, the heart pendant bouncing there with my pulse, at least, I think it's my pulse moving it.

Danger, danger, danger.

Rue had tried to tell me, and I didn't listen. She wasn't talking about the lioness but the panther, this killing machine that rests patiently on top of me, tail flicking over the edge of the mattress. He raises a paw, and I draw in a breath. Our eyes lock as he washes the pads, then pins me again, eyes boring into mine. He leans forward, whiskers brushing against my face. His breath is full of blood, rancid with his last meal. He sniffs at me cautiously, little hot puffs of air tickling along my neck.

"Where've you been?" I ask him, and the cat's upper lip curls, showing me his teeth.

My what big teeth you have, Grandma, I think, then bite down so that I don't giggle. I'd raided our Oxy stash before coming to bed and taken another hit off the joint in the living room, hoping to find some comfort there. Instead it's made me slaphappy, and that isn't good with two hundred pounds of wild cat sitting on your chest.

But Grandma did have big teeth, I think. *Big enough to tear off Cecil's balls.*

Okay, that *is* funny. A high whine of amusement escapes me as I try to laugh, not laugh, and breathe at the same time. The cat pulls back, unsure what to make of me. His nose trails down my arm, finding the wound. His ears lie back at the smell. I guess scent translates across language barriers, and death doesn't know any strangers.

"You got me good," I tell the cat, and his ears come forward again, catching my sounds.

A deep rumble resonates from his chest as the cat settles in across my body, purring. He's warm and comforting, the thrum of his purr carrying me off to sleep. I twitch once, twice, and give in to unconsciousness as his tongue licks at the edges of the duct tape, cleaning my wound.

My alarm goes off in the morning, the sound drumming through my brain, pulling me up out of sleep. I sit up suddenly, my body reacting—way too late—to the memory of danger.

But I'm alone, and there's no hint of the panther in my room.

"Oxy, you bitch," I say, digging my palms into my eyes. No wonder my clients keep coming back for more. Apparently, you get a free safari along with the high. But my relief is gone along with the cat, and my arm is a deadweight beside me. I roll over, snagging my hoodie off the floor with my good hand. The tea bottle rolls out, coming to rest label up, accusingly.

"Yeah, I know," I tell it. "Danger."

But I can't worry about loose panthers or PETA or the fact that the Allan house went down into the ground and the Usher house is on the way. I can't do those things because those are the big picture, and the last time I tried to ask hard questions and understand the larger scope of the world somebody died, and I got halfway there in the process.

What I need to do now is get away with it. I need to get up and go to school. I need to be as normal as

possible, avoid suspicion, not draw attention, and hope-
fully not die in the hallway. The half-heart pendant
slides across my skin as I roll over, reminding me that
the other half will never see daylight again. I can't take
back what I did, but that doesn't mean I have to give up.
Felicity Turnado may not have known what happened to
my parents, but someone does. What happened Friday
night doesn't mean everything is at a dead end.

Nope. Just Felicity.

Shit, I'm still high. I'm still high, and I need to go to
school.

I haul myself out of bed and inspect my bandage. The
red streaks of infection haven't moved, but there's some
pus leaking out around the edges of the tape. Better
out than in, I suppose. I find a pen and make a slash on
my arm, marking where the red lines end. The skin is
bloated and swollen, and even the slight pressure from
the tip of the pen makes me wince.

Cecil is unconscious on the couch, one arm thrown
across his eyes.

"Hey." I nudge him with the baseball bat I keep in
the living room for exactly this purpose—waking Cecil
from a distance.

He grunts and pushes the bat away, makes a move to
roll over, but I won't let him.

"Do you have any pills leftover from your surgery?"

When the cat got his eye Cecil had come home from the hospital armed with a platoon of orange bottles. The painkillers we'd sold, but there were more than a few antibiotics in that pile, too.

"Bed," Cecil says, waving his arm in a gesture that might be an attempt to point toward the hallway. "Under the bed."

I lift his mattress—surprisingly clean, since he passes out most nights on the couch—to find a handful of prescription bottles. As I expected, there's a few outdated antibiotics, an unmarked bottle of Oxy, and . . . oh, nice. Some Viagra. I'm about to flush it down the toilet but reconsider. I bet I can sell it pretty easily, and not just to older dudes, either. People get bored in Amontillado.

I pop a few antibiotics, chasing them down with a handful of water. I wash my hair in the sink and put on some deodorant, adding a little body spray for good measure. Then I check myself out in the mirror. My eyes are bloodshot, I'm green around the gills, and the tips of my fingers still smell like pot. But I'm cleaner, and I don't look like I killed someone.

Whatever that looks like. I've been searching the faces of Amontillado since fifth grade, wondering if I can pinpoint it. Wondering where my parents are.

"Shit," I say to my reflection.

Then I hang my head, and I cry.

Chapter 14

Ribbit

Monday

They're waiting for me in the library. I take a second to relish that. *They're* waiting for *me*.

Hugh Broward, Gretchen Astor, Brynn Whitaker, and David Evans are gathered around a table, looking like an American Eagle ad. Huge and David are in their football jerseys, the dark wings of our mascot—a raven—spread across their chests. Brynn is wearing her volleyball uniform, and *damn* those shorts are definitely not dress-code appropriate. I became a big supporter of our volleyball team right about seventh grade. Never missed a game.

Gretchen rounds out the group in her cheerleading uniform, the deep V of the neckline drawing me in, as I know it's supposed to. Tress had ticked off the ancestral families of Amontillado yesterday, pointing out our

blood ties to three of them. The fourth—the Astors—
is represented by Gretchen, and if I really wanted to
make Lenore happy, I'd use my newfound fame to worm
my way into her heart. But in the game of Fuck, Marry,
Kill, I know exactly where Gretchen lands for me.

And I don't think she's the marrying type.

"Ladies," I say, nodding to Brynn and Gretchen as I
walk in.

"Ribbit!" Gretchen squeaks, and jumps to her feet,
eager to welcome me. She goes in for the hug, which I
certainly won't reject. Over her shoulder, Hugh frowns,
watching my hands. I nod at Brynn, but she barely glances
up from her phone, her thumbs flying across the screen.

"Great news," Gretchen says, one hand resting lightly
on my chest. "We're going to clone William Wilson."

My smile stays in the same place and so does her
hand. But I'm definitely confused. "You're going to
what?"

"William Wilson," she laughs, tapping at me.
"Remember, my pupper?"

Oh yes, her *pupper*. Which was eaten by something at
the party. My tongue flicks across the back of my lip
where the remnants of a silky, raised scar can be felt.
William Wilson gave me that. I hope whatever ate him
chewed slowly.

"Yeah," Gretchen goes on, pulling out a chair to sit
down. "There was enough DNA in his tail that this big

company in the city said they could clone him, if I want. So there's going to be a second William Wilson."

"Too bad they can't do that for Felicity," Brynn says darkly, eyes still locked on her phone.

"Dude." David's hand clamps down suddenly on Huge's shoulder. "Two Felicitys." His eyes are bright with the possibilities, and I doubt that any of them are G-rated. I keep the smile on my face, even though I know it's stretched too thin, now.

Felicity isn't for him.

"Right now I'd settle for one Felicity," Brynn says. "They just updated the Facebook page. The search party is on for today, after school."

"Cool," I say, then realize it's the wrong thing to say as Brynn frowns.

"I'll be there. I'll help," I quickly amend.

What do you need from me? What can I do for you? How can I make it better?

"Good." She nods tightly, avoiding my eyes. "We'll need everyone. They're starting out at the Allan house—"

"Okay, look," Gretchen says, clapping her hands together. "I'm just going to say it. Felicity probably ran off with some guy. Has anyone checked Patrick Vance's bed?"

"That's over," Hugh growls roughly, but Gretchen rolls her eyes.

"Whatever, Broward," she says. "If Patrick said, *Jump*

on my junk, she'd say, *How hard?*"

"Seriously?" Brynn says. "I thought Felicity was your friend?"

"Uh, yeah. She is my friend," Gretchen insists, somehow sounding insulted. "And I know her better than you do. Weren't there a couple of dudes from Prospero at the party? If one of them had pills, they could've just left her a trail, and Felicity would have followed. She's probably zonked out in the woods somewhere. I just hope she can get her underwear back up before the search party finds her."

"Some friend," Brynn says, her tone more biting than ever.

"What?" Gretchen asks, eyes wide. "I'm not slut-shaming. I'm supporting her. Go, Felicity! Bang it out all you want. In the meantime, I've got a spirit week to plan."

She turns to me, eyes still shining. "And I've enlisted the celebrity of the hour to help. Fame has done something for you, Ribbit," she says. "You look . . ." Her gaze wanders up and down my body, but her confidence has sputtered out, and she can't quite put her finger on what's changed about me.

It's hard to pinpoint *acrimony*.

"I have an idea," I announce to the group. "Something to make this week's homecoming the best yet. The school board, the village council, everyone is trying to push past all the negativity and accentuate the positive. Homecoming is the best way to do that, and Gretchen and I came up with a great way to make it memorable."

I nod toward Gretchen, even though the extent of her contribution was a string of emojis when I told her my plan. They were (in order)—a smiley face, flames, a 100, and a heart. I silently agreed with all of them.

"Accentuate the positive?" Hugh repeats, looking at me as if he'd like to squash me. And he could, like a bug. People call him *Huge* for a reason.

I smile, I nod. I do what I'm good at.

"Sure," I say. "We all know Felicity had . . . problems." (*Drinking, Oxy, boys who were mean to her.*) "But everyone is assuming the worst, when the reality is that Felicity is probably just fine."

I don't know that. I don't know anything. In truth my heart leaps and my stomach flips every time someone says her name, but that's not a new development in my life. The flame of panic is . . . the deep conviction that if I find her, she'll finally see me. Realize that I've been here all along, patiently waiting for her to assume her rightful place, the spot I'd carved out and sealed for her one night in fifth grade. The night I claimed her as mine, and made a pact with Mother in exchange for her life.

A life which could very well be in danger right now.

Felicity could have been eaten by Tress's panther. Or, maybe she received an emergency booty call from

Patrick and hasn't worn out her welcome yet. There is part of me—the heart emoji part of me—that wants to play the hero. But there's another part—the fire emoji part—that sees an opportunity. And when people don't like you—but they *need* you—you have to always be on the lookout for opportunities.

And right now, I've got to rank my priorities.

"You don't know the half of Felicity's problems, man," Hugh growls at me.

"I'm sure that's true," I say, because Huge has two hundred pounds on me and it's important I agree with him. "However, let's assume she's all right. Let's assume she drank too much and got lost in the woods. Let's assume we find her today during the search party."

"Yes," Brynn says, nodding her head vigorously, like saying so will make it so. "Let's assume that."

"So . . ." I hold up my hands, looking helpless and innocent. "What if we don't make any plans for homecoming, because we're all sad, and distracted? And then we find her, and everything is okay, and nothing is ready for Wednesday night?"

"Wednesday?" David looks to Hugh, confused. "What's Wednesday?"

"Bonfire night!" Gretchen shouts, popping out of her chair like a firework. "Seriously, guys—c'mon. It's the same every year. Monday is spirit day." She points at their coordinated sports uniforms, as if to congratulate them all once again on being part of the in-crowd.

I don't think it even crosses her mind that I have nothing Amontillado High related to wear. Not a sports uniform, not a marching band T-shirt, not a jersey with numbers flaking off the back because at least I have a boyfriend or girlfriend who will loan me theirs from last year. No, the master of these ceremonies will go without, moving behind the scenes. And that's just fine.

Honestly, that's for the best.

"Tuesday," Gretchen goes on, "is twin day. So twin up!" She claps her hands together, making Brynn jump and drop her phone. I swoop down and pick it up for her, and I notice that she's been texting Felicity. There's a string of unanswered texts, all marked as *undeliverable*.

"You two." Gretchen points at David and Hugh. "Twins. Not football stuff. Get creative." She turns to Brynn. "You and me, twinkies."

"Um, how?" Brynn asks, her forehead—much darker than Gretchen's—furrows. "You're the whitest girl I know."

"Think outside the box, Brynn!" Gretchen says. "Besides we're all one, really."

"And you're both pink on the inside," David says, holding up a fist blindly for Hugh to bump it. He doesn't, but I get the tap in, and David blows it up, winking at me.

"Whatever," Brynn mutters.

"I found the cutest little tanks that say *twin* this summer at—"

"We should do a vigil," Brynn interrupts her.

Gretchen, mouth still forming the name of whatever upscale store she shops at, stammers. "A what-il?"

"Vig-il," Brynn says, delivering each syllable succinctly. "You know, for Felicity?"

"Yeah," Gretchen says, nodding. "Totally. But how does that tie into homecoming?"

"Um, it doesn't," Brynn bites back. "It's more like a someone-we-care-about-is-missing-and-in-danger thing. Sorry it doesn't fit your theme."

"Oooohhh!" David says, suddenly animated. "Murder week!"

I hide a smile as Brynn erupts. "Fuck you, David!"

"Wait, wait, wait, wait, wait," Gretchen says, waving her hands like she can dispel the dark cloud that's fallen among us. "Brynn, if you want to do a . . ."

"Vigil," Brynn says tightly.

"Vigil," Gretchen says with a nod, "you should absolutely do that. That can be your thing."

"Okay." Brynn nods. "I was thinking maybe sell candles in school colors, like a dollar a candle. We'll donate the proceeds to help with the search."

"That's sweet, but the Turnados don't exactly need charity," Gretchen says.

"I. Have. To. Do. Something," Brynn says, biting off each word.

"Cool," Gretchen agrees quickly. "Then you totally should. And if you can tie it into homecoming somehow for continuity, that would be great."

Brynn's mouth falls open like she's about to fire back, but she changes her mind, dropping her head back to her phone. This girl knows how to choose her battles.

"So . . . Wednesday!" Gretchen announces, clapping her hands together. "School colors—purple and black. Then the parade and bonfire in the evening. That's where Ribbit comes in." She steps aside as if making room for me on a stage. I clear my throat, and I tell them my plan.

David gives me a fist again, blowing it up.

Gretchen continues to talk about her plans for Thursday and Friday—pajama day and funny T-shirt day, respectively. I don't tell them they shouldn't work too hard for pajama day and funny T-shirt day. They won't be getting a Thursday or a Friday. And Saturday, more than likely, is going to be funeral day.

I smile and I nod when I'm supposed to. And when David asks me to, I blow it up.

Chapter 15

Tress

Monday

There are "MISSING" posters all over the school. As if the entire town doesn't know (1) that Felicity is missing and (2) what she looks like. Her name has been on everyone's lips, and her face isn't easy to forget. Whoever made the posters had their heart in the right place, but their head was decidedly up their ass. They'd used a template for a lost dog or cat, and so Felicity's "MISSING" poster also states that she has been spayed and is up to date on her rabies shot.

I laugh. I don't mean to, but I can't help it. I try to cover it by pretending it's a sneeze and bury my face in my elbow.

"It's not funny." Meg Cofflero is beside me, posters in one hand, a roll of tape in the other. She stands on tiptoes to stick one to the wall outside the girls' bathroom, stretching as if the higher she puts it, the more likely it is Felicity will be found.

"No, it's not funny," I agree, quickly pushing my sleeve back down to cover my arm. The red of infection hasn't receded past the line I drew this morning, but it hasn't climbed higher, either.

"Are you helping with the search party?" Meg asks. "It's after school. I mean . . ." She pauses, considering her words. "I mean, I know it might be hard for you to do that, and all."

And all. That's a nice way to neatly summarize my own parents' disappearance, the lines of people walking in tandem, yelling their names, finding nothing. Me, standing next to the drink station, refilling water glasses for volunteers because maybe, just maybe, if I'm a really good girl and I do the right thing, I'll be rewarded.

Rewarded by having a family again.

That search party didn't end well, and neither will this one. I already know this, know what nobody else in Amontillado does. But I still reach for the stack of fliers that Meg is carrying.

"I'll help," I say. I follow her, keeping my injured arm close to my chest, pulling a sheet off the top with my good hand. Meg tears tape with her teeth, putting a flier every five feet down the hallway. It's overkill, and pointless. But I let Meg work. I know how it feels. The need to do something will lead you to do anything, every fiber of your being saying to God, fate, or what-ever cosmic force, *See? See? I'm trying. I'm working. Please, let it matter. Please, make it count. Please tell me everything isn't futile.*

The thought is so hard and bright, sharp like a dia-mond, that I feel tears pricking my eyes as I hand the last poster to Meg.

"Hey," she says softly, resting her hand on my arm. "It'll be okay."

It won't be, but Meg doesn't know that. Meg lives in a nice part of town with a mom and a dad and a sister and drives a cute little Kia Soul and probably has a dog and a cat that are hypoallergenic. Meg has the freedom to think that things will be okay because she doesn't know the things I know. She hasn't lived in a world where it isn't.

"Looks good!" Lisa Johnson—Meg's bestie—walks up behind us, surveying our work. She smiles like the sheer number of posters will tip the scales and Felicity will come walking out of the bathroom, and say, *That five hundredth poster, that's the one that did the trick!*

"Tress, you okay?"

Now Lisa is touching me, and I can feel the pressure of her hand on my shoulder. Pressure like the dirt set-tling on top of Felicity's body, taking up more space as she takes up less. Decomposition might be the first time that Felicity Turnado loses at something.

"Shit," I say, taking a pained breath as Meg's grip on my arm tightens. The soft, swollen skin pushes back, and deep within my arm, something pops. My knees go out from under me, and Lisa grabs my other arm. Together they ease me down to the tiled hallway floor.

"Tress? Tress?" Meg's face is inches from mine, but the distance is too far for my words to cross. My tongue is dry and heavy, and I don't know what to say anyway. Maybe, *I think you broke an abscess in my arm.*

But *abscess* is a hard word to say when you're about to pass out.

"Lay her down, put her legs in the air." Meg is calmly giving instructions to Lisa, who is dutifully positioning me. Then Meg's face is back over mine, and I can feel sweat running down my torso, pooling at my back, and man, this is going to be one funky mess for the janitor to clean up.

"Tress?" Meg says. "I need you to focus on me."

I do, amazed at her confidence, and suddenly I remember that her little sister has MS and that she's probably handled all kinds of first aid situations and she probably *doesn't* have a hypoallergenic cat and she definitely *does* know that things aren't going to be okay.

She's just choosing to believe that they will.

"Get me up," I say. "I'm fine."

Meg blinks, then must reassess the set of my mouth. Because even though things aren't going to be okay, Tress Montor still has to be fine. If I'm not, people will notice. And the last thing I want is to be noticed right now.

"Get me up," I say again, and Meg and Lisa each put a shoulder into one of my armpits—which is a true sacrifice on both their parts, at this point—and haul me to my feet.

"I'm okay," I say, leaning against the wall, absorbing the coolness of the tile. "I just . . . I didn't eat anything yet today."

Which is totally true. Ever ready, Meg pulls off her backpack, digs around, and hands me a granola bar.

"Thanks," I say, blinking back tears. I promise myself I will eat this. I will not make Meg's granola bar as pointless as her "MISSING" posters.

"You sure you're all right?" Meg asks, just as the tardy bell rings. Lisa tugs on her elbow.

"I'm fine." I wave them both off. "Just going to wash my face."

I duck into the bathroom, pulling a stall door shut behind me. There's a dark stain forming at the edge of my hoodie sleeve, a yellowish-brown color, tinged with pink. I push the sleeve up to survey the damage.

There's some seepage, which I expected. I mincingly press on the bandage, and more liquid wells up from between the seams of tape, dots of my sweat adding to the mess as my forehead drips. Visually, it's horrific. But the smell is what has me truly worried.

Under that shiny tape, my arm is rotting.

This bandage is going to have to come off, and the wound is going to have to be thoroughly cleaned. And the truth is that if one doesn't kill me, the other probably will.

"Shit."

I rest my head against the back of the stall, staring at the ceiling, reading graffiti upside down. A lot of it has Gretchen's name in it, some has Felicity's. The only place the queen bees can be run down is inside this tiled hive, anonymous drones venting their bile.

Except, a hive can only have one queen, and in nature, all the drones are male.

"Yeah, Montor," I correct myself. "Get a grip."

It's good advice, and I should take it. But the problem is that I gave the advice to myself, aloud, alone in a bathroom stall, with a fever spiking and while trying to validate my own analogy.

I'm delirious.

"Shit," I say again, and close my eyes.

Because no matter how many times Meg Cofflero insists that everything will be okay, I have a sneaking suspicion that it won't be.

And, the bitch of the thing is—I'm usually right.

Chapter 16

Ribbit

Monday

School is a shit show, and not just your average, every-day, run-of-the-mill shit show. This is a five-star shit show, and two names are being repeated over and over, nonstop, ad nauseum. Mine . . . and Felicity Turnado's.

Everyone wants to find Felicity. Her parents jumped the gun in a major way and are offering a $50,000 reward to whoever finds her. Everyone knew the Turnados had money, but the fact that they can drop a cool $50K without blinking has sent tongues wagging. In Amontillado, you're allowed to have money, but you're not allowed to show it off. Felicity's parents just did, and the gyrating pinball machine of public opinion doesn't know whether to feel sorry for them or not.

On the other hand, it's not hard at all for people

to decide what to think of me. The legacy of my last name combined with a squandered fortune and awkward appearance means that I am a person to be pitied. And the pity party for Kermit Usher just gained a lot of attendees. They're all adults, and they're all worried about me. The clip of me explaining how, when, why, and where I jack off has a million views on YouTube, and I guarantee that half the adults who feel sorry for me boosted that hit count. But they are rallying to protect me, forming a human cordon of button-up oxfords and silk blouses around the last Usher. I'm old blood, brought low, waded through by teenagers with smartphones and good Wi-Fi signals.

"Like I said," I explain to Mrs. Febrezio, the guidance counselor, "my mother already spoke to the police, and we're not interested in pressing any charges."

Her lips come together in a tight line, creases of worry (*For my benefit; that'll leave a mark—find a new sympathy face or you'll have crow's-feet*) stretched across her forehead.

"Yes, I spoke with your mother," she says. "But outside of law enforcement, I'm wondering what else can be done for you?"

Oh, a hell of a lot. But that's not for an army of adults to decide.

"Really, I'm fine," I say. "You know how Mrs. Anho is always talking about our choices?"

"Yes . . ." Febrezio's face stays carefully controlled, her voice so adamantly neutral that I know she's seen the video, specifically the part where I say I'd bang Anho. Shit . . . did I say I'd tap Febrezio, too? I can't remember. But I definitely would.

"Well," I go on, matching her neutral with a resigned martyr tone. "I made a choice that night. I made the choice to drink. I made the choice to let others lead me somewhere unhealthy."

God, I sound like a pamphlet, like an after-school special, like the poster hanging directly behind Febrezio's head. And with good reason. I'm basically reading it aloud, grabbing good pull quotes and filling in my personal details.

Hello, my name is Ribbit and I have a drinking problem.

I bite the inside of my cheek. Now is not a good time to start laughing.

"I chose to drink. No one made me. I'm choosing not to punish others for my decision."

The word *punish* comes out a little too enthusiastically, like my tongue is tasting it, relishing the syllables. Febrezio doesn't seem to notice.

"Okay," she agrees, tapping her nails on her desk. "But you didn't agree to be filmed, or to have . . . personal details shared with the entire world."

Like my dick. My actual, naked-ass dick, swinging

like a pendulum counting down the seconds to . . . what? So many things. Wednesday. Felicity Turnado's last breath. Tress's parents being declared legally dead. A bonfire. I feel like I need more dicks in order to keep track.

That causes another burst of hilarity, this one deep in my gut. I cover it by standing and stretching, readjusting my backpack. Febrezio stands as well, disconcerted. I ended the meeting, not her. She feels like she hasn't helped me, hasn't fixed things, hasn't made it all better.

Adults. They think they have so much impact.

"I'm fine," I tell her. "I have been fine. I am fine. I will continue to be fine."

She still hesitates, biting her bottom lip, unsure. My phone buzzes in my pocket and I reach for it, thankful for the text message from my cell phone company letting me know I've used up all my data. I smile at the text, like it's a message from a friend, and type out a reply.

STOP.

"I've got to go," I tell Febrezio. "I'm meeting a friend."

"Oh?" She brightens at that.

"Yeah," I say, feeling a weird lift in my stomach at the thought as well. "Brynn Whitaker. I'm her partner for the search party."

Febrezio smiles further, the ends of her mouth lifting

up. Yes, I'm sure it seems perfect in her boxy little mind. The social outcast and the only Black girl in school teaming up to find the lost sheep.

"Well that's lovely," Febrezio says, her whole face alight at the idea. "I hope you two have a good time."

She catches her statement at the last minute, like we probably shouldn't be having a good time while searching for Felicity, the lost sheep who has wandered away before. Felicity, who was spared. Felicity, who doesn't know who saved her. I tighten the straps on my pack, and send a text to Brynn.

This time, Felicity will know exactly who to thank.

And I will get my just rewards.

Chapter 17

Rue

My girl goes, FoundChild, gone now.
Hours without her, no apples
Or handwords.
Her hair in my hands, let me know.
Scared. Hurt. Broken.
Cannot help, over this distance.
Cannot say, Danger, danger, danger.
Fingers, still and bored, empty-arms.
Another girl, that one from my body.
LostChild. Taken.
Empty-arms. Empty-arms. Empty-arms.
(CAREFUL! SHE'S GOT A LONG REACH.
THE BACK ACRE, YES.)
OldCat, SadThing, NearlyDead,

Does not move, from her mess.

A bad sign.

GrayMan, OneEye, DrinkSmell,

Walks slow, small stumble.

His trip to the box on the road

Today takes time.

(IT WAS TAKEN FROM US. STOLEN. CHEATED.)

My words to tell her, so she

Can hear with eyes.

FoundChild, see my words.

Danger. Danger. Danger.

Chapter 18

Tress

Monday

"You know what I would do with fifty grand?"

A male voice floats above the others, hot bodies jostling as we weave our way out of the school. The buses stand, sentinels in a line, doors open, waiting. Younger kids from the other buildings are pressed against the windows, hands and noses leaving smudges, watching us, most of them probably scanning the crowd, hoping to spot Felicity and scream, "Found her!"

"You know what I would do if I find Felicity? I mean, *before* I let anybody know I found her?"

Another male voice responds, and I spin, ready to punch somebody. I've thrown a few good hooks in my life and have stress fractures in both wrists to show for it. But nobody looks overly guilty as I try to determine who said it, and pretty soon the flow of traffic makes all the faces blend. That and the Oxy I popped right after sixth period.

Why couldn't Cecil and I deal in black-market antibiotics? My life would be so much easier right now. A face separates from the crowd, makes its way to me.

"Tress? You helping with the search party?"

I blink. Once. Twice. Try to identify the planes of these particular cheekbones, these blue eyes, this five-o'clock shadow. "Hugh," I say, my sluggish brain catching up. "Yeah, I'm helping."

"Cool." He turns toward the parking lot, where most of the student body has filed out to. There are a series of tables set up where you can register, get your instructions, grab a T-shirt, and be assigned to a grid. I follow Huge over to a table and put my name, age, address, and cell phone number on a list.

"Tress Montor?" The woman looks up when I hand the clipboard back to her, and I barely suppress a groan. It's Gretchen's mom, Jill Astor. She's wearing yoga pants that end below the knee and a cute little knotted tank. I hope she gets poison ivy. Like, in her vagina.

"How are you doing, hon?" Jill asks. "This must be hard for you."

"No, it's really easy," I say, words spilling out before I have time to double-check them. "Been there, done that. Have the T-shirt."

I totally do. It says, THE MONTORS ARE MISS-ING! and has my parents' faces silk-screened on the front, along with a hotline to call. I dialed it once, in seventh grade. Back when I used to have hope. An Officer Riley had answered, halfway through his retirement-day bottle of whiskey.

"C'mon," Hugh says roughly, pulling me away from Jill Astor, who is still trying to put together a response to my less-than-sympathetic comment. Hugh leads me through the crowd, checking the numbers we were handed. Somebody has pulled their monster truck up at the edge of the parking lot. April Turnado is standing in the bed, her ponytail neatly pulled through the back of a baseball cap, brick red with white embroidery that shouts FIND FELICITY! She's got on sneakers, and they flash brightly as she climbs onto the cab of the truck. They're brand-new, probably the first pair of sneakers she's bought in a long time. Because April doesn't go for walks in the woods.

I'm sure she's got 100 SPF on. From a designer brand. I hope she gets poison ivy in her vagina, too. Then she can have a calamine lotion douche party with Jill Astor.

"Everyone!" April shouts into a megaphone, her voice amplified and roaring across the citizens of Amontillado. "Thank you for coming!

"You've all been given a number that is assigned to an area on this grid." She pulls a cord and a map unrolls from the side of the truck, like a scene change in a play. But I guess it kind of is a scene change for the Turnados. They were parents; now they're not.

"Check your numbers for your grid area and make your way independently to that place. Once you're there you'll cover the area together, moving slowly, arm-width's distance from one another."

Whoever is on my left side will likely want to be more than an arm-width's distance from me, given the putrefaction of the arm in question.

"If you see anything of interest, the police have instructed me that you are not to touch it! Take a picture with your phone, and text it to me."

April recites her phone number, and cells pop out of pockets all through the crowd, thumbs hastily recording the information. I'm betting she gets at least three dick pics by midnight.

"This is what Felicity was wearing the last time she was seen," April goes on, and another poster unrolls, this one attached to the side of a school bus. It's a larger-than-life Felicity, in her smaller-than-socially-acceptable Halloween costume she wore to the party. She's a pink-and-purple jester, with little bells on the pointy tips of her hat. It's shorter than it needs to be, tighter than it needs to be, and Felicity has one hip cocked, making both of those things more obvious than they need to be.

Somebody wolf-whistles.

"What the fuck?" I say under my breath, and Hugh turns to look at me.

"You okay?"

"Yeah," I say. "I'm fine. What the fuck is wrong with everyone else?"

And then it hits me. I'm the only person who knows Felicity is dead. To everyone else, this is an Easter egg hunt with only one egg. A big one worth fifty grand.

Hugh and I get in line to check out where on the map our numbers correspond with. It's a patch of woods in the middle of nowhere but near the Allan house.

"Oh, thank God," someone behind me says, and I turn to find Brynn and Ribbit standing together, holding their numbers.

"We're on the same grid," Brynn says. "I'm glad I'm with someone who will take this seriously."

Normally, I'd agree with her. The search for Felicity has become some kind of weird attraction. Amontillado might like it so much we do it again next year. Guys are lining up to take close-up pics of the poster of Felicity, acting like they want to make sure they've got all the necessary information. Not, you know, a great shot of her cleavage.

But I don't necessarily want people taking this too seriously, either. If they get intense about finding her—and if they actually succeed—I'll have more problems than my court-appointed lawyer will know how to deal with. There's a chance I might be spared a long sleep on a gurney, but the alternative is a life in a cage.

Like Rue.

"Yeah," I say, shuddering as I stick my grid number into my pocket. "I hope we find her."

And I mean that. I hope we do. I hope we find Felicity alive and well, wandering around in the woods, her jester cap skewed sideways and a big, dumb grin on her face. I know it's impossible. I know what I did. But I can also stare into a void and hope to see a flash of brightness, the same way I stayed at my bedroom window in fifth grade, looking for Mom and Dad's headlights, waiting for them to come home.

They didn't. And now I've just switched one void for another.

"We're on the same grid, want to ride out together?" Ribbit asks Hugh, who gives my cousin a once-over. He's never trusted Ribbit, but the fact that Lenore Usher isn't going to be slapping him upside the head with multiple lawsuits has probably won Ribbit more goodwill than allowing himself to be mistreated ever did.

"Sure, I'll drive," Hugh says. The four of us pile into his car, Brynn and I in the back seat.

Hugh turns on the music and rolls the windows halfway down. It creates a helicopter effect, a distinct *thwup,*

thwup, thwup that makes it impossible to hear anyone else. I catch a few words from Hugh, directed at Ribbit.

Sorry . . . tried . . . didn't want . . . too far . . . my bad.

And my cousin, in response, his lips stretched thin and pale pink over his teeth.

Cool . . . okay . . . we're good . . . homecoming.

"Who the fuck cares about homecoming?" I ask, glowering at the back of the driver's seat.

"Right?" Brynn says, popping out an earbud. "But to actually answer you—Gretchen, that's who. She cares a lot. With Felicity out of the picture she'll be voted queen, no doubt. She's going to make sure it's one hell of a homecoming and she's wearing the crown."

Ribbit turns around and says something like, "It'll be a night to remember!"

"What?" I shout back, the wind *thwup, thwup, thwup-ping* in my ears, but he waves me off, shaking his head. Oh, that's right, I forgot. He's in on the homecoming planning, one of the cool kids now. Whatever. I mean, I guess I should be happy for him. It's what he's always wanted, and all he had to do was debase himself thoroughly while I neglected my duties to keep him sober.

Hugh checks the pin he dropped on the map and slows down, finally pulling over along the edge of the woods. Behind and in front of us, other cars fan out. We're all wearing our FIND FELICITY shirts that we picked up at the appropriate table in the parking lot, the word VOLUNTEER emblazoned across the back.

"I'm the only person who can find her," I say under my breath.

"What?" Brynn asks, unclicking her seat belt. At least, I think that's what she said, there's still a thumping in my ears, even though the car has stopped. I shake my head and get out, jamming my fingers into my ears, hoping to stop the *thwup, thwup, thwup.*

I walk away from the car quickly, panic rising in my throat. It's not stopping. It's not stopping, and it's not the wind. It's a pulse. A heartbeat.

And it's coming from the necklace around my throat.

Chapter 19

Ribbit

Monday

"I'm going to find Felicity," Brynn says, with an absolute confidence that makes it almost impossible to disagree.

But I do. I disagree.

Because *I'm* going to find Felicity.

We line up with a few feet in between the four of us and start walking in a line, eyes scouring the forest floor. I see, in order—a leaf, a stick, a beer can. I do not see Felicity, or anything she might have been wearing that night, or her footprints, or her hair, or her eyes or her teeth, or anything that might even be remotely related to Felicity Turnado.

And I would know. I have been watching her for years, studying her, learning her likes and dislikes, taking notes and marking time. I didn't need her mom to have a bus-sized poster of Felicity printed in order to know what she was wearing Friday. I remember. There wasn't much to it, and what there was . . . let's just say it wouldn't have kept her warm in a light breeze. I could feel every inch of her through it.

She'd touched me on Friday. Accidentally, sure, but a guy gets what he can get when and where he can get it. Someone had jostled her, and she'd fallen forward. I'd caught her, and we'd stayed like that for a moment, chest to chest, belly to belly, and I know—I know—I wasn't the only one who felt something.

I mean, there's no doubt she felt *something*, because yeah, that outfit was thin as paper and I might have had jeans on, but denim can't hide my feelings for her.

But it was more than that. It was beyond that. It was the moment when the socially acceptable mask that Felicity always wears fell away because she was in my arms. It slipped, and I saw it go, and for a moment . . . Felicity Turnado was flustered by me. Did she remember in that moment, another night? A night when I pulled her from the water and defended her life? A night when the two of us became a bonded pair? A sacred, special moment when the universe imploded on itself and became the size of two children who contained everything that ever mattered?

I'm not a child now. Neither is she. And when I find

her, I'm going to make sure we're together. The way we're supposed to be.

"Felicity!" Brynn calls, her voice slicing through my daydream.

To my left, Tress winces. "Are we supposed to be yelling?" Her hand goes to her head, as if she's in pain.

"They didn't say *not* to yell," Brynn says, and sucks in another big breath, cupping her hands around her mouth. "FELICITY!"

Broward—resident genius—weighs in, bellowing, *"FELICITY!"*

In the distance, echoing through the woods, we get a response.

"WILSON!"

"Oh my God," Brynn says, her hands falling in disappointment. "People are so fucking horrible."

Huge kicks at a twig, sends it reeling out of sight. "Why aren't the cops doing more?"

"They can't," I tell him. "They can't use resources unless they have reason to believe there was foul play. And as of right now . . ." I shrug.

"Right," Brynn says. "So the Turnados use their"— she makes air quotes—*"resources* instead."

"Foul play," Tress repeats. She's staring straight down, transfixed by something. Maybe she dropped an Oxy. "How do they decide that?"

"Probably go through her phone," I say, moving forward. The others follow, and I have a moment of intense pride. I'm a leader. Their leader.

"What if they can't find it?" Tress asks.

"I don't think they need the actual phone," I tell her. "They can just get the phone records."

"But would the records actually show what a text said?" Tress asks, frowning, "Like, she sent a text to this number at this time, or would the records actually have what the text—"

"Who the fuck cares!" Brynn suddenly halts in her tracks, screaming up at the sky. "It doesn't matter, you guys," she says adamantly, scanning our faces. "It doesn't matter who she texted, or when, or what she said, or where in the ever-living hell her phone is. Because we're going to find her."

She's stabbing a finger in the air now, pointing at each of us in turn. "We're going to find her, and none of this will matter, okay? Not foul play, not stupid phones or what she drank or what she was wearing or who she was fucking! Okay? It doesn't matter. None of it matters if we find her. And I'm going to. I'm going to find her."

Her voice cracks on the final *her* and tears are running down her face. Tress just stares at Brynn dumbly as Hugh moves in, enfolding her against his barrel chest. She sobs against him, and it would all be very moving except for the fact that Brynn isn't going to find Felicity.

I am.

I am, and Felicity's going to know it was me this time and I will be rewarded. And not just with fifty thousand dollars, thank you very much, but with Felicity herself. Like it's supposed to be. Like it was decided, a long time ago, in the dark, in the night, both of us wet and her bleeding, clinging to me. Needing me.

I sigh. God that was a good night.

She could count on me then. A young Ribbit Usher standing tall, shivering, water running down my goose-bumped skin. Staring down my mother. Defiant. For the first time, ever . . . and the last. I stood in between Felicity and a dark fate, and my will was done.

Not like Friday, when I couldn't even stand. When my will was bent and twisted for the entertainment of others. While my tormentors unspooled me on a livestream, something happened to Felicity, and I wasn't there for her. As her white knight I had only delayed the dark fate from fifth grade, and it had come for her with a gaping maw while I was not there. Not standing watch.

I trip over a stick and stumble forward, only to have a strong arm pull me back.

"You all right?" Tress asks.

"Yeah, I'm . . ." But what am I? Confused. Lost. Directionless. Felicity has been my true north for so

long that I don't know what to do with this rearranged
compass. I'm spinning, searching, waiting for the mag-
netized power of *us* to draw me to her. Then I can tell
her. Explain. Yes, I failed her. But there are reasons.

And one of them is next to me right now.

"Do you know the last time you saw her Saturday?" I
ask Tress. I remember the three of us standing together,
under the makeshift lights, Felicity colorful and vibrant,
her body vibrating with life, filling the air with the
music of bells. Tress, dark and quiet, her hood pulled up
around her face, eyes darting around the room. Watchful. Waiting.

For what?

"Tress?" I ask again, snapping my fingers in front of
her face.

She looks up, seems to struggle to focus on me.
"What?"

"Saturday," I repeat. "When was the last time you saw
Felicity? Your *friend*?"

I hit the last word hard, like maybe she forgot
why we're out here in the middle of nowhere, wearing
T-shirts with a hotline number across the front. Tress
is staring at the ground again, her fists curled inside of
her sleeves.

"The last time I saw my *friend* Felicity was in fifth
grade, through my bedroom window," she says.

A shiver crawls up my spine, quickly chased by a flash of anger. "Stop fucking around," I snap at her.

She raises her head, eyes locking with mine.

"She waved goodbye," Tress says.

That's when I realize Tress is as lost as I am, unfocused, scattered. She was this way on Friday, too. Edgy. Reserved. Not fully present. And then not present at all, when the wolves came for me. The shiver finishes its journey up my spine, hitting my brain stem with a jolt.

I'm asking the wrong questions.

"Where were you?" I ask Tress.

Not *Where was Felicity?* Not *When is the last time you saw her?*

Where were you, Tress? And why did you let that happen to me?

Because the truth is that we wouldn't be out here if I hadn't been piss-ass drunk that night. The truth is that I would never have let anything happen to Felicity if I'd been sober. The truth is that if anybody is to blame for this, it's Tress Montor.

"I was selling," Tress says. "I was doing what I always do."

I accept that with a nod but don't point to it as a half-truth. Because she didn't do what she always does. She left me alone, out of the equation. And that's where things went wrong.

"It's okay," I say out loud, and Tress nods as if she's

been absolved of something.

But she hasn't. Not even close.

I just happened to realize that it's going to be much easier to kill her by Thursday. And that's more than okay. My slate is about to be clean. I'll do my duty to Mother, avenge myself on my enemies, and save the girl. All in the same week. And after that, fate locks into play, sealing Felicity to me.

The combined power of the Usher name and Turnado money will make us a true force in Amontillado. I'll reinforce the crumbling family mansion, fill it with children—all Ushers. Mother will be happy with me, finally. And once Lenore is gone and the children have left, it'll still be me and Felicity, like it's supposed to be.

And everyone else . . . well, everyone else can just burn.

Brynn steps away from Hugh, wiping her eyes dry. She smiles her thanks and he lights up like a candle. A motherfucking candle.

Yes, I think, still watching Huge. *They can burn.*

Chapter 20

Tress

Monday

There's a goddamn pawprint between my feet.

At least, I think there is. I also thought a panther was sitting on my chest last night, so I have reason to doubt my sensory inputs in my current state. And I want to. I want to doubt them severely, because the half-heart pendant resting against my chest is beating—that sound, *thwup, thwup, thwup*—insistent in my ears. I'd like to believe these things aren't true.

My fingers stray toward it, looking for confirmation, and it takes real effort to force my hand down so that the others won't notice. I also hope they don't notice the panther print, because there's a lion with no teeth painted black back home, and that is not going to go over well with anybody if the real panther shows up and we're outed as lion painters.

It's like a lion tamer, but not really.

Oh shit, I'm definitely delirious. I'm not in my right mind, and everyone else around me is. I'm like the drunk at the party who is trying really hard to appear sober by overenunciating. I make a list in my mind of words not to say aloud—*panther, lion, murder.*

Well, that went off the rails.

My hand wanders back to the beating heart at my clavicle, and I force it to reroute, to touch something else. It goes to my head instead, finding the divot where my skull is dented in from falling down the old well in the back of the Usher property when I was little.

I'd landed hard, cold water up to my hips and warm blood running down my neck. Ribbit had been an outline, a shadow high above me, a high voice that yelled, "Are you dead?"

Not *Are you okay? Are you all right? Are you alive?*

No, my cousin had asked me if I was dead.

"I'm not dead," I say now, under my breath, pressing against the irregular spot on my head. Inside my chest, my heart beats in confirmation. Outside, the necklace answers. Between my feet, the panther print remains adamantly real.

"Foul play," someone says, and I look up, my hand falling away from my head. Ribbit—who always seems

to know things, how can he know so many things?—
explains what it takes to determine if foul play was
involved in a disappearance, and suddenly I don't care
about the pawprint. Because it may or may not be there,
but Felicity's phone is a real and physical object. One
that has texts from me and to me, measurements in
ounces and milligrams, meeting spots and drop-offs.
Plus one last, and very final, drop-off.

And I'm an idiot because it never occurred to me to
take Felicity's phone, but I don't think she had it anyway, because that outfit didn't exactly have pockets. And
I'm asking the right questions and Ribbit is answering
them and I am listening but Brynn is very upset and I
can't see her being upset, because I am upset, too. And
Felicity wasn't supposed to die, anyway, and how the
fuck did this all even happen?

Brynn is crying now, and I'm about to cry, too, and
I don't even know why, so I decide to look up instead.
Look up and hope that my tears don't fall out of my
eyes, and suddenly I forget all about crying and my tears
evaporate because I'm staring at the panther.

He's above Brynn and Hugh, sitting idly in an oak,
regal as shit and looking like he should be flanking the
steps of the New York Public Library, not relaxing in
the woods of Amontillado, Ohio. But he is, he's here
(or at least I think he is), and I've got to get Brynn and

Hugh and Ribbit away and make sure nobody else dies because of me.

I do the simplest thing. I walk forward. I put my right arm out to the side, and I steady myself against my cousin, like we were supposed to, like we were told, like I am just following directions and not running from a wild animal (because you don't run, you should never run, it engages the prey drive) and they are following. Our arms are stretched out and our backs are turned to the danger, and we move together, calling a dead girl's name.

I squeeze my eyes shut, and I call for Felicity, and I hope not to hear anything behind me.

Chapter 21

Tress

Monday

Cecil unloads a shotgun at me when I walk through the front door.

I know it's real because there's too much happening simultaneously for me to have imagined it. There's a deafening *bang*, the smell of ignited powder, and the feeling of gritty linoleum against my face as I hit the floor at just the right time.

"What the fuck, Grandpa?!" I yell from the floor. Funny, I pretty much never call him that. For some reason now seemed like a good time.

"Sorry," Cecil says from the couch, calmly loading another round. "Thought you were the cat. Did I get you?"

"No," I say, rubbing my shoulder, which aches from

the impact against the floor. Thank God the only gun Cecil has access to is a .410. I hid his twenty-gauge last summer when he threatened to shoot Rue because she kept making masturbating gestures at him while pointing and laughing. I figured he'd be happy enough to find any gun if he got in a shooting mood, and Rue would be quick enough to get out of the way of a smaller spray of destruction.

"You dead?" Cecil asks, leaning forward to get a better look at me.

"Nope," I say, dragging myself to my feet to confirm it. I'm not, but I'm going to have a hell of a bruise, purple and black at first, then fading to blue and green, finally a sickly yellow. I pull my injured arm to my chest, my pulse beating there, hot and heavy, stirring around who knows what kind of infectious soup.

On second thought, I doubt that bruise gets a chance to reach the yellow stage.

"You went down hard," Cecil observes. "Good reflexes. You're an Allan, girl."

I groan at this old argument. Cecil has thrown it at me more than once, insisting that anything smart I do is because of his blood, while anything stupid is blamed on the polluting Usher influence. The Montor name goes unmentioned, my dad having no part in the genetic battle Cecil imagines being fought inside my bones, the only fight with my grandma he ever had any chance of winning. And maybe it's true. More than once I've caught myself resting my chin in my hands, like Cecil does, or rotating the double joints in my elbows, an Allan mutation we share.

"I saw the cat," I tell him.

He pumps the shotgun, his single eye alight. "Where?"

"Out in the woods, about half a mile from the Allan house," I say, rotating my arm in small circles, shrugging my shoulder to make sure everything still works.

"You do anything about it?" he asks.

"Yeah, Cecil," I say. "I dropped cat treats behind me all the way back home. We're friends now, and he agreed to a lifetime in a cage with no personal benefits whatsoever."

Cecil rests the shotgun across his knees, debating whether I'm being sarcastic or not. It's never been his strong suit. Finally, he grunts.

"If that cat's not in his cage, he best *get* into it. You hear me?"

Honestly, it's a valid question. The thump of the heart is a constant rhythm, one I can't escape. It's low and deep, a pulse not my own, a buried harmony in my bones like white noise.

Thwup, thwup, thwup.

Cecil tightens his grip on the shotgun. "You hear me, girl?"

I open my mouth to reassure him that yes, I can hear

him, but that has no bearing on my inability to retrieve a loose panther, when a car horn blasts from the driveway. It's long and insistent, and whatever argument was about to erupt between us dies with it. I glance out the door—still open, gunshot holes decorating the wall beside it—to see Hugh.

"I got it," I mutter to Cecil.

"It the Feds?"

"No, it's not the— You know what? Get up off your ass and see for yourself!" I yell behind me as I walk to Hugh's car. He rolls down the window, mistrustfully eyeing the painted lion, still lying on her side in the cage.

"Cat's still here," he says, almost to himself.

"Yep," I agree. Technically it's not a lie. "There's a cat here."

He's quiet for a second, staring ahead, over the steering wheel. Hugh doesn't want to look at me, and I know why. A muscle quivers in his jaw, and he's going to say it. Right here, right now.

"Let's go for a ride," I say, beating him to the punch. He nods stiffly, and I get into the passenger seat. Hugh sniffs once, then shoots me a glance.

"Gunpowder?"

"Oh . . . yeah. Cecil took a shot at me."

Hugh choke-laughs. "Holy shit, Tress. Your life. I don't even know."

I start to laugh, too; it's a silent one, rising from my belly and shaking my shoulders. "I don't even know, either, man," I tell him. We're quiet for a moment as Hugh navigates the bridge and we pass the Usher house, cattails from the pond in front blowing their seeds into the wind.

"Ribbit . . . ," he begins, but I hold up a hand. My good one. Well, my better one. The shot didn't get me but my shoulder hurts like hell.

"Don't worry about it," I tell him. "I heard you apologize to him earlier. He's cool with everything, and that's his call. Not mine."

Hugh clenches his jaw, and I realize maybe that wasn't what he was going to say. Maybe it had nothing to do with the party Friday night or the streaming video. The beat of my heart picks up, the necklace fluttering at my collarbone.

"You said you knew where she was," Hugh says.

I take a deep breath, ignoring the specks of black floating in my vision.

"I talked to you on the phone that night and you said you knew where Felicity was."

"Yes," I say. I don't want to lie to him. Hugh is my friend. He's protected me in the past, gone with me to drug drops and handoffs to make sure I was safe, never asking for a cut or anything else in exchange. But he was also dead-ass drunk when we talked, so maybe I can tell a lie without feeling like too much of a liar.

"I did," I tell him. "I knew where she was when we talked."

"I checked my calls," he says. "It was 3:05 a.m."

He turns left, and we're rolling through the middle of town, the one stoplight set to flash orange because it's evening and all the people of Amontillado are at home, eating dinner with their families.

They have those.

"So we know where she was at three in the morning," Hugh goes on. "Which means we only have to narrow down a small window to try and figure out what happened to her."

A small window. Hugh's time frame measures in hours and minutes—after 3:05 a.m. and before eight, when her parents realized she hadn't come home. My timeline uses pain and injuries—after I broke her ankle but before she died and I laid her down in her own puddle of piss and puke.

"Where was she when you saw her?" Hugh asks. He's driving by rote, his hands and feet taking us to his house while his mind is elsewhere. Elsewhere, like mine.

"The basement," I say, and his tight line of a mouth goes a little tighter. I'm sure Brynn has told him that she saw me coming up from the basement, and they both assumed I was dealing down there. And, I kind of was, but we weren't trading cash for drugs.

"Did you see her leave the basement?" Hugh asks now as we pull in to his driveway, the engine idling. The curtain flickers as pale fingers draw it aside. His grandma, who he lives with.

"No," I tell him, eyes still on the window. "I didn't see her leave the basement."

Technically true.

He kills the engine, his eyes wide and on mine. "Oh my God, Tress . . . You don't think . . . ? I mean, they would've checked before they knocked the house down, right? Like they would have made sure there wasn't still some kid in there, passed out."

"I'm sure they would have checked," I say. And I am. And I am also sure they saw nothing in the basement except a nicely laid wall of brick. I finished it before I left, tucking my mortar pail and trowel neatly into the corner. Sloppy work gets you killed around wild animals, and my good habits extend to when I'm the danger in the room.

"Okay . . ." Hugh's hands relax on the wheel, the imprints of his thick fingers left behind when he pulls away. "Well, that's a relief."

I'm sure it is. I'm sure it's nice to have horror removed from your world so easily.

"What did you sell her?" Hugh asks. "Do you think she OD'd?"

"No," I snap. "I would never sell her enough to kill her."

He doesn't have a response to that. Hugh's seen me sell enough to kill an elephant to a lone dude, but he won't call me out on it. His phone rattles in the cupholder, and he looks down at it. It's a text from Brynn, but I can't see what it says. He thumbs through the phone, cracks his door.

"Me and Brynn are going back out," he says. "Want to come?"

"Where?" I ask, thinking of the cat. Patient and waiting.

"Different quadrant," Hugh says, scrolling through Brynn's text. It's a huge rectangle on his phone, a massive diatribe. He smiles to himself.

"She says Gretchen and David were probably just fucking where they were supposed to search so we should go there. I gotta get a shower. You want to come in?"

Not really. No, in fact. I don't. I don't want to make small talk with Hugh's grandma while he showers and then return to the woods as a dynamic duo, dedicated to finding something they're never going to find. But the front of Hugh's shirt is still stiff with Brynn's tears, and I don't want to be more of a detriment to the world than I already am.

"Sure," I say. But Hugh doesn't move, instead goes back to staring out the windshield, his wrist loose and bent across the top of the steering wheel.

"She has seizures," he says quietly. "Did you know?"

"Your grandma? Yeah, you've said before."

"No." Hugh shakes his head. "Felicity. She's an epileptic. I guess . . . she must not have told you."

No. She hadn't told me. She hadn't told me because we weren't friends anymore. But that's not why I thought he was talking about his grandma when he mentioned the seizures. It's because he used the present tense. And I'm the only person who knows Felicity Turnado should only be spoken about in the past tense.

Now, and forevermore.

Chapter 22

Rue

HorseStripe complains, long-winded,
from the pasture. LongBird yells
a song, not pleasant.
Another sound—BANG—from the human cage
my girl, FoundChild, falls.
No-you-cannot-take-her
No empty-arms for me again.
GrayMan, OneEye, DrinkSmell,
New handwords, hand to throat.
(KILL HER. SMELL THAT? LIAR.)
Watch and learn the
human things. All bad.
Dirty things. Filthy creatures.
(MAKE IT QUICK. GOOD KID. BAD
LUCK.)

Metal comes, car sound. Man-thing.
Big. Like me. Lip curl, smile, handwords.
Hello, I love you, I am me.
FoundChild goes, but it is near dark,
Time for BlackSmoothShine
And quiet steps.

Chapter 23

Tress

Monday

"Grandma?" Hugh yells when we walk in the house, but nobody answers. I remember seeing the ghostly white hand at the curtain, but I don't mention it when he says she must be asleep. It's totally possible I hallucinated it.

He tells me he's running upstairs to hop in the shower—a phrase I used all the time, too, until Felicity teased me about it. (*Are you actually going to hop in the shower? That sounds dangerous. You might slip.*) Hugh takes the stairs two at a time, the whole house shuddering as he does. I sit on the couch, thumbing through my own phone. There's a missed call from a number I don't recognize right away, but then it hits me. It's April Turnado. Felicity and I used to sing her number to the tune of the Russian Dance from *The Nutcracker*, a show we'd seen together every Christmas, Felicity entranced by the dancers' tutus, me laser-focused on the painful contortions of their feet. April's number flashes at me now, Tchaikovsky running through my head (*five, five, five, one, one, one, one / five, five, five, one, one, one, one*).

It's not one missed call from April; there three. All right on top of one another, but she didn't leave a voice mail. That means she's panicked enough to call me but not desperate enough to leave a message. I'm guessing the well-put-together woman from this afternoon got a dose of reality and has come to the conclusion that her daughter might not be so easily recoverable after all. I doubt there are more megaphones and white sneakers in her future. More like Xanax and some triple sec.

"Annabelle?"

I look up, startled. Hugh's grandma is standing in the doorway to the kitchen, holding on to the frame like she might collapse. I remember her from Amontillado Elementary, back when we had a school nurse. She would dole out Band-Aids and suckers to kids with scrapes, let us rest an extra fifteen minutes on the cot if we asked nicely. I jump up to help her, but she backs away, clawed hands holding her robe closed at the throat.

"Annabelle?" she says again, eyes searching my face.

This isn't new to me. I know I look exactly like my mom, and Cecil has been drunk enough to call me by her name more than once. But Hugh's grandma doesn't have the decaying breath of an alcoholic, so I'm guessing dementia might be an issue.

"No, Mrs. Hannah," I say. "I'm—

"You fucking whore," she says, her face pulling into a sneer. "Annabelle Usher, get your filthy, cock-sucking mouth out of my house!"

I'm stunned. My stomach bottoms out, and my heart skips a beat, pitter-pattering in my chest. The disembodied beat continues, unperturbed. *Thwup, thwup, thwup.* My hand goes to my neck, pulling out the charm, holding it as if for comfort.

"What?" I ask, the one word dry and fluttering.

"What?" she mimics back at me, high-voiced and mocking. "I'm Annabelle Usher, and I don't understand bad words."

"I'm not . . ." My dry tongue sticks to the roof of my mouth. I swallow and try again. "I'm not Annabelle."

But she's not listening. Her eyes are on my hand, where the heart pendant dangles. "You took it!" She backs farther away, one bony finger pointing in accusation. "You took it back!"

"What? I don't . . ."

"Best friends forever!" She's doing the high, singsong, mocking voice again, her mouth twisted into a horrible grimace. "Shared everything, didn't you?" She moves in closer, not scared of me anymore, her apparent rage outranking it. *"Didn't you?"*

Her breath is hot in my face, weirdly pleasant with

the smell of butterscotch, the thin disc of a dissolving Werther's on her tongue. Upstairs, I hear the water turn off, the sound of Hugh rolling back the shower door. His grandma moves eerily fast, my hand suddenly in her firm grip. She twists my wrist, but I'm angry now, too. And I'm not giving up this necklace.

It beats in my hand, stoically. We stare each other down, her eyes old and rheumy, mine burning with fever.

"Fine." She snaps in disgust. "Keep it. But you should have the rest." She backs away from me, finger stiff and accusatory again. "You should have all of it!"

She slips past me, careful not to turn her back as she goes, disappearing down the hallway and ducking into a bedroom. Hugh comes thundering down the steps, water still running from his hair.

"Ready?" he asks me, quickly followed by, "What's wrong?"

"Nothing, it's . . ."

His grandma is back, hustling down the hallway and carrying an old shoebox. "Here," she says, shoving it at me. "Take it. I don't want it in my house!"

"Grandma," Hugh begins, but she turns her fury at him.

"I don't want it in my house!"

"Just take it," he mutters to me, and I do, tucking it under my arm. We turn to leave, and he puts himself in between me and her, a hand on my shoulder, guiding me to the door, even though I can see well enough where I'm going.

In the car, he rests his forehead against the wheel.

"Sorry," he says. "Must be one of her bad days."

"It's okay," I say, looking down at the shoebox in my lap. It's for a pair of LA Gear high-tops, pink and white. Ladies size 9.

"You can just leave it in the car," he says, following my gaze.

"No." I run my finger along the edge of the cardboard. Frayed and discolored. Somebody opened this box a lot. And came back to it. Again and again. "She wanted me to have it."

"Whatever, dude," Hugh says, backing out of the driveway. "I hear the nineties are back. Hope they're your size."

"Can you just take me home?" I ask suddenly, and he shoots me a look. "I don't think I want to . . ." (*be in the woods, look for a dead girl, pretend to be okay*).

"Sure," he says. "No problem. Sorry about . . . sorry about that."

He thinks it's his grandma that spooked me, and he's half right. What's really got my attention is the weight of the box in my hands. I don't know what's in it, but it's not a pair of shoes.

And whatever it is, she wanted Annabelle Usher to have it.

Chapter 24

Ribbit

Monday

I didn't find Felicity.

It's a failure, one that sinks like a stone into my gut as I make my way down to the river. A scree goes out from under my feet and I snag a tree to keep from falling. Once I'm steady, I start out again, more carefully this time, picking my way like one of Tress's wild animals.

The search for Felicity had started like some kind of bizarre game sponsored by the local printer that had donated the T-shirts. All of Amontillado had spanned out, trusting that goodwill and group effort would save the day. Snacks had been distributed, goodie bags that had included a laminated sticker that read *I Helped Find Felicity!*

But a pall had fallen by the evening, as the sun sank and grids were crossed and recrossed. The snacks had been digested, and the energy they divested spent, no goal in sight as Felicity refused to surface. The gift bags rest in the bottom of trash cans now across the homes in Amontillado, and most of the stickers had blown away on the wind, to be used by squirrels and birds to line nests. They'll provide some comfort this winter, a little bit of warmth declaring that wildlife helped find Felicity. And I have to admit that as the clock ticks, it's possible that they might be the only ones that ever do.

Shit. SHIT.

Panic spikes in my chest, hot like vomit. I take a deep breath, analyze the loss of the day and the role I played in it. Granted, I'm not the only one who failed. We all managed to *not* find Felicity, and Brynn had been heart-broken, burying her face against Huge a second time while Tress and I looked at our feet.

It was hard for Brynn, I know. She's a good person, and she truly loves Felicity. But it didn't hit her the way it hit me. Felicity is my future and my fate, and I can't be rewarded by her if I can't find her. I get down to the river and make my way to a large, flat boulder that juts out from the water, a place for turtles and snakes to sun. A place to haul a soaking body, have a rest, catch your breath. It's twilight, and I slip my sandals off, the rock still warm from the sun. It's stupidly sentimental to come here, as if I can save Felicity twice in the same place, just because I will it.

But the will of an Usher is an unbendable thing.

I take a deep breath, calming myself, diving deep within to access my true center, which always points to Felicity.

"Where are you?" I ask.

I close my eyes and think, calling up Felicity's face, the curve and planes, the perfect geometry of it. Her hair, each curl. The dimple in her left cheek, no . . . that's as she's facing me, so it's her *right* cheek. There . . . there. That's Felicity, I can see her in my head so clearly that the world seems empty and useless when I open my eyes and she's not there.

Someone else is, though.

"Hello!" the woman calls to me from the other bank, and I jump, one foot skidding off the rock and into the water.

"Jesus!" The cold current sends the word hissing through my teeth.

"Didn't mean to startle you," the woman says, and I wave her off, hoping that she didn't catch the stark moment of pure rage that undoubtedly crossed my face. She caught me off guard, threw me. Saw me as I actually am.

That's not good.

And neither is this woman. One glance and I know

she's not from around here, and not only because I don't recognize her face. Her clothes are all black, and she's wearing pumps in the woods. I glance up at the bridge and see a silver BMW idling there.

"Are you Kermit? Kermit Usher?" she asks, taking a step closer to the river. One heel sinks into the mud, and I get about two seconds to pull myself together while she struggles with it.

"Why are you asking?" I call back, retreating to my bank, leaving the rock behind. Mud squishes between my toes, but I don't look down for my sandals. I keep my eyes on her. Because unless she's here about my Harvard application—and I doubt that—this woman is trouble.

"I need to talk to you," she says. "It's about your cousin, Tress."

Oh. Fuck. She is definitely not here about college applications if she wants to talk about Tress. I grab my shoes but don't put them on.

"I can't talk to you," I tell her, trying to keep an *apologetic* tone in my voice. And I am. I'm extremely sorry that somebody probably smelled an acre of marijuana and called the Feds. Because that land might belong to Cecil, but the acre next to it has things on it that nobody needs to know about.

And I mean, *nobody.*

"I'll only take a minute of your time," the woman

calls, taking a step closer, out into the water. She's got her pumps in her hand now and damn if she isn't dead-eyeing me. I wouldn't be surprised if she jumped in the water and baby-sharked over here and took my head right off my body, just like Cecil's crocodile.

Oh, shit. The animals.

Maybe it's not about the back acre. I remember the black tea bottle Tress had turned in her hands, questioning who was monitoring their property. I thought she was stoned at the time, but this woman looks like she might be exactly the type to pay top dollar for non-GMO, responsibly sourced tea, and then toss it into a country ditch for some 4-H trash basher to pick up later.

"I don't have a minute," I tell her, scrambling up the bank. "I can't talk to you."

"Why not, Ribbit?" she calls, her voice lingering on my nickname. A flush heats my neck, and I turn to face her, grabbing a tree for support.

"Because . . . because . . . you're a stranger."

Jesus. I sound like I'm fucking five. But she's got me by the balls, and I'd much rather have my balls under my own control.

"Cecil keeps Tress on a tight leash, too," she says, ignoring my comment. "I haven't been able to speak to her. I was hoping you could help me with that."

"No, no, I can't help you," I say, turning again and lunging my way up the ravine. Leaves and rocks slide out from under my feet, and I go down onto my belly, knocking the wind out of me. Rage swells, hot and heavy, bulging up into my throat. I am going to be in so much trouble. Mother is going to be so mad at me.

I can't mess things up again. Can't be the reason everything goes wrong, *again*. I screwed up—badly—in fifth grade, and I've been failing at my job ever since, and I didn't find Felicity today and dammit, I am so tired of being wrong. Of being a failure. Of smiling while I do it.

I see the edge of my roof as I struggle for the top of the ridge, and a calm spreads through my body at the sight. I can make it. I can make it to the Usher house and rush inside, like Tress and I used to do whenever we heard a car coming. We were so accustomed to our solitude, to having everything to ourselves, that the sound of an engine sent us panicking, diving for cover. No one could see us. No one who wasn't family.

We told each other it was a game. We laughed while we hid.

I'm not laughing now, and the woman behind me is not an Usher. I crest the hill and turn to tell her to go away, that she is not welcome here, but she's gone. On the bridge, the BMW comes to life, lights flicking on. She drives away, past the house, giving me a jaunty, high-pitched, expensive-sounding toot of the horn.

I wave reflexively, every cell of my body trained to be polite, do the right thing, be helpful. I hate myself for it. As the red taillights fade away I put my hands to my mouth and yell, "Littering is a five-hundred-dollar fine!"

It's a terrible comeback. Tress would have told her to fuck herself with her expensive shoes and put them back on. I pulled out village code.

I wipe the dirt from my knees, straighten my shirt. Exhale once, sharply, to get the river out of my nose, clear my senses. I have to go inside and talk to Mother. Tell her someone is asking questions.

Mother will know what to do.

She always does.

Chapter 25

Tress

Monday

I check out my bruised shoulder in the mirror, but the damage doesn't seem to be more than skin-deep. My left arm is a different story. It pulses bright and hot, my skin warm and puffy around the silver edges of tape. I tell my blue-tinged fingers to move, and they do, but barely. The red streaks of infection have begun their march back to the line I drew, advancing faster than before.

I scour Cecil's room and find all kinds of things (porn, a rubber-band ball, a molar with the filling still in it), but no more antibiotics. I won't be much use to anybody, and soon, if I don't get some medical attention for my arm.

I take the shoebox Mrs. Hannah gave me and head

out to the pens, knowing the animals respect my privacy far more than Cecil does. I slump to the ground, my back resting against Rue's cage, box across my knees. Her strong hands reach, feel my shoulders, flutter to my hair.

"Hey, Rue," I say quietly. "Hey, pretty girl."

She finds a knot in my back and begins to work on it, easing out my kinks. I take a deep breath and open the box. Inside I find four journals. They are small and spiral-bound, with hearts, unicorns, rainbows, and a Pegasus in a violent array of colors. It's so visually jarring I have to wonder if I stepped on a tab of acid in Cecil's room. But the hearts aren't pulsing and the unicorns aren't talking to me, so I figure I'm good.

Next to the journals is a flat, green, velvet-covered box. My hand goes back to the necklace at my throat, and the steady beat there seems to have increased, *thwup, thwup, thwup.* I hold the jewelry box, my hands shaking. I fumble with the clasp, flipping it open, but I don't raise the lid. I can't.

Rue's arms reach around me, take the box, and open it.

My hands fall into my lap. Useless.

It's empty, all that's left is the thin, filmy green outline of a cheap charm. The other half of the Best Friends necklace I'm wearing. Why would Hugh Broward's grandma have this?

Rue tosses it aside, uninterested.

To her, it's an empty box.

To me, it's another piece of a puzzle I've been trying to solve since I was eleven.

Hugh answers on the first ring.

"Change your mind?" I hear brush crackling, and Brynn asking who it is.

"What? No," I say quickly. I forgot they were going back out to look for Felicity. Back out into the woods where I saw a panther just a few hours ago.

Shit.

"Listen, your grandma—"

"Yeah, sorry about that . . ." There's a lot of rustling, and I imagine him walking farther away from Brynn, dropping his voice.

"No, it's fine. But weird question, did your mom know my mom?" I ask, which is a dumb question. Everyone knows everyone in Amontillado. I try again, am more specific. "Were they friends?"

This time the silence stretches longer. When he speaks, it's just the one word. "Why?"

"Nothing, never mind," I say. "I gotta go. Stay close to Brynn. And you guys should get inside."

I don't know why I tell him to stay close to her. Hugh might be massive, but the panther doesn't care how much he can deadlift.

"Tress, wait—"

I hang up. Rue takes my phone from me, an old game that stopped being funny when she used one of my burners to dial a repeat customer and screeched at him for ten minutes. I get up, dusting the dirt from my knees. Rue puts my phone to her ear, mimics listening really hard, then looks at me intently, and draws a finger across her throat.

"What?" I ask, alarmed. "Why would you . . . Rue—why did you do that?"

Rue reaches out, gently touches my left hand, brings my arm up to the cage. She sniffs it, then signs at me—*Danger, danger, danger.* She draws her finger across her throat again and signs, *Danger, danger, danger.* Then points at the cat cage and signs again.

"Yeah, I know. He's still out there," I tell her. "And so are Hugh and Brynn. I've got to go back out, got to . . ."

Got to what? Offer myself up, instead? Have a heart-to-heart with the panther? The last time I tried that he opened up my arm.

"I don't know," I finally say, raising my eyes to meet Rue's. "I don't know what to do."

But there's a heart beating at my chest, one that isn't in rhythm with my own.

I grab the dart gun from the storage shed, checking my shots. I've got three. With shaky hands and a fevered gaze, trying to hit a panther in the dark is about as likely as my parents materializing out of the woods to tell me everything is okay and they're here to take me home. But it's what I've got to do right now.

I tuck the shoebox underneath the passenger seat of Cecil's truck and take off without telling him what I'm doing. There's no need. He knows. I'm doing what I usually do. I'm doing my job. I'm looking after the animals—and if that means hunting a hunter, then I'll play the game.

I rest my arm on top of the steering wheel and head out to where I spotted the cat this afternoon, the grid that the four of us had been assigned to. I'm an idiot. This is stupid. It's probably how I die. I glance at my blue fingers, feel the thump of my pulse in my arm.

At least the cat will kill me quick.

Chapter 26

Rue

Find her pain, with my hand

Felt in hair, before. Now, real skin and muscle.

Touch the pain, smooth the ache.

(HOW MUCH? LIFE'S CHEAP. DEATH AND TAXES.)

Tell my girl, use GrayMan handwords

Hand to throat

Danger, danger, danger

(I DON'T KNOW. BASTARD ALMOST GOT ME. SOON.)

FoundChild goes again, away.

Far, like the one, from me.

Inside me, then gone.

LostChild. Empty-arms.

A man took her.

A man.

Fire inside. Fingers on cage.

Curl and scream.

Rage and ruin.

Danger, danger, danger

A man cannot have my girl.

Not again.

Chapter 27

Tress

Monday

He's waiting for me, like he knew I'd come back.

The moon is out, brightly painting everything silver. He sits at the foot of the tree, tail curled around his front paws, ears flicking at my approach. I stop twenty yards away, and raise the dart gun, sighting him in. The cat makes eye contact with me and yawns.

"I'm not fucking around," I tell him, and he raises a paw to clean it, teeth digging in between the pads.

"Fine," I mutter, raising the air rifle to my shoulder, wincing a little as the butt settles against the bruise. There's not a ton of recoil from a CO_2 cartridge, but this is still going to hurt.

"You're an asshole, you know that?" I tell the cat. He stares back at me, right down the barrel. I pull the trigger and there's a metallic click that makes one of his ears flick toward me, but nothing else. The CO_2 cartridge must be empty.

"Shit," I say, looking at the gun in my hands. Unless I want to try throwing these darts, everything I brought with me is useless.

The cat comes to his feet, stretches, his back arching and every hair standing out brightly in the moonlight. He strolls toward me silently, each movement smooth and supple, his shoulder blades rising and falling. I back up a few steps, and the cat slips past me, sparing me a sidelong glance. He pauses, looks back over his shoulder.

"What?" I ask. He takes a few steps, turns again, to see if I'll follow. I look down at the pawprint beneath my feet, each pad standing out distinctly, the weight of a two-hundred-pound killing machine pressing it into the earth. I step over it, matching the panther's stride. He moves forward again, no longer checking my progress.

Against my skin, the heart beats faster, and the panther speeds up, easing into a lope. I clutch the heart, feel the cheap copper quivering in my fist. I break into a run, following the cat as he moves through the brush, rifle slung over my shoulder. My breath is ragged and sharp in my throat, bile rising in my stomach.

"Wait," I call to the cat, but the heart in my hand is pushing incessantly against my fingers, urging me on and forward. Ahead of me, the cat breaks into a clearing, and I follow, stopping to catch my breath when I emerge from the trees.

A bulldozer and a backhoe stand, still and ominous, sentinels in the dark. In the woods, something cries out and is suddenly hushed by something larger. I edge forward to where the cat sits, patient at the edge of a newly filled hole. I stagger to him, falling onto my knees, the heart beating so loudly I can hear nothing but its rhythm. Fanatic. Insistent.

Thwup, thwup, thwup.

This is what's left of the Allan house, a still-settling hole filled with bricks, shattered remains of abandoned antiques, and at least one massive grandfather clock. I wonder if it chimed as it fell, still tolling backward as it had on Friday. I settle on my knees across from the cat, useless and burnt out. The rifle slips from my shoulder, and I let it fall, clattering to the ground like a child's toy. His gaze flicks to it, then back to my face, the moon burning in his eyes.

I'm mesmerized, staring and lost, the heart pounding against my chest, a pace no human could match without exploding. The cat is utterly still but I'm falling, slumping to the right and coming to rest against the side of the Allan house, the bricks cool and solid against my cheek.

But it's gone, these bricks are under the ground at our feet, buried and forgotten, Amontillado moving on with forced smiles and plastered goodwill. But they're also here, solid and insistently real. The cat holds my gaze, unmoving, and I try to speak, look for words to form questions. But I have none, despite the inexplicability of the situation. The Allan house is both here and not here, two parallel and contradicting realities.

Last year Cecil and I had fallen into the habit of turning the TV on in the dark winter evenings to catch the national news. We watched the screen together, not talking, relishing the only escape from Amontillado either of us would ever know. There had been a piece about NASA scientists in Antarctica who believed they had found a parallel universe that mirrored ours, only with time running backward.

Cecil had grunted, draining off the last of another beer. "If I could go there I'd find myself, tell him not to marry your grandma."

My own thoughts had been bleary and half-formed, the neck of my own beer warm in my hands. I didn't usually drink, but Zee the zebra had stepped on my foot at feeding time, and alcohol took the edge off. I'd run my thumb over the label, fanning the thin paper. "But if you didn't marry Grandma, I wouldn't exist," I'd argued. "My mom wouldn't exist."

Cecil had twisted the top off a new beer, relishing the first swig. "She doesn't exist now, kid."

"But I do," I say now, my face grinding against brick, the words echoing back to me, reaffirming the presence of both me and the wall, two things that should not be here together, at this time and in this place. The cat lowers his head, eyes still on mine, his massive skull almost touching my knees. He chuffs once, disturbing the dirt and sending a dark cloud into the air. Coal dust.

"No," I say. "No."

But the heart pushes back, insisting with each thump—*yes, yes, yes.* A matching rhythm finds it, one that rises from the coal chute, Felicity's necklace pulsing in time with mine. It's down there, with her. But only one heart beats in that darkness.

"I didn't mean to," I tell the cat. "I didn't want—"

Something cracks in the woods, and the cat jumps, startled. His eyes break with mine, and the house is gone, the heart quiet in my hand. The moon bounces madly off machinery, bright pinpoints of light that my eyes attempt to follow, trying to understand.

"What?" I ask, but the cat is gone, bounded silently away to leave me here, on my knees, next to the old coal chute that my friend lies at the bottom of.

"I'm so sorry," I say quietly, my voice odd and alien here in the woods. I fall forward, shaking, my face pressed against the ground. My mouth is stuck open, a black cave for my grief and guilt to pour out of, and it does. Retching, I scream.

"*I'M SORRY, FELICITY! I'M SO SORRY!*"

And very quietly, her voice rises. "Tress?"

Jesus. Jesus fucking Christ. I scuttle backward on hands and feet, fresh agony tearing up my arm, but I don't care, can't care. There is nothing in the woods but me and madness, and I have to leave this place, have to escape before I lose my mind completely. I hit the brush at a run, brambles tearing my hair out at the temple, blackberries snagging my legs and leaving scratches behind that circle my legs like decoration.

I run blindly, madly, catching a glimpse of the panther keeping pace beside me, long velvet-black legs eating distance. I stumble onto the road and throw myself into the truck, panting behind the wheel.

The cat does not follow, if he was ever there at all.

Felicity does not appear from the woods, pale and ghostlike, a pointed finger accusing me.

"It's okay," I tell myself. "You're okay."

But against my skin, the heart picks up a beat.

Chapter 28

Ribbit

Tuesday

I have so, so many things to do today.

First, I need to find Tress. I didn't want to risk calling or texting her about the woman I saw at the river. Tress has not exactly been reliable lately. She zoned out entirely during the search for Felicity, her eyes blank and staring. And I noticed when I drove past Amontillado Animal Attractions on the way to school this morning that Zee—usually impeccable in presentation—definitely needs a brushing. If Tress is letting the animals slip, something is not right. And I am not relishing the fact that I get to tell her there's more wrong in our world than whatever is going on with her. But also, she has only two days to live, so what's a little more stress?

I've also got to figure out who I'm twinning with today. I didn't bother asking anyone to actually be my twin, because that stuff gets figured out days ahead of time, and I wasn't the kind of guy anyone wanted to be mistaken for before this weekend. My newfound viral fame might have helped me land a twin for spirit week, but the timing was all wrong. So instead I've got a handful of old Amontillado Ravens jerseys I found at the thrift store. I can scan the crowd, find someone else sporting the same year, and pop it on, claiming them as my twin if someone asks.

As always, I will be condoned, but not included.

I spot Tress making her way to the girls' bathroom and snag her arm before she ducks in. Her backpack slips off her shoulder to land awkwardly in the crook of her elbow, and she yelps in pain.

"Sorry!" I say, immediately backing up. She's pale under her tan, with the flush of a fever just rising on her cheekbones. "Jesus, Tress, are you okay?"

"No," she says simply, honest as always.

"Sorry, but I've got something to tell you that won't exactly make your day better."

Tress nods, unsurprised. Her life has taken so many turns for the worse I guess at some point you just don't expect the road signs to offer you anything better. We duck under the stairwell, near the lost-and-found box. There are a handful of dead cell phones, some hoodies with plenty of wear left in them, a pair of expensive earbuds with nothing wrong other than a little earwax. My classmates lost these things. Lost them and didn't even care enough to check in, just bought replacements and moved on. I glance down at my shoes, at the spot where my big toe is close to busting out the front.

Fuckers.

"What?" Tress asks. "Hurry up, I've got to—"

"Someone's looking for you," I blurt out, and her irritation evaporates instantly, her eyes narrowing and the dullness of them replaced with a snap and a spark. There's Tress. There's my cousin. There's a girl that just never fucking quits or gives up. Or fails. Or dies.

Mother is going to have my hide if I don't take care of that soon.

"What do you mean? What did they want?" she asks.

I give her a quick rundown, her fever spots burning brighter as I explain about the woman, her city clothes and expensive car, her questions about Tress, and the statement that Cecil keeps her on a tight leash.

"I don't have a damn leash," Tress growls, and I immediately nod, acquiesce, show my belly. *I am beta, please don't hurt me.*

"Totally," I say. "But I got the idea she wants to talk to you without Cecil around, you know?"

It's Tress's turn to nod, slowly. "And he hardly ever leaves the property," she says, almost to herself. Her eyes cut to the side, charting out the hallway, as if she expects the woman to materialize there. "I don't think she can talk to me unless I agree to it, or have a lawyer or an adult present. I'm a minor."

"For a little longer," I agree. I think of Thursday, marked in red on my calendar at home. With a bull's-eye.

"I don't have to talk to her and she can't make me," Tress says again, eyes closed, like she's giving herself a pep talk. "Did you tell Lenore?" Followed quickly by "What did she say?"

Because of course I talked to Mother, and Tress already knows that. Knows that I went running to Mommy the second I got scared.

"She said the woman wasn't police or she would've flashed a badge," I tell her.

"Or a Fed?" Tress asks, her eyes begging me to say the right thing, know the answer that will make her feel better. I can do that, can repeat Mother's reassuring words. My chest puffs out a little, happy to be leaned on, to be needed. Even if I am just a repeating puppet.

"Mother said if the woman was law enforcement of any type she can question you if she thinks you're involved in a crime, minor or not. But she said—"

Tress has gone white. She leans against the wall, and slides to the floor, accidentally tearing free a spirit week poster reminding everyone about the bonfire tomorrow night. I don't need to be reminded. I know exactly when it is, and how much time is left.

"A crime?" Tress repeats, looking up at me, her eyes

huge and round in her face.

"Tress, it's okay. Calm down." I crouch next to her. "Mother said she's probably just a reporter, following up on the—"

"Yeah." Tress waves a hand, dismissing my utter internet humiliation with a wave. Anger spikes in my gut, bright and flaring. She was supposed to spare me that. "But what if that's not it?"

"I don't know," I tell her. And it's true.

There's a running list, constantly updated, of things I know and things I don't. I keep a similar tabulation of things Tress knows, and things she doesn't. For example, she doesn't know about the back acre of Amontillado Animal Attractions and what it hides. I do. She doesn't know if her parents are alive or dead, or where they might be. I am well aware of both of these things, and keeping them from her has been a relatively simple matter throughout most of childhood. Wide eyes. Somber nods. An offer to help search the vernal pools on the Usher property in seventh grade, ending badly with both of us covered in leeches. Mother's exasperated sighs as she tore them from our bodies, bloody mouth suckers, spinning, searching for purpose.

So great has my grasp been on forbidden knowledge that it has never occurred to me that Tress might know some things I don't. But suspicion had prickled my skin when she slid to the floor, already pale face slipping into gray as she went. Tress doesn't act like this. Tress doesn't waver and fall, sink to the ground or look to me for reassurance. Tress means what she says and does what she wants, without apology.

Except, she did apologize. Sunday. She said she was sorry for leaving me to the masses, letting me get drunk. She's always bailed me out in the past, pulled me away before things got out of control. Except for the major exception of Friday night, when all the shit hit the fan and Tress wasn't there to help with splatter control.

And why is she so worried about this woman? I knew it might ruffle her, but Tress Montor just literally collapsed at the word *crime*, and she's been committing them on a fairly regular basis since she was thirteen, so unless something major happened—

Wait.

Something *did* happen. My spine straightens. My eyes narrow. I become Ribbit from fifth grade, cold and wet. But not scared. Not at all. Not of Mother, and not of Tress. Not anymore.

"Tress?" I ask, my voice a thin wire. "Did you—"

A shriek emits from farther down the hallway near the entrance; a crowd suddenly gathers. Laughter swells, rolling toward us. I immediately flush and smile, drop my shoulders instinctively. It takes a moment for me to realize they're not laughing at me. Can't be, as I huddle here with Tress in the corner beside the bathrooms.

"I didn't mean to scare you," I tell her, sliding back in my role of outwardly assuming I am slightly wrong at all times. "I just thought you should know about this woman looking for you. It could be about the cat; it could be . . ."

"The weed, yeah." Tress waves her hand again, blithely, like an acre of marijuana is not that big of a deal.

"Okay." Tress nods, pulling herself together. "It's probably either a reporter or some animal-rights person, then." She exhales once, sharply, like I did after leaving the river behind me. I wonder what smell Tress is trying to clear from her mind, and how long it's been lodged there. Since Friday?

"I don't have to talk to her," Tress says, but the words are only for herself. Her eyes are unfocused again, her hand going to clutch at something under her sweatshirt.

"*What the hell is this?*" someone—I think it's Brynn—shrieks. Phones are coming out near the front doors, and whatever is going on has everyone's full attention. I hold out a hand to help Tress up from the floor, but she comes to her feet on her own. She's wobbly, but she manages.

"I'm going to puke," she informs me, and ducks into the bathroom. Moments later, Principal Anho's voice comes over the loudspeaker.

"*Tress Montor, please come to the office. You have a visitor.*"

Chapter 29

Tress

Tuesday

I lose my breakfast in about twenty seconds.

Not that there was a ton in my gut to begin with. I ate something because Rue mimed it at me from her cage and then threatened to throw shit at me if I didn't. I carried a bowl of oatmeal outside and sat in front of her so she could watch me eat it. Then she told me *Danger, danger, danger,* and acted like she was using a phone again. I didn't understand then, but I think I do now.

Rue was trying to tell me about the woman.

I also understand that oatmeal really is the worst thing to vomit back up.

I flush the toilet and rock back onto my heels, pulling my backpack around and unzipping the front pocket. The brightly decorated journals fall out, brilliantly harsh under the fluorescent lights of the bathroom. It's the only reason I came to school today. Cecil would be way too curious if I stayed home and shut my door. This is the only place I can assume some privacy. The only place I can figure out why Hugh's grandma wanted my mom to have these notebooks. These notebooks that she kept next to the empty jewelry box that once held the other half of my heart necklace . . . both of which my mother gave to me, already old, used, copper and cheaply green at the edges. I'd kept one and handed the other to Felicity Turnado the night my parents disappeared.

"Who had the other part of your mom's necklace?" Felicity had asked, pulling hers over her head. "And why did they give it back?"

I didn't know then and hadn't cared. Today, I know who had it—Hugh Broward's mom. And I care about why she gave it back.

I care a lot.

I've got study hall first period and already told the monitor I was going to the library—which had been my original plan until Ribbit hijacked my morning and made the bathroom my new study hall. I lean back against the stall and grab a spiral-bound notebook at random. It's the one with a Pegasus riding on a rainbow, a trail of multicolored hearts rising from her back for no discernable reason.

I'm hit with a wall of beautifully looped handwriting. Cursive. My mother's. I'd recognize it anywhere. It takes my breath away, recalling birthday cards with puppies blowing air horns, kittens wrapped up in streamers, a folded twenty-dollar bill inside and the words: *Happy Birthday, Tress! Mommy and Daddy love you!*

These words are in the same handwriting, but they are very different.

Did you see that fucking bitch? What the hell is she wearing? What a hoochbag.

"Hoochbag?" I say aloud to myself.

"Tress Montor, please come to the office. You have a visitor." Anho's voice fills the bathroom, bouncing off the stalls. I snap the journal shut, but not before catching a glimpse of the next line, written in a different hand.

Don't bug out on her. Devon just kicked her to the curb.

I fan the pages, looking for dates, but there's nothing. It's just a notebook that apparently my mom and Hugh's mom passed back and forth. I remember Hugh's grandma shoving the shoebox into my hands, telling me to *take it.*

"Oh . . . ," I say, figuring it out. "It's like they were texting."

I imagine our moms passing each other in these same hallways, handing off the journals, jotting notes to each other in class.

"Tress Montor, please come to the office."

Anho does not sound nearly as calm as she did the first time, and I hear a high-pitched yell before she cuts off the comm. My phone vibrates in my hand. It's a text from Hugh.

Dude. Brynn set up a vigil for Felicity outside, like with candles in school colors and shit.

That's nice and all, but I couldn't care less right now.

Gretchen hijacked it. Said each candle sold was a vote for homecoming queen. Black for Gretchen. Purple for Brynn.

I stare at Hugh's text, at a loss for words. I tap out something, then give up and just dial him instead.

"What is actually wrong with her?" I ask.

"I can't diagnose her, because I'm not a doctor. But I'd say that she's a bitch," Hugh says. "I don't know if there's a medical term—"

"Listen," I interrupt him. "Can you do me a favor?"

"Yeah, sure. What?" Hugh asks, and I love him so much for not hesitating.

"I need you to walk past the office and tell me if there's a woman in there."

"Like, other than Anho?"

"Yeah, smart-ass," I say. "Like someone that doesn't belong."

"Sure, hold on." He keeps his phone out, and I pick up snippets from the hallway.

"*—cannot believe—*"

"Did you see Brynn's face?"

"—thought she was going to lose her—"

"So shitty."

"Yep," Hugh comes back on. "City clothes. Looks bitchy."

"Thanks," I say, and hang up on him, immediately dialing Ribbit.

"Tress," he picks up on the first ring. "You're not going to believe—"

"Gretchen tried to make Brynn's vigil for Felicity into a homecoming queen contest," I say. "Big surprise. She's a fucking hoochbag."

"Hoochbag?"

"Are you near the office right now?" I ask.

"Yeah, I'm running attendance slips. I guess the Wi-Fi is down and Febrezio asked me to—"

"The woman from the river is here, asking about me," I tell him.

"Fuck." The single word leaves him in one breath, like it's winded him. I silently thank him for letting my shit bother him as much as his own does. "Is that why Anho—"

"Tell her I'll meet her at the library at three," I say, cutting him off. "Tell her I don't want to talk at school. People might see us."

"People will see you at the library, though," Ribbit

says. "I mean, she kind of sticks out like a sore thumb. She's carrying a Coach purse and . . ."

I let him spin his own wheels, figure it out on his own.

"Oh . . . ," he says, finally hitting it. "You're not actually going to meet her, are you?"

"Nope," I say. I hear the heavy office door swing open, the high-pitched wail of Gretchen defending herself.

"I'm trying to lift school spirit, Anho!"

Then the principal, tersely. *"Did you stop to consider how this would look?"*

"Yeah, that's why I made the purple candles a vote for Brynn, not the black ones."

I hang up, very done with Gretchen. The bathroom door swings open, and I hear someone crying, deep sobs that sound like they're catching in their throat, gagging them.

My phone vibrates with a text from Ribbit.

Done. She said she'll see you there at three.

Thanks, I shoot back.

You won't be able to dodge her forever.

I think of the notebooks in my bag, three of them, writing scrawled on both sides of every page. Messages from the past, flying back and forth between my mom and Hugh's. I pull up my hoodie sleeve, check the red progress of infection, burning a path to my elbow.

I'm not worried about forever, I text back.

Brynn is hunched over the sink when I leave my stall, her shoulders heaving as she splashes cold water onto her face. She's wearing a silver tank top with the word TWIN bedazzled in pink across the chest. I'm betting Gretchen has on the same thing, but any similarities between these two people stop there. Wordlessly, I put my hand on her back. She looks up, red-rimmed eyes meeting mine in the mirror, water dripping off her chin.

"Fuck Gretchen," she says.

"Fuck her to death," I agree.

Chapter 30

Tress

Tuesday

Brynn gets herself together quickly, squaring her shoulders and staring into the mirror, like she's giving herself a silent pep talk before hitting the field of battle. I back off, allow her some space, until her eyes cut to mine.

"Got anything I can borrow?" she asks.

"Huh?" My mind is slow, like blood is coagulating in my brain.

"Clothes," Brynn repeats, pointing to her tank top. "I don't exactly feel like twinning with that bitch."

"Yeah." I nod. "I've got you covered."

I always carry around a change of clothes in my backpack because I never know when I might discover a wad of zebra snot, stray ostrich spit, or an orangutan turd that Rue had launched at me before leaving for school.

I hand over a T-shirt from a Tom Petty concert from the nineties that had been my mom's, along with an old flannel. On me, this outfit would look like it belonged to a homeless person. On Brynn's volleyball build, it seems like she couldn't care less but still knows she looks better than everyone else.

"Thanks," she says, and I watch as she fists her tank top into a ball, stuffing it into the trash can. "I owe you one, Montor."

I nod, but any favors I need in the future will probably include immunity from a felony, and I don't think Brynn can grant me that. I glance at my phone after she leaves. I've only got thirty-five minutes until second period. Thirty-five minutes to look at the journals, thirty-five minutes to flip through the pages of my mother's life and try to piece together a picture of who she was and why Hugh's grandma hated her so much. I remember how Mrs. Hannah's lip curled when she spotted me, the instant rage that had flared up, years of vitriol finally finding its spark.

She'd called my mom a *fucking whore*.

Was she? When I called the Montor hotline as a little kid, Officer Riley had told me that I might learn some things I didn't want to know if I kept asking questions, that I'd hear some things that would make my parents come off as not the best people. He'd also said that those things were probably true. I fan the pages of the notebooks, smelling the last remnants of what must have been scented ink. My mother signed her entries with big loops, her writing large and feminine, using a vibrantly pink pen. *Annabelle.*

Hugh's mom's entries are more concise, her letters printed and slanting to the side, like she naturally writes in italics. Her name is a series of slashes. Confident, a deep purple. *Heather.*

I hesitate, checking my phone to see if I have any texts. I don't. I flip through the hashtags I'd saved on various platforms—#HonestUsher, #TrueLoser—but the traffic has faded to almost nothing, just the remnants of people who weren't there for the livestream, following up on a story that is burning out as quickly as it flared up, Ribbit's fifteen minutes already over.

I consider calling Cecil and just asking him if my mom was a *fucking whore.* My thumb hangs over his number for a second before I decide against it, already imagining the answer.

All women are fucking whores.

Thirty minutes. I've got thirty minutes now. I fan the pages again, my thumb resting in a well-worn spot where someone else did this. Someone else who pored over these words. The paper is frayed and feathered here. I am not the first reader.

I take a deep breath, and dive in.

* * *

Finding out you wouldn't have been friends with your mom when she was in high school kind of sucks. And no, it's not because she was a fucking whore.

It's because she was fucking stupid.

"Are you serious?" I ask myself for the tenth time, staring down at the second journal.

As best I can tell, Annabelle and Heather started their epic note writing sometime in the middle of their junior year. And it's about as interesting as the regurgitated oatmeal I flushed down the toilet twenty minutes ago. I started skimming their entries, conversations about who was wearing what, who had been at a party, who made out with who and whether they were allowed to, something someone had said about someone else. It's all the same shit I hear every day in the hallway, but without any pics or screencaps, which seems to make it a lot easier for he-said, she-said.

And it's not even entertaining . . . until my mom starts dating my dad.

And then I puke again. I don't know if it's the rapidly deteriorating state of my health or that I just read a very detailed account of their first time together, which apparently was "amazing." But I really didn't need to know about that.

Apparently, Heather wasn't all that interested, either.

Hey, that's cool. I mean, I'm happy for you. I just don't really get into that kind of stuff.

It's a terse response to three pages of exuberantly worded man-worship, and I can almost feel my mom's disappointment when she writes back, a tinge of passive-aggressiveness imbued in hot pink.

Awwwww . . . I'm sorry. Maybe if Jason was better in bed . . . Train your man up!

Heather's response, in regular black ink now, the scented purple ballpoint abandoned as she jotted off something quickly, her pen flying so fast as to leave little feather marks between the letters, barely lifting off the page.

Jason is fine. We're happy together.

I imagine the handoff in the hallway, Heather coldly passing over the journal, avoiding eye contact.

You can't be all that happy! Four inches doesn't do much. If you ever want to try out a real man, just say the word. Lee thinks you're hot.

"Shit, Mom!" I sputter. There's a smiley face drawn after that, an emoji from another time but still just as hard to interpret. The eyes bulge, the tongue hangs out. Is it like *Just kidding?* Or *No, really, I'm into this?*

I flip the page, and find an enormous bloodstain.

Chapter 31

Tress

Tuesday

Years of working around animals has taught me a lot about shit, vomit, and blood. I can't exactly put that on my college applications, but it does come in useful in odd situations. Like when I'm trying to determine if someone died while reading this journal.

It's not drops of blood. Those fall in circles, sending out little splashes around them. I can't tell myself that someone just had a bloody nose and didn't grab a tissue in time when they went in for a little light reading. This is a spray, fanning out from the bottom corner and sending long, thin fingers of blood all the way up into the top left. It completely obscures the light pink of my mother's handwriting, with only some words still showing on either side of the splatter.

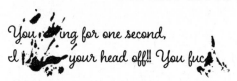

You [...]ing for one second,
I [...] your head off!! You fuc[...]

I hold the page up to the light, but it's useless. The blood has soaked through to a few pages, and the ones after that are blank, the friendship apparently over.

"What the fuck?" I ask, just as the bell rings. I get to my feet, jamming the journals back into my bag as I make my way to anatomy.

The halls are quiet, the mood subdued. Teachers stand next to their classroom doors, their mouths in thin lines, gazes challenging anyone to push them, just a little. So much for pepping everyone up for spirit week. That has taken a turn for the worse, with one of the noms for homecoming queen turning a monument to the missing into a popularity contest.

Gretchen slips past me in the hall, nose in the air. Gretchen Astor doesn't give a shit what people think. She doesn't have to. She's Gretchen Astor. If she cares about anything, it'll be that the move might have cost her the vote for queen, her bid for power backfiring. Voting doesn't happen until tomorrow, with the winner announced at the bonfire.

We used to do it on Friday nights at the football game, after all the candidates were paraded around the track, riding in convertibles—or, barring the availability—a nice Jeep with a sunroof. But that whole method of presentation got canned about five years ago when one of the losers lost her shit and took over the steering wheel of a Mazda Miata, heading right for the queen, who was still dismounting from her 4Runner. The entire football team had piled onto the Miata until it gave up, sputtering to a halt on the thirty-yard line.

Apparently, it was quite the sight. I don't know. I wasn't there. I was brushing a zebra, standing on a stool so I could reach Zee's back. Cecil didn't exactly allow me to have much of a social life growing up.

He keeps her on a pretty tight leash. . . .

"Fuck you," I say under my breath, and Gretchen turns to look at me, alarmed. I brush past her into anatomy, not caring if she thinks it was meant for her.

"Good morning, everyone!" Ms. Nabowski says, clapping her hands together to illustrate how excited she is to see us. Maybe she didn't get the memo that spirit week just turned into spite week.

"I thought today we'd do something fun," she goes on, and everyone audibly groans. Last time Nabowski wanted to try something *fun* we'd all had to lie down on long pieces of paper while someone drew a human outline, and then we had to fill in the organs with Sharpies and a minimal amount of artistic talent. The penises and breasts had been the most realistic, I'm sure due to hours of long study on my classmates' parts.

No pun intended.

"Blood typing," Nabowski finishes, not above scanning the room in victory while everyone's mood switches from *disengaged* to *full-bore into it*. There's really nothing like handing a bunch of teenagers lancets and permission to go to town on each other to make them perk up. I just hope Nabowski is smart enough not to partner Brynn up with Gretchen. She's much more likely to go for the neck than the thumb pad.

Which . . . shit. I pull my bad hand farther up into my sleeve and scan the room. I need a partner who isn't going to be too curious about my injury, someone who is distracted, not into this project, or both. Someone who . . . my eyes land on Hugh. Nabowski moves between the desks, handing out sheets of paper and lancets. I huddle over my phone, madly googling with one thumb.

Is there DNA in human blood?

"Want to be my partner?" a voice says, and I look up from my phone to find Meg Cofflero giving me a wobbly smile. I guess we're best friends now that I helped her hang up posters stating that Felicity is spayed and microchipped.

"Um . . ." I shoot a glance over my shoulder, but Hugh is already following David over to a black-topped table. "Sure," I say when I see that Lisa—Meg's actual bestie—has taken Brynn by the arm and is leading her to a corner far away from Gretchen. Smart. I should give those two more credit.

Except they just royally fucked my plan to get some of Hugh's blood.

Meg does not want to prick me. She hesitates, stabbing halfway down and then pulling back at the last minute, eyes full of apology.

"Here," I say, "let me do you."

I take her hand, pinching together the skin at the tip of her finger, letting it turn red as blood gathers. Gretchen lets out a screech when she's pricked, bringing a not-at-all-hidden smile to Brynn's face. Meg jumps, and my lancet misses, skidding off the side of her hand.

"Sorry," Meg says, and I wave off her apology, pinching her finger again. I can feel her pulse in my hand, heavy and regular. My own beats, sluggish, pushing thick, infected blood through my body. At my neck, another beat keeps rhythm with a different heart, one buried in rubble, surrounded by decaying flesh—*thwup, thwup, thwup*. Meg doesn't jump when I stab her, and once she realizes it's fairly painless, feels less guilty about lancing me.

"Here, I'll toss them," I say, holding out a gloved hand for our lancets. I slip mine into my hoodie pocket, then head for the trash can and make the rounds, offering to gather everyone else's used materials.

"Hey, Tress, looking a little trashy," David Evans says as I approach his and Hugh's table. "Maybe lay off the garbage weed?"

"Hey, David, looking a little bit like an asshole," I shoot back. "Maybe lay off the rim jobs?"

Hugh sputters a laugh and hands me their lancets. "Thanks."

"No problem," I say, sliding his into my pocket.

After class I duck into the bathroom and shoot a text to one of my clients, Henley, who graduated a few years ago. He's a decent guy who will roll with it if I come up short on Oxy, letting me stiff him rather than other more dangerous clients when I'm in a bind.

Need a favor. Something in it for you.

Is that something in your pants or in a bottle? The answer comes back immediately. *I'm game, either way. What do you need?*

What I need requires him to call in a favor of his own to a cousin who works at a genetics lab. But since Henley had talked his cousin through NARCAN'ing his wife out of an OD with no questions asked last month, I doubt it will present much of a problem.

I take a chance and dial. He picks up on the first ring.

"I've got an old bloodstain from an unknown person and two fresh blood samples," I say, skipping the greeting. "The bloodstain likely belongs to the mother of either Sample A or Sample B. I need to know which it is. Can your cousin do that?"

"Maybe, but the *something in it for me* better be a bottle after all, and not in your pants. I mean, I think you're cute, Tress, but that's a big ask—"

"Two bottles of Oxy," I tell him. "Eighties. And I need to know the answer, like, *now*."

There's silence for a moment as Henley weighs the cons against two bottles of escape. "I don't know. I'll have to drive to the city after work and that traffic—"

"No," I tell him. "You're going to drive to the city now. Leave work and meet me in the library parking lot. You're going to take what I have for you straight to your cousin, and you're going to stay there until you've got an answer, and then you're going to call me. You got it?"

"Tress, that's—"

"Two bottles," I repeat. "And a pound of weed," I throw in.

"A *pound*?"

"Hey, man, I've got weed to burn. You in or not, 'cause I can call—"

It's a bullshit threat. There is literally no one else I can call who has ties to a genetics lab, but it gets him moving.

"I'm in," Henley says. "Library parking lot. When?"

I glance at the clock. We're barely halfway through the morning, but with Felicity's disappearance and Gretchen's stunt, I doubt anyone comes looking for a truant drug dealer.

"Now," I say.

"Okay. Uh . . ." His voice wavers, uncertain.

"What?" I snap.

"Does this have anything to do with your parents?"

"Yeah," I say, feeling the weight of the journals on my back, their spiral edges digging into my spine. "I think I might have finally caught a break."

Chapter 32

Ribbit

Tuesday

Getting out of class is easy when you're on the homecoming court.

I, of course, am not. But I am the master of ceremonies, and with the combined powers of the court hitting the front office with the full wattage of their camera smiles, we're allowed to leave the building to work on homecoming preparations. The material for the bonfire—mostly wooden pallets—is stacked on the mowed expanse of the side lawn. I tell the others I'll meet them out there, and I head for the parking lot. The additions that are going to make tomorrow's bonfire extra special are in the back of my truck.

I drive out to meet them. David, Hugh, and the third king candidate—a wide receiver named Cody

Billings—unload the stuff from my truck. The girls—Gretchen, Brynn, and Maddie Anho—cluster to the side, Brynn keeping her distance from Gretchen while Maddie flutters between the two of them, unsure where her loyalty lies.

"What's all this for, anyway?" Cody asks.

He's a low-lier, the dark horse for king who wasn't in on the initial meeting and has no idea what is about to go down. He's also kind of dumb and wouldn't understand what collateral damage is, even if I tried to explain it to him. Which of course, I'm not going to do.

"This," I say, putting my hand on the frame and door they just unloaded, "is part of the ultimate homecoming bonfire."

"Escape hatch," David says, holding his hand out for a fist bump from Huge.

"What?" Cody asks, looking from one to the other.

"We're going to build it into the pyre—" I cough. "Sorry, *fire.* We're going to build it into the bonfire stack. It'll be to the back, so no one can see it."

Typically, the crowd would circle the bonfire, but I've already taken the steps to ensure that there will be signs directing people, and school staff on hand to make sure onlookers are kept to the front. When I'd explained everything—well, not *everything*—to Febrezio, who is in charge of homecoming, she'd been impressed. I'd also seen a hint of caution around her eyes, but the fact that Ribbit Usher, internet bullying sensation, had come up with this plan hand in hand with his tormentors, seemed to outweigh any concerns.

"You'll make sure the steps are foundationally secure, right?" she had asked, eyebrows coming together when I showed her my quick pencil sketch.

"Absolutely, I'll even have the shop teacher double-check us," I'd reassured her. "The steps will not be a problem." And it's true. The steps most definitely will *not* be the problem.

I whip out that sketch now, and the homecoming court huddles around me.

"The guys will be inside the structure," I explain. "The stairs are going to go up the back, and the doorway will open underneath it. The girls will be standing in the back with me. When the head of student council announces the queen, she'll ascend the staircase, wearing this."

I pull a garment bag from the cab of my truck, laying it on the ground. The girls gather in more closely as I unzip the bag and carefully pull out my new creation.

"Oh. My. God," Gretchen says. Her hand is on her chest like her heart might stop beating.

Just wait a little bit, I think to myself.

It's a full pair of human-sized wings, buzzard feathers

attached to a wire frame. "You'll put on these wings." I
illustrate, running my arms through the leather circlets
attached to either wing, one at the wrist, one above the
elbow. I hold my arms out, the wingspan topping eight
feet, easily.

"And *voilà*," I say. "Congratulations. You're the queen
of the Ravens."

"Damn," Brynn says. "That's . . . pretty cool."

"Okay, but I mean, you'll, like, get us down before
you light the fire, right?" Maddie asks.

"Uh, duh," Gretchen says.

"Why you worried, Maddie?" David asks. "It's not
like you're going to win."

Cody laughs, while the girls all sheepishly avoid looking at each other. Homecoming royalty isn't supposed
to *want* to win. And you're supposed to act surprised
when you get it.

I slip out of the raven wings, carefully folding
them back into the garment bag. "Guys," I go on.
"You'll be inside the structure, and when the queen is
announced—" I pause a second and wait until I have
everyone's attention.

Then I set my arm on fire.

The girls screech, and all the boys jump back, grabbing at each other for balance. No one comes close to
me. No one tries to put it out. No one is worried about

Ribbit Usher, on fire. Not a surprise. Again, that's for tomorrow.

"I'm fine," I say calmly, approaching the girls, which makes them screech again.

"Completely fine," I repeat, waving my arm quickly. The fire sputters out, and I see that Brynn had been tearing off her flannel, ready to tackle me.

"Dude," Cody says, grabbing my arm and pulling it closer for inspection. "What the shit?"

"Stunt gel," I tell him. "Like they use on movie sets. Wanna try?"

"Yes," Cody says immediately. I coat his hand in a thin layer of the gel, and light him up. Gretchen whips out her phone, but I motion at her to put it away.

"Gotta keep everything under wraps for tomorrow," I say as Cody waves his arm, extinguishing the flame.

"Damn, bro," he says, looking down at his still-smoking skin. "That's kick-ass."

"It doesn't hurt?" David asks, moving closer.

"No, I mean, like, a little," Cody admits. "Just really warm, but it doesn't burn."

I scoop another handful of gel from the container. "Wanna go?" I ask David, and he shoots me a look. He has to, and he knows it. Cody manned up and came out on the other side unharmed, if not entirely unsinged. David holds out his arm, and I slather on the gel, igniting him.

He puts his hand in front of his face, entranced. "Yeah, it's not so bad," he says, a muscle in his jaw ticking. I can see him counting down the seconds to ensure that he stays on fire longer than Cody had. He barely makes it, shaking out his arm.

I look at Hugh, but his eyes are on the bonfire, and the center pole I'd already sunk for it. "So," he says. "The queen will be on top—"

"With my wings on," Gretchen adds, then cuts her eyes to where Brynn and Maddie stand. "Sorry, I mean, with *her* wings on."

"And the guys will be inside?" Hugh asks.

"Right," I say. "I'll have a bucket for you with the stunt gel. You can put it on your arms, legs, whatever. But I probably wouldn't put it on your head."

"Not this moneymaker!" David says, drawing an air circle around his face.

"There will be lighters for you, inside," I go on. "You'll light yourselves, and come out the back door when we announce the king candidates."

"People are going to freak out," Brynn says, shaking her head. "They're going to think the guys are actually on fire."

"I'll make an announcement about pyrotechnics being used in the show," I say. "I'll let everyone know not to be alarmed and that it's all part of the plan. And I'll have this, just in case."

I hold up a fire extinguisher, with what I hope is a reassuring smile on my face.

"And Febrezio approved this?" Brynn asks. "She's okay with—"

"She wants this to be the best homecoming yet," I say. Which is absolutely true and is a direct quote from Febrezio. It also is not an answer to Brynn's question.

"Look," I say, putting down the extinguisher. "I know everyone is upset about Felicity."

Brynn immediately ducks her head to hide real tears. Gretchen scrunches her face together to bring about an approximation of crying, while Maddie does nothing. Which is no surprise. If Felicity were here, Maddie wouldn't even be on the court.

"But I haven't given up on finding her," I say, and Brynn's head comes back up, eyes locking with mine. I feel a little tremor in my spine. Shit, that girl is good-looking.

"I'm not going to let anything happen to you, Brynn." I say.

And it's true.

I'm not going to let anything happen . . . to Brynn.

Chapter 33

Tress

Tuesday

Your dad was cheating on your mom.

It's one of the last things Felicity Turnado said to me, right before I killed her. I'd denied it, screamed at her, thrown a trowel that had bounced off the wall next to her head, ricocheting and breaking our only light bulb. Things got dark after that, literally and figuratively.

I uncap a bottle of my water and suck down half of it as I sit in the library parking lot, sweating in Cecil's truck. The school secretary had taken one look at my pale, gray skin and let me sign out when I said I had a doctor appointment. Given that most of the student body was puking up everything from dinner to their own stomach linings only a few days ago, it wasn't a difficult lie to float.

Your dad was cheating on your mom.

I hear Felicity's voice as clearly as I did last night at the ruins of the Allan house, the coal chute sending it up to me, along with the pulse pound of a beating heart. I couldn't outrun that rhythm, and now her voice has found me again, too.

"So what?" I say.

And really, seriously—*so what?* People cheat. Like, all the time.

But do they go missing?

That's not Felicity's voice. Annoyingly, it's my own. I rest my head against the steering wheel, let the cheap rubber burn against my forehead.

What do you control?

That's my mom, her voice low and sincere. Probing. This was her trick, one that undercut any problem, any difficulty, and all the drama. If I came home from school upset because there hadn't been room for me at my friends' lunch table, Mom would listen, hands on her hips and then say, "Tress, what do you control?"

And my answer, the only possible one. "Myself."

"That's right," she'd say, kneeling down. "The only person you can control is yourself. You can't make someone do what you want them to do. You can't *make* a girl get up to create a space for you. You can't *make* anyone go with you to a new table."

I'd sniffed, knowing this was all true, and hating the finality of it.

"But the good news is," Mom had said, cocking her head, "is that this means no one else can control *you*, either. People can do things to you, Tress. But only you decide how you react."

"How'd you get so smart, Mom?" I'd asked, looking up.

Her smile, tight and thin-lipped. "Experience."

I pull back from the steering wheel, the imprint of it a red half-moon on my forehead. The journals lie on the seat next to me, pages fluttering in the light breeze coming through my open windows. The girl in those journals didn't have experience, and she *had* controlled people. Page after page was filled with schemes to break up couples and friendships, put people who stepped out of line back in their place. Annabelle Usher had run Amontillado High during her stretch there, and the evidence is in a bloodstained pile on my passenger seat.

What changed? At what point did my mom realize that the control was an illusion? Right after she encouraged her best friend to hook up with her boyfriend, and maybe those two found out they couldn't control themselves, either? And how long did that last? Into adulthood? Long after the women had ceased talking to each other?

I don't know, and there's no one to ask. My parents are gone.

And so are the Browards.

There. There it is. There's the messy bit that I can't quite wave away, or explain without doing some pretty phenomenal mental gymnastics. Hugh's parents went through a divorce—by all accounts an ugly one—right after my parents went missing. They'd both skipped town, leaving Hugh behind to be raised by Heather's mother.

Your dad was cheating on your mom.

I grab a journal, the one with the bloodstain, running my finger over it as if expecting to feel a thrum of recognition. Is this my mom's blood? Was she poring over the past, trying to determine where things went wrong? Did Heather find her like this? Want the journals back? Or maybe she just wanted my dad to herself?

Or is it the other way around? Is this Heather's blood, my mother coming after her in a fit of jealous rage, no longer able to face the fact that the only thing she could control was herself, and her grip was slipping? If so, did Jason come after Mom for hurting his wife? Did Dad get in the way?

The heart pulses next to my skin—*thwup, thwup, thwup*—the beat stronger than my own, reminding me of Felicity's plea, begging me just to listen. I hadn't. Instead, I killed her. I close my eyes, whispering, "I'm so sorry, Felicity."

When I open them, I see a long black tail disappearing around the corner of the library.

Shit.

I get out of the truck, letting the door click quietly

shut behind me. I circle around to the back of the building, but there's no cat in sight. What I do spot is a shiny
silver BMW.

Double shit.

It throws me, and I stutter step, trying to look casual
as I walk past the rear parking lot, glancing to make
sure the car is unoccupied. I told this woman I'd meet
her after school, so why is she here now? I picture her
inside, maybe scrolling through microfiche and asking
the librarian what she knows about Amontillado Animal
Attractions. Asking if she's ever caught the scent of pot
up on the ridge, knows anybody who traffics in pills
that help make the pain go away.

Or if she knew Felicity Turnado . . . or anyone who
might have wanted her dead.

I slip down the alley at the thought and lean against
the side of the library for support, the bricks cool in the
shade, reminding me of the Allan house, the cat, and
Felicity's voice rising in the darkness, accusingly.

I might have convinced Ribbit that I'm only worried
about this woman digging for information about exotic
animal trafficking or maybe doing an exposé on hill-
billy heroin and the fall of small-town America. But the
truth is that I doubt the Turnados are relying solely
on the goodwill of the community and reward money
to find their only child. Hiring a private investigator
would be another tool in their arsenal, and I'm willing

to bet that April Turnado traded in her eyelash crimpers for a personal cop when she discovered that her usual weapons weren't getting the job done.

The real bitch of it is that I have no way of knowing what the BMW woman wants with me—*tigers, marijuana, and dead girls, oh my!*—until I talk to her. And that is just not going to fucking happen, because all three of those topics implicate me in felonies.

"All right, Montor," I say, squatting down, the leaves of a climbing ivy vine brushing against my face as I rest my head against the bricks. "What are you gonna do?"

My phone vibrates with a text from Henley.

Here.

"Okay," I say, not bothering to text an actual response. This is something I can do. An immediate action I can take that will move me forward. I stand up, brush the ivy away from my face, and circle back around the library, pretending to be texting as I pass the rear parking lot, my hair falling in a dark sheet between me and the BMW. It's still there, empty, rims shinier than anything I've ever owned in my life.

Henley has pulled up next to my truck, and I give him a little up-nod as I reach inside my cab to grab the journal and the baggie with the two lancets. I slip into his passenger seat, and the smile that he'd been wearing dissipates.

"Shit, Tress," he says. "You look like—"

"Like I'm dying, yeah," I agree.

"You want me to take you to the hospital? Or maybe urgent ca—"

"No," I say, handing off the baggie and tearing one of the bloodstained pages from the journal. "I want you to do what I said. Take these to your cousin and call me back as soon as you know the answer."

He holds the Ziploc up to the light, like maybe he'll be able to spare us both the trouble and answer the question right now using his grocery-store-cashier abilities and UV rays.

"Henley!" I say, and he jumps, almost dropping the baggie. "The lancets are marked A and B. A is mine, and B belongs to someone else. I need to know—"

"Yeah, if the blood on this"—he waves the journal page, the paper leaving a faint trail of smeared blood, tinted with pink and purple ink in the air behind it— "is from the mother of one of these." He lifts the baggie in illustration, but my eyes are still following the colorful trail, now dissipating in the sunlight and falling like dust motes.

Shit. I'm hallucinating.

But I've spotted something strapped to Henley's visor that I'm pretty sure is actually there.

"I'm taking your bowie knife," I tell him.

Chapter 34

Ribbit

Tuesday

The Montors have a mausoleum in the center of the Amontillado cemetery, stones still tightly notched, the moss that grows in the cracks seeming to bind everything together, nature bestowing her blessing on what Montor hands had built. Meanwhile, the Usher house has ivy climbing the walls, each green grasping finger digging more deeply into crevices, passively destroying the work of my ancestors as our stones fall onto soft soil, then sink out of sight over the years, Mother Nature slowly obliterating us.

But on a long enough timeline, we all die.

And fuck mothers, anyway.

Hugh, David, and Cody have no idea what they are building. They think they do. They think it's homecoming week and we're teaming up to make everything better, gloss over the loss of Felicity, pat Ribbit on the head, and move forward like good, stalwart Midwesterners, hanging onto the deliverance of our Protestant work ethic through clenched teeth. We're going to put our heads down and plow forward, take it on the chin and pull ourselves up by our own bootstraps. *Go Ravens! Fly high!* So fucking high that you can't see what's right in front of you.

Damn these people are stupid.

But they are also well built, and that counts for a lot in high school. All three of them had stripped down to the waist once we started working on the bonfire. Even though it's early November the days have held on to their heat. Truth is, I've seen these guys toss off their shirts in forty degrees, so apparently human vanity operates on the Celsius scale. Me, I don't take my shirt off in public.

I've been teased about it plenty, with theories running from me having everything from a chicken chest to a third nipple. No one would ever guess that it's because of scars. Tress wears hers like badges of honor, well won on the field of battle. She doesn't know how right she is, and that she's been winning a war since we were kids, fate smiling down on her. The current not strong enough when I dared her to wade out into the river after a flood. A lightning strike that sizzled inches from her bare feet when she was sent out into a storm to see to the animals.

Apparently, Mother Nature loves Montors, and Ushers . . . well . . . Ushers have mommy issues. That's where my scars come from, not blithely trotting through life but holding firm to the stair railing while a belt buckle landed on my shoulder, striking just right, flaying to the bone, Usher blood falling on Usher floors and Usher tears soaking back into the wood. Mine, and Mother's, if I'm being honest.

She always felt bad, after, if she got too "carried away."

Life is hard, she always said. *Life isn't fair. Do you want the world to teach you, or me? Stop looking at me with that face.*

(My father's face, not an Usher face, nature failing again.)

Don't just stand there, do something. Do I have to tell you to do everything? Would you stand still all day if I didn't give you directions?

Probably, yes. Because I am terrified of doing it wrong (*your way, the right way, the only way*). I would stand still and immobile, a puppet with no puppeteer.

Take some initiative, for Christ's sake.

"I am," I say as I lean back against my truck, watching my own puppets build their pyre. They move at my behest, following my orders, dutifully fitting a screw here, a board there. My word is law, and they are quick to enforce it, muscles that will soon stop moving, delivering the fruit of my labor, breathing heavily and filling the air with carbon dioxide.

I suck in my own breath, filling my lungs, pulling in Amontillado molecules. Something like 15 to 40 percent of carbon dioxide stays in the atmosphere, cycling around for two thousand years. Am I breathing in Usher exhalations? Their spent breaths finding me on the wind, attracted by our shared blood? Or—even better—can Felicity feel me, needing her, wanting her? Is her breath slipping into mine, are we already one, still bound from a night in fifth grade? I let my air out in a gasp, not realizing I'd been holding it. Holding it close, keeping it sacred, pretending it was a connection to Felicity.

Maybe I can use this, after. Tell her I caught her trail in the air, her molecules and mine, blending together inside our lungs. Parts of me and parts of her communicating, tangled, like her hair had been that night, catching in my fingers, gold strands that I would allow to hold me forever. Binding us.

But it's been four days, and no matter how mystical a force might connect us, Felicity is ultimately made of flesh and bone. Flesh can tear and bones can break and if Tress did something to her . . . I don't need more reason to kill my cousin other than Mother wants it done. But if exerting a little pressure on Tress before finishing her off helps lead me to Felicity, well . . . it's about time something worked out for Kermit Usher.

"—cops coming in tomorrow." I catch the end of David's sentence, his breath low and panting as he hefts a beam over his head, moving it to the bonfire.

"Heard about that," Hugh responds, their half sentences and small nods to each other forming a conversation I am not a part of.

"You in trouble?" David asks, but Hugh shakes his head.

"Nah." He throws a quick glance at me, but I've got my head in my phone, buds in my ears. They are playing nothing, and my screen is showing only my to-do list, but I seem lost to the world. Or they are lost to me. Whichever.

"Ribbit didn't press charges." Hugh's voice drops low, the spike of a hammer hitting nail almost overriding it. "They already talked to me, wanted to know when I'd seen Felicity last, all that stuff."

My heart picks up a beat at her name, my biology expressing its interest.

"Yeah, my mom said they aren't worried about the drinking or anything," Cody jumps in. "Like all that other shit just doesn't matter now."

Me. Stripped. Exposed. Reduced to "all that other shit."

I pull in another deep breath, hoping Felicity is in there somewhere.

"You okay, bro?" Cody calls, making a trip back to

the bonfire, his arms loaded with wood. An old barn had collapsed, and the farmer had brought the refuse here, happy to be rid it. It splinters and cracks, dried and ancient, perhaps protesting its fate. It had a purpose, once. The hands that built it meant for it to shelter and protect. Those hands are gone, and its purpose has changed dramatically.

"Yeah, I'm good," I tell Cody, willing myself to breathe normally. He nods and continues working, the bonfire growing under my direction, nails and screws, wood and skin, all coming together to create something memorable.

My revenge.

And after that, my reward.

"Hang on, Felicity," I whisper. "I'm coming."

Chapter 35

Tress

Tuesday

The tires on a BMW are just as easy to slice as the tires on a beater piece of shit. But I will say the puff of escaping air might smell a little better. Either that, or I'm still hallucinating.

I've slashed a few tires in my life, mostly because I wanted to, but occasionally at Cecil's bidding—people that owed money, someone who had made him angry. The tires I slashed were always by-blows of a personal insult, my pride reinflating as their car sank lower to the ground. I don't feel that way now. I feel like a criminal as I scuttle back to my truck, shoulders hunched, Henley's bowie knife tucked inside my sleeve, an animal hiding from the world.

I snap the door shut behind me and start the truck, pulling up my shirtsleeve. The skin around the duct tape is swollen, puffed up far above the silver edge of the tape. It looks like I jammed my arm into a finger trap, the hand coming out the other side a sickly shade of gray. I turn left out of the library, checking my light three times before I'm reasonably confident it's actually green, and I'm not imagining it. I confirm my blinker is on before taking the turn, careful as a drunk driving home on New Year's Eve.

But I've seen those drunks sliding all over the streets, their extra levels of care only mattering in the dark recesses of their mind as they clutch desperately for small actions they can take to mitigate their mistakes. Believing that an excess of caution as they drive home from a binge will wipe their slate clean, not realizing that in reality they're already in the weeds, broken pedestrians behind them and a telephone pole jammed up next to the engine.

I'm doing that now. Denying the danger of the red lines climbing my arm, the flutter of movements in my vision that aren't actually there, the mania settling into my brain, the beat of a heart not my own resting against my chest. I'm gone, and I know it. I can either resign myself to that, or I can dig in and stand up, tell death it's going to have to come a little farther down the road if it wants me, because I'm not in a rush to meet it.

In other words, I need to see a doctor about my wound. But no doctor in their right mind would take a look at this and see it for anything other than what it is. I've been mauled by a wild animal, and nobody is going to let that slide. Not when Amontillado has been looking for a reason to come after me and Cecil since forever, and there's a missing local beauty to be accounted for.

Luckily, I know just the right person to fix me up. Not a doctor in their right mind, but a school nurse who most definitely isn't.

I come to a full stop at the light, check my rearview mirror, ignore the flashing lights exploding in my vision, the constant thrum of the heart against my skin.

I turn left, and head for Hugh Broward's house.

Hugh's grandma comes to the door hesitantly, as if a visitor here is not something to be celebrated. As soon as she spots me her mouth goes tight, twin flames igniting in her eyes.

"Annabelle," she says stiffly. "Heather isn't home right now, so you might as well climb on back into your tower, little princess."

"Mrs. Hannah," I say. "I'm hurt, and I need help."

That gets her attention, whether because of the Hippocratic oath or a deeper, dark sense of curiosity, I don't know. And I don't really care, either. She unlatches the screen door and opens it, clicking her tongue at me as I slide past her.

"Not pregnant, are you? I don't do that kind of work."

"What? No!" I say. "I'm—"

"A girl like you gets herself in trouble, that's usually the cause, and I won't apologize for my words," she snipes, taking me by the wrist and drawing me into the living room, where the TV is playing *General Hospital*. There's a miniature ironing board set up on the coffee table, steam escaping from the upright iron next to it. A pile of laundry sits on the sofa, the middle cushion permanently dented in what I assume must be the shape of Mrs. Hannah's ass. A crossword puzzle book has been tossed aside, a magnifying lamp with a swinging arm lights up her unfinished puzzle brightly, the dark smear of eraser marks exposing her frustration.

Ironically, the clue that seems to be giving her the most trouble is 5 across: *nurse.*

My mom did crosswords in ink, but now probably isn't the time to share that.

"So, what have you done to yourself?" Mrs. Hannah asks, plopping onto her spot on the couch. "I can't prescribe medications, so if it's gonorrhea—"

I sit on the floor, tucking my legs under the coffee table, and pull up my shirtsleeve.

"Oh," she says, suddenly flustered. "Oh my."

Judgment is momentarily suspended as she pulls the magnifying light above my arm, cool fingers probing gently at the skin. She might be crazy, and she might hate me, but she still has the deft touch of a healer.

"What happened?" she asks, pulling at the edges of the tape. "What's under here?"

"I was mauled by a panther," I tell her, feeling a measure of relief just by telling the truth about something for the first time in a while.

"Those panthers," she says, shaking her head. "Bastards. You know we lost the league pennant to them in 'sixty-six?"

I dismiss the comment as her wallowing in dementia, until I remember that Prospero's mascot is a panther. "What sport?" I ask.

"Bear baiting," she says simply, then raises her head to look at me. "Who put this tape on here?"

"I did," I tell her.

"Well, you're an idiot," she says, shoving the lamp away. "Taking it off will just tear the wound further, and you've got an infection that would make a stripper blush."

In my pocket, my phone goes off. It's a text from Henley.

He said he can do it. 8 hours or so.

I hope you brought something to read, I shoot back, and his response is immediate.

Nope. But we've got the lab to ourselves. I'm sharing the weed, spreading the love. He said he'll check me for all kinds of stuff. Nerd party with pot.

I slide my phone back into my pocket and glance up at Hugh's grandma, who is glaring at me. "You kids and your phones," she huffs. "Once Heather got hers, that's all it was all day, all night. Talking in her room with the door shut. Needed her *privacy*."

There's poison in her words, and it's personal. A deep wound. "Was Heather on her phone a lot?" I ask.

"Was Heather on her phone a lot?" she parrots back at me, a replay of the other night. "Asking like you don't know the answer, Annabelle Usher. Like it wasn't you on the other end. You had your claws so deep into her she—"

Mrs. Hannah stops, pulls back from me, poking at the edges of the tape. Some liquid seeps out, rolls down my arm to be soaked into the ironing board, staining a light pink peony with a sickly green tinge.

"Taking this off is going to hurt," she says grimly, looking up at me. "It's going to hurt a lot."

"I already hurt a lot," I tell her, but my mind is elsewhere. If my mom and Heather got cell phones when they were in high school, that would explain why the notebooks came to such an abrupt halt, tech surpassing their scented ink. But it still doesn't explain the blood-stain.

Mrs. Hannah switches off the TV, rocks back and forth to gain some momentum, and gets to her feet. "I'll be right back," she says, sticking a bony finger in my face. "Don't move, and don't touch anything."

I do as I'm told, and she returns with a pint of whiskey and a sewing basket.

"This is for me," she says, holding up the whiskey.

"And this"—she flips open the basket, pulls out a wicked-looking pair of scissors—"is for you, Annabelle."

"Can I have some of that, too?" I ask, pointing at the whiskey.

Mrs. Hannah spins the lid off, and tosses back a shot like a pro. "Not yet," she says, switching the magnifying lamp on and pulling it into position over my arm. "You ready?"

I close my eyes, feel the beat of my heart, and the extra rhythm of the other.

—*thwup, thwup, thwup*—

My phone vibrates with a call from April Turnado. This time, she leaves a message. The red indicator pops up, telling me there's a voice from my past inquiring about the current whereabouts of her daughter.

"You ready?" Mrs. Hannah asks again, scissors poised to strike.

"Yes," I say.

And she makes her first cut.

Chapter 36

Tress

Tuesday

The tape on the underside of my arm comes off easily enough, Mrs. Hannah slicing lengthwise across my homemade bandage, separating the section stuck to my wound and efficiently stripping off the layers. The last few take off all the hair on my arm, the tape tossed aside where it lies upside down like an obscene caterpillar, dead legs raised to the imaginary sun that is the magnifying lamp.

The past few rips have taken the wind out of me, even though the air feels cool against my exposed skin. We learned in biology that our skin actually breathes, but I never truly understood until I felt it suffocating. It's gasping now, gulping in fresh air. But I can only feel a measure of relief. I know there is worse to come; much worse.

Three dark, open mouths are under what's left of the tape. I saw them Friday night, had half a moment to witness the inside of my arm, muscle and tendon, white flash of bone, exposed layer of fat. Then the blood came in a rush, and I covered it all, spinning and spinning the roll of duct tape, trapping dirt, flecks of glue, tape fiber, and whatever mess of bacteria lived under the panther's claws.

Drops of sweat fall from my brow, collecting on the ironing board cover. Near my elbow, the iron hisses, a jet of steam releasing from the top. Mrs. Hannah leans over my arm, trimming away pieces of tape with her scissors, no hint of madness in the dexterity of her hands.

My phone goes off, and I pull it from my pocket, set it on my lap so that Mrs. Hannah can't see it. It's another text from Henley.

Good news! I don't have the gene for Alzheimer's.

I flick the message away, checking the time. School will be out soon, and I don't want Hugh to find me here, hovering over my mangled arm while his grandma plays surgeon with her sewing tools.

"All right," Mrs. Hannah says, studying the scraps of tape that are left, little silver rectangles that are keeping my insides where they're supposed to be. "Are you ready?"

I nod, bracing my other hand against the floor,

pushing back against something solid just to know it's there. She gently lifts a corner of the tape with her fingertips, pressing down on the skin with the flat edge of the scissors as it tries to rise with it. Flesh and fiber separate and pus rolls out, the black mouth of a slash vomiting out infection.

It hurts. Hurts in a whole new way. I've had rocks fall on my head, accidentally caught parts of myself on fire, fell down a well, been mildly electrocuted, and smashed each of my fingers and toes more times than I can count. But this is searing pain, a crescendo with no peak. A smell rises with it, rot and ruin, the sickly-sweet scent of death that draws vermin and vultures. I close my eyes as my throat clenches, willing myself not to get sick and add to the mess on Mrs. Hannah's coffee table.

There's a soft noise as she tosses the strip of tape aside. It rolls from the edge of the table and falls into my lap, leaving a warm, wet feeling in its wake.

"Oh dear," she says, voice oddly calm.

"What?" I ask, opening my eyes, but focusing on her, not my arm.

"Sweetheart, you've got maggots."

She sounds almost joyful, as if the fact that a fly laid eggs in my wound is proof that I'm truly rotten and deserving of her scorn. I glance down, the pervasive itch explained by an army of white worms crawling around inside of me. I look away as one crawls out, inching toward my elbow.

"I'm going to puke," I say, and Mrs. Hannah twists my wrist, getting the first utterance of pain out of me.

I try to pull my arm back. But it's no use. She's got me clenched, the small bones of my wrist grinding together. I'm too weak to fight her, so I stop struggling and rest my head on the ironing board, forehead to peony. She pulls the magnifying light closer to my arm, the heat of it adding to the fever in my skin, her eye huge and distorted.

"I'm getting my tweezers," she says, rocking back and forth again until she gains her feet. I give an approximation of a nod, but I don't know if my head actually moves. My cheek is against the board, my gaze following little white maggots as they fall from the wound to explore this new, cleaner world.

"They're making a break for it!" Mrs. Hannah sweeps in with a paper towel, blotting them out of existence with one swipe. She crushes the towel in her hand and it falls next to the wad of tape near my legs.

"This is my splinter tweezers," she explains, and I lift my head dutifully, scared to displease her. She's holding a long-tipped tweezers that looks like it's made for popping balloons rather than digging in human skin. I sit up, push my hair back from my eyes, and straighten my spine.

"Okay," I say, meeting her gaze. "Go for it."

She smiles, tapping the metal against her thumbnail. "I don't like you, Annabelle," she says. "But you've got some grit in you."

"And some maggots," I say, which gets a chuckle from her. It starts low and deep, like it's something that hasn't happened in a while and isn't sure how to get out. She goes to work, each infuriating itch now replaced by a bright pinprick of pain. I lick my lips, willing some strength into my voice.

"Why did Heather leave?" I ask.

Mrs. Hannah's mouth goes thinner over the light, the creases near her eyes deepening. "Heather's not home, I told you that," she said.

"I know," I say. "She left after the divorce. Her and Jason both. Why?"

"They needed to go," she says. "People were talking. They left me Hugh." The flat lips curve now, a real smile exposing false teeth. "He's a good boy."

I don't argue. I've always liked Hugh, but the truth is that he's spread more legs in this county than the gynecologist, and Mrs. Hannah's rankings of people's relative goodness seems to be directly tied to their sex life.

"Was Heather good?" I ask.

"Mmm-hmm, till she got in deep with you," she says, not missing a beat, eyes still on my arm, a growing pile of bloodied, twitching maggots building on the table.

"They were swingers," I hazard the guess but get little reaction.

"Sinners," she corrects me, glancing up to pin my gaze, a speared maggot on the tweezers as she points it at me. "They were sinners and didn't care who knew. I set her down once, told her the things people were saying, the words I'd hear repeated about my own daughter in the grocery store. Where was her shame? Where was the knowledge of right and wrong?"

I'm silent, letting her rage spill, hoping to catch details in the flood.

"She wasn't raised that way, I'll tell you," Mrs. Hannah says, shaking her head. "When you four took a honeymoon together, don't think the whole town wasn't talking."

"What?" I ask, my heart jumping, a hot pulse pushing back against the tweezers as she goes deep into my arm.

"Married a week apart and matching cruise plans," she says. "Best friends forever," she singsongs, a nasty parody of nice words. "Some thought it was sweet. Others . . ." She shakes her head again, mouth back to a thin pink line of disapproval. "Others knew. I told her. Told her it couldn't last. Somebody would get hurt. And they certainly did. Hurt to death."

She turns my arm in the light, investigating the slash

for any missed maggots. "Ushers," she snorts. "You think your shit don't stink, and if it does, others ought to be grateful to get close enough for a whiff."

I'm picking apart her words while she fishes for maggots in my arm, my brain sorting and categorizing as quickly as it can, operating inside a fevered head.

"Ready for the next one?" Mrs. Hannah asks, her fingers already playing with the edge of the second strip of tape. I nod, and the process begins again, the release of pus, a puff of decay, and the frantic, squirming maggots that have never known daylight.

"Who got hurt, Mrs. Hannah?" I ask, repeating her words. "Who got . . ." My mind spins, searching for what she'd said. "Who got hurt to death?"

"You did, Annabelle. You and your pretty man, Lee."

She scrapes the edge of the scissors across the second slash, like she's taking the head off a beer. Maggots tumble to the side, lost and squirming.

"Did Heather kill Annabelle?" I ask Mrs. Hannah, watching her for a reaction. She grimaces, her teeth pushing past lips thinned from years of being pressed together, a lifetime of resentment.

"People thought it, and plenty of them," she says. "Heather couldn't take it, said she wanted out. Wanted to go somewhere nobody knew her face. Jason told her . . ."

She lifts her gaze from the wound, looks at me with tear-filled eyes. "Told her she could go somewhere nobody knew her easy enough but that people could still spot a whore."

Mrs. Hannah sniffs, wiping her nose with a clean tissue. "Can you imagine, a man saying that to his own wife?"

I want to tell her that's not any worse than a woman's mother saying the same thing, but she's got the tweezers poised above my arm. In my lap, my phone vibrates.

Low risk of heart disease! The g/f won't believe it. She says mine is already dark and shriveled.

"But did she do it?" I ask. "Did Heather kill Annabelle?"

Mrs. Hannah grips the edge of the third piece of tape and tears it off fast, like a Band-Aid being pulled from a screaming toddler. The slash underneath yawns open, fresh blood squeezing past the rotting lips, a stream of pus rolling out. Black spots explode in my vision and my tongue goes dry, sticking to the roof of my mouth.

"You can have some whiskey now, Annabelle Usher," Mrs. Hannah says.

And dumps the bottle over my arm.

Chapter 37

Ribbit

Tuesday

The stairs on the bonfire will be the most difficult part, because of (as Cody says)—*math*. Luckily for him I already calculated rise and run and have everything cut to size. I haul the pieces from the back of my truck and give the group a once-over.

The girls took off a while ago, Gretchen claiming asthma once sawdust had started to fly when we drilled the doorframe into the back of the structure. Brynn had dutifully checked her phone every few minutes so as not to be late for a volleyball game, and Maddie had evaporated once the other girls were gone, fading into the breeze without the support of someone else's light to reflect. David and Cody made vague excuses about *dinner* and *chores*, then disappeared in the direction of the high school gym. I have no doubt they are sitting in the bleachers now, with a great view of the volleyball game, and Brynn's legs.

Only Hugh stayed to help me unload the stairs, and we're driving nails, securing the steps, hammers falling rhythmically as the light fades. We're silent, our lips bristling with nails as we finish up. There's a code here, some essence of masculinity I have never been a part of. The first few times I tried to drive a nail I'd struck it at an angle, and it pinged off the wood, brushing my earlobe as it flew wildly through the air.

"Dude," was all Cody had said, shaking his head and going off in search of the fly-by nail, muttering something about it puncturing a mower tire if it wasn't found.

"Here," Hugh had said, offering me his hammer. "This one is heavier," he'd explained, his lips tight around a bunch of nails. "Easier to drive with weight behind it. And try to hit it square. It's not as easy as it looks."

His hammer did have more heft, although I imagine having a couple hundred pounds of muscle behind the tool also makes a difference. But there are some things I am good at, too—*listening, watching, learning*—and as the others skulk off into the evening, Hugh and I are working in tandem, my nails driven as straight and true as his. If I were to stop and consider, it's almost like I fit in. But, if I were to stop and consider, it could be construed as a need for a break, to pause, to catch my breath. As weakness.

Weakness is my old role, the part I played Friday night at the Allan house, prey to Hugh's predator, a jester for their jokes. Each nail I drive is building a new Ribbit Usher, one who will be worthy of Felicity Turnado . . . when I find her.

I drive the final nail, running my tongue over the dent in my lip where it had rested. Below that, the silver smooth scar from Gretchen's horrible dog, William Wilson.

"These'll hold her, right?" Hugh asks, giving the stairs a cursory shake. They wobble but don't collapse.

"Yeah," I say. "Gretchen weighs what—all of a hundred pounds?"

"Right," Hugh says. "Gretchen . . ." He shakes his head, digging a palm into his eye. "For a second there, I just kind of forgot, you know?"

I nod, following his thoughts. His may have wandered with the work, but mine are always on her. On Felicity.

"Four days," he says. "It's been four days. Could she even . . . I mean . . . ?"

Once again I find myself in a situation where Hugh Broward is asking me questions. This time, there is no livestream. This time, I choose not to answer. Instead, I turn the tables, a late move in this, my long game.

"What do you think happened?"

Hugh sighs, steps back from the bonfire, taking in

our creation. "I don't know," he says, all of his normal energy gone. In front of him, the bonfire rises, casting a long, dark shadow. Near it, even Huge seems small. He shrinks further with every word.

"I know she was there at the party," he goes on, not looking at me. "I saw her. I remember."

I nod, agreeing but unable to confirm. I remember very little from Friday, except for that one bright, burning moment when Felicity's body was pressed against mine.

"And she was . . ." His eyes flick to mine, gauging my reaction. "She was with Tress."

My ears perk up, but I will my eyes to remain dull, my expression vague. "Felicity was with Tress?"

"Until, like, three in the morning, yeah," Hugh says. "I can't believe . . . I mean, Tress wouldn't *do something*, would she?"

He looks to me, like I should know. He looks to me, as her blood, to discern her depths. The truth is that Tress is part Usher and, yes, Ushers will eventually *do something*.

You just have to push them hard enough.

But if Tress does hold the answer to where Felicity might be, I don't want Hugh Broward sniffing down that path. Hugh has saved the day for many girls and been rewarded by all of them. I have waited patiently, for the best of all.

I have waited for Felicity.

"No." I shake my head. "Tress wouldn't."

On the outside, I behave as expected, say the right thing. Externally, I encourage Hugh to believe what makes him feel good. I do my job. I make it better, for those who believe that they are better than me.

Inside, I wonder.

I have a list. It's a new one. The old one is mostly accounted for, only a few check marks waiting for the rest of this week to unfold. The new one carries a different sense of urgency, my need that connects to it slightly more wild, due to the unknown factors.

It's been four days.

Those words have been on the mouths of Amontillado, echoing down the hallways at school, lighting up phones with texts, spat out around a mouthful of nails while Hugh and I worked. Brynn is the only one who seems to grasp the true gravity of the situation. The rest of them tighten their lips and double down on the idea that things will be okay if we just have our homecoming. We've been raised on happy endings and defy reality to comply.

But . . . it's been four days.

So while Brynn keeps insisting that we will find Felicity, the other girls nod in agreement, then check their stock of waterproof mascara and make sure they have good funeral clothes. The guys, I imagine, are doing mental calculations on whether it's okay for them to cry in public or not. The ramifications of not crying versus crying, what the perfect balance of tears is to mark them as sensitive, but not a pussy.

I don't have time to cry. I've got shit to do.

After I leave the bonfire, I consult my list. Like most things I write down, it would look like senseless garble to anyone else.

Where I saw her first

When she touched my shoulder

The smell of her hair

The smile that broke me

I sit very still behind the wheel of my truck, waiting for a pull, a magnetic resonance, Felicity's self reaching out for mine. Needing me. But all I feel is a hard clump of fear, lodged deep in my gut, heavy and hot.

I drive to the elementary, find the merry-go-round in the back by the old, overgrown kickball field. The playground equipment near the school flashes brightly, the last rays of sun bouncing into my eyes as I run my hand over the dilapidated rejects, ignoring the signs telling me that there is danger, that I should not play here.

The merry-go-round can spin no more, its axle removed. It's inert and sinking into the ground, the wooden boards splintered, metal handrails almost entirely stripped of paint. Except for this one, here. Light blue.

It had matched her fingernails the first day of kindergarten, when we hadn't assessed each other's clothes for
labels and quality. When we had just been five-year-olds
entranced by centrifugal force. She'd leaned against me,
physics pushing us together, shoulder to shoulder, her
pinkie against mine. Her hair, sprayed across my face.

"Felicity," I say, pulling in a breath, wondering if any
of her exhalations are still here, twelve years later. If
they are, they tell me nothing, don't coalesce with the
center of me.

She's not here. The paint that matched her fingernails chipped almost entirely away.

Next is the gym, easy to sneak into as the volleyball crowd leaves, someone—an adult from visiting
Prospero—holding the door open for me, first with a
quick glance, then with a longer look, an assessment, a
whispered *That's the guy . . .*

I duck my head, slipping into the gym as the janitor
runs his wide mop, sweeping away the sweat of the volleyball players, their extreme efforts of the past hour lit
brightly on the scoreboard, vanishing in a second as he
flips the switch in passing.

"Lost my hat," I say, pointing to my head.

He just nods, makes a turn, accumulating dust and
dirt as he walks.

I make a show of looking around, pretending to be
in search of something. It's not like I think Felicity will

actually *be* here—although what a colossal embarrassment for the Amontillado PD if she were. Instead, I find the spot where she touched my shoulder freshman year, during a pep rally. The cheerleaders had been shooting T-shirts into the crowd and one had hit me directly in the eye. I hadn't been paying attention. It's a hard sell to divert my eyes from the bouncing, emphatic cheerleaders, but a string of texts from Lenore had come in, and I knew better than to ignore them.

Then a balled-up T-shirt hit me in the face, and Felicity was beside me, her mouth in an apologetic O, tiny beads of sweat on her forehead, her hand resting on my shoulder. She was so sorry. Was I hurt? Could she help?

My mouth, wired shut. My eyes, searching her face, looking for a spark, the oneness of her seeing the oneness of me, realizing the combined weight of us, the memory of that night. Her hand had twitched on my shoulder then, a muscular reaction that I hoped would travel up her arm, past her perfectly curved shoulders, up the slender neck, letting her brain know what her body already did.

Ribbit Usher is your savior.

But then Gretchen had yelled, "Go Ravens!" into a megaphone and everyone around us had screamed, "Fly high!" And our moment was lost, Felicity headed back to the gym floor, her rightful place. Where the attention was centered.

I breathe in, asking the question. "Where are you?"

"C'mon kid, quitting time," the janitor says.

I nod and walk to the exit, dutiful. I don't tell him he's wrong.

It is nowhere near quitting time.

The smell of her hair does not linger in the library, on the second floor, near the study carrel in the back. I'd found her there freshman year, head down, Patrick Vance lurking in the background, a wolf scenting a lamb. She'd glanced up at him, then me, and I'd waited once more for that moment, my moment. The moment she knew. Instead, she'd left with Patrick. And I'd sat in this chair, aware of what was left of her.

It's gone now, and the seat is cold, as the librarian wanders upstairs, spots me, jolts in surprise.

"I didn't know anyone was here," she says.

"Nobody is," I tell her.

The smile that broke me happened at Gretchen's house, somewhere I cannot simply appear. I drive to the back acre with my lights off, ignoring the danger of the falling dusk and the light mist that has risen. An old dairy barn, a crumbling hay mow, a dilapidated orchard—the remnants of what made the Astors who they are—stand alone, darkened. I slip into the woods silently, find the rock so many have used to consummate short-lived passions.

She's been here, I know. I've seen her leaving with Hugh. I did not follow in those moments, did not want to see the depth of her betrayal. But once she had gone alone, her walk uneven, her breathing stilted. My duty to keep her safe pulled me to follow her, to warn off others, flash my teeth if they saw this weakened one, strayed from the fold. But I'd lost her in the shadows and cursed myself, stumbling in the dark, no longer a protector but simply another lost sheep.

There was a light sound, a gurgle, perhaps a laugh. I'd followed, found her on the ground, hair luminous in the moonlight, eyes wide and blank.

"Felicity," I'd said, falling to my knees beside her.

She'd turned, her head crackling the leaves, eyes locking to mine, a smile spreading.

"Hey," she'd said, her voice light and thready, breath like my dad's, thick and rich with drink. A flicker passed, a light in her pupils, a question rising, recognition dawning. Her hand rose from the ground, dirt on the palm, to cup my cheek.

"You," she'd said. The word I'd needed. What I'd wanted.

"Yes," I said, equally breathless, heart beating fast, lowering to her.

But that smile slipped, realization faded, her body tensed, the hand against my cheek going cold as her brows drew together, concern rising in her eyes.

And then, "Where's Hugh?"

"He's not here," I say now, kicking at the rock. Although he had been, I'm sure. Been here, with her in ways that I've never been. Their shared history may outweigh mine in time and touch, but Felicity and I are anchored together in depth and desperation. Bonds that hold.

A sound builds, crawling over the horizon, a dull *thwup, thwup, thwup.* In the sky a helicopter rotates, spinning slowly, missing nothing. An intense beam of light cuts the ground below, dissecting, bisecting, searching in all the ways that they know how, the Turnados' money illuminating the night. Their methods have failed, for four days.

It's time for mine.

"I'm here," I tell Felicity as I sit on the rock, staring at where she had lain, and for a moment—I'm sure of it—*knew.*

Knew the strength of it, our connection. Knew our fates, tied.

I breathe deeply and wait for us to come together.

Chapter 38

Tress

Tuesday

I wake up to the opening credits of *Wheel of Fortune.*

I've lived with an old man long enough to do the math; if *Wheel* is on, I've been out for hours. I roll onto my side to see Mrs. Hannah's thick-soled shoes, tapping along. There's a hiss as the iron releases some steam, and I grab the edge of the coffee table, pulling myself up to a sitting position. The floor around me is clean, tissues and squashed maggots cleared away, all evidence of our impromptu surgery gone, except for three lines of stitches marching across my arm.

She used the school colors, purple and black, alternating. The skin around them is red and puffy, pressing back against the fabric teeth, bursting at the seams as it swells. The line I'd drawn on my arm is gone, erased in a wash of whiskey. But I remember where the red streaks of infection had stopped. They're past that now, wrapping my elbow and journeying toward my upper arm, a tattoo of pain.

"How you feeling?" Mrs. Hannah asks.

"Like shit," I tell her, my dry mouth struggling with even those two words. I spot the whiskey bottle still on the table, a thin line of amber resting at the bottom. I swig it down without asking permission, the fire in my belly matching the one in my arm.

"Is it going to be okay?" I ask, pulling my sleeve down.

"Do you mean in general, or your injury?" Mrs. Hannah asks, muting the television. "My experience of life so far—and I've been around—is that no, more than likely, things are not going to be okay. As for you . . . honey, you're dying. The infection's in your veins, tied in with your blood. Nothing I can fix with a scissors and a needle."

I close my eyes and nod, almost relieved. I hear the pulse of the heart at my neck, quieter now—*thwup, thwup, thwup*. Lighter. Is it mine, after all? Fading to nothing?

Under the table, my phone buzzes, insistent, unaware that it holds no relevance after an announcement like that. My arm throbs in time, sharper pain now, the itch of the maggots replaced by hundreds of tiny lacerations in my tissue, spots where Mrs. Hannah dug deep and purified with Jack Daniel's.

"Why'd you bother?" I ask. "Why clean me out and sew me up if I'm going to die?"

"Because I wanted to hurt you, Annabelle," she says, glancing up from one last piece of ironing—Hugh's Ravens jersey.

My phone vibrates again, this time with the quick, staccato beats of my ringtone. I flip it over to see it's Henley calling. There are a series of missed texts from him, their tone changing rapidly.

> **Don't have Huntington's! Don't know what that is but cousin says it's a bitch.**
>
> **Have the alcoholism gene. A surprise to no one.**
>
> **Cuz says another hour on your bloodstain, FYI**
>
> **Won't get breast cancer—bullet dodged!**
>
> **Hey Tress . . . you around?**
>
> **Got your results. Don't really want to text this.**
>
> **Hey—you getting these?**

His call goes to voice mail just as headlights flash across the living room wall, sending Mrs. Hannah into a fit.

"Hugh's dinner!" she cries. "You naughty girl! I spent all my time working on you when I should have been—"

She doesn't finish, only brushes past me in a huff while I stare down at my phone, another panicked call from Henley coming in as I struggle to my feet.

"Hey, Grandma, why is Tress's truck—"

I watch as Hugh comes into the kitchen, sawdust clinging to his hair, confusion on his face. I answer Henley's call.

"What's the verdict?" I ask.

"Tress, Christ . . . ," Henley says. "I don't know how to say this—"

"Use words," I suggest. "One in front of the other. Whose blood is it?"

"Tress?" Hugh spots me, comes into the living room, bringing a chemical smell with him. Something dark and charred. "Tress, what are you doing? Why are you here?"

"The blood is from the other person's mother," Henley says. "But listen to me—"

"Wait." I hold up my hand, stopping both Hugh and Henley. One with my words, the other with my motion. My heart stops, the one clue I've had in all these years fading into nothing, going out with my pulse.

"It's not my mom's? It's not her blood? You're sure?"

"Yes, we're sure! But listen, Tress—"

"Blood?" Hugh asks, coming farther into the room, his eyes searching my face. "Tress, who are you talking to?"

"The other sample . . . Okay, look—I'm really sorry, Tress. Please don't kill me."

"I won't kill you," I say, my voice dull and low, the promise kept in the simple sense that I lack the energy to even speak louder.

"The other sample you gave me—it belongs to your brother."

"My . . . ?"

The world fades out, the yellowing wallpaper of Mrs. Hannah's front room infiltrated by black, creeping in on all sides. The silent, spinning wheel on the television blurs together, all the colors fusing into monochrome.

I stumble forward, dropping my phone. Hugh grabs my shoulders, pulling me against him to break my fall. I collapse into his chest, where I've seen so many girls before. Brynn. Gretchen. Felicity. (*I'm sorry, Felicity.*) But never me, never a flirtation or a wandering hand. Not even a crude joke or allowing others to make them at my expense. Always, Hugh has protected me. Always, like a brother.

I raise my face, look up into his. See my father's eyes there, for the first time.

"You knew," I say.

"I'm sorry, Tress." He rests his forehead against mine, and I press back against it, my heart finding a cadence, picking back up.

Refusing to quit.

Chapter 39

Tress

Tuesday

"Your dad and my mom."

It's the most Hugh will say on the subject, but it answers a lot of questions. If Hugh is my brother—half brother, anyway—then yes, my father was putting his dick somewhere it wasn't supposed to be. Hugh pushes a glass of water toward me across the kitchen table. He'd talked his grandma into watching the news, settling her onto the couch with orange juice and the remote control.

I switch the water glass to my good hand, experimentally twitching the fingers on my other one. They still move, everything still works, even if it hurts like hell. The heart at my neck beats lighter now. In freshman biology we had to collect bugs, capturing them in mason jars and dropping alcohol-soaked cotton balls in after them, screwing lids on tightly. The butterfly I'd caught had scrambled desperately at the glass sides, gaining no purchase as the oxygen evaporated, fumes taking it over as its wings beat, ineffectually, shuddering to a slow halt.

The necklace feels the same, the desperation gone, an acceptance of the inevitable slowing it, easing it away from life and smoothing the way toward death. I clutch at it, understanding, the smooth edges of the half heart cutting into my palm, the two pulses meeting, both flagging.

—*thwup, thwup, thwup*—

"My dad and your mom," I repeat, and Hugh nods. I take a sip from the glass. It's lukewarm, tasting slightly of eggs, the sulfur of a hand-dug well infused with the water. I'm familiar with the taste. Cecil refuses to pay for a hookup at the trailer, says he won't pay people for what God gives for free.

"I think it had been going on for a while," I say, my eyes on Hugh as I talk, careful to avoid any words that might cut. *Adultery. Cheating. Infidelity.*

"Grandma says . . ." Hugh's gaze goes to the door, like he'd rather not bring her into the conversation, which I appreciate. He finally convinced her that I was his friend Tress and not Annabelle Usher, although she continued to throw me dirty looks, as if both could be true at the same time. And maybe they can, just as the Allan house can be both there and not there, just as a heart can beat in my hand and in my chest simultaneously.

"What does she say?" I prompt him.

Hugh sighs, rakes his hands through his hair, knocking bits of sawdust to the table. "I don't want to hurt you, Tress," he says.

"Not knowing is what hurts," I tell him. "And I've not known long enough."

"All right." He glances again toward the living room, but Mrs. Hannah's head is moving in time with the theme song for the national news, lost in larger worries than the long-past happenings of Amontillado.

"They were friends," I begin for him. "But something went wrong."

"Good friends," Hugh says darkly. "Maybe too good. They shared everything."

"Even boyfriends," I say so he doesn't have to.

"Yep." He nods. "And that kept up after they got married. I guess a lot of people knew what was going on, but nobody said anything."

No, of course not. Not with an Usher and a Montor in the mix. Money and power both coming down on your head like an anvil from the sky.

"But something went wrong," I say. "I read the journals. Even back in high school. My mom was pissed off about . . ."

About what? Her boyfriend sleeping with her best friend, when it was her own idea? Or was it something that started out sounding fun and went south fast?

"Your mom wasn't . . ." Hugh tries to meet my eyes and can't, his gaze bouncing off mine and landing somewhere more comfortable, the Formica tabletop, a nonreflective surface. "After we were born your mom said it had to stop. Said it was time for all four of them to settle down and be parents."

"Did she know that you were . . . that you were my dad's kid?"

"I don't think so." Hugh shakes his head. "But *my* dad did. And I think people have put it together, as I got older. I . . . Tress, when I go to the grocery store I feel people looking at me, trying to decide if I look like a Broward, or talk like a Montor."

I can imagine. I've felt eyes on me my whole life, dark wells of pity ready to swallow me if I would just wade in, give myself up to their compassion. I've always walked away, showing them my back and straight spine.

"But they didn't stop," I say. "After we were born."

"My dad and your mom did, but . . ."

"Okay," I say, not needing more. "But there was a falling-out before that, in high school."

"Yeah, I guess that happened a lot," Hugh says, a small smile forming on his lips. "I mean, hasn't anyone ever told you that you're just like your mom?"

"All the time," I say. "It never feels like a compliment."

"I wouldn't say there's not admiration in it," Hugh says, but his jaw clamps shut and his eyes move to something over my shoulder. I turn to find Mrs. Hannah peering around the doorframe, empty juice glass in hand.

"You didn't get your temper at a garage sale," she says. "That comes natural."

Her mind is in the right place for now, seeing me as Tress and not my mother. I jump at the opportunity. "But why was there blood on the journals? Heather's blood?"

"That's my fault," she says, moving to the sink to rinse her glass. "Caught Heather reading them once, after your parents went missing. Jason had left her on account of Hugh looking more like Lee every day. She was living here, brought Hugh and all her stuff along. I thought a fresh start was in order. But all she wanted to do was wallow in it, moon over things from her past. Anything connected with Annabelle or Lee. She was paging through them books, crying about something or other—*What I've lost*, she tried to tell me.

"*What you've lost is your damn mind*, I told her," Mrs.

Hannah says. "And smacked her a good one with my coffee mug, right on the temple. She always was a bleeder, and more worried about saving those bits of paper than what was dripping all over my new carpet. I told her if she knew what was good for her she'd get rid of all that stuff, wipe the Montors away like the stain they were, and get the hell out of Amontillado before her name got tangled up in something it shouldn't."

"Their disappearance?" I ask.

She nods, wiping the glass. "My girl had nothing to do with it, her man, either. They told me as much, and I believe them. But you do one wrong in Amontillado, you carry it with you, and are more liable to be condemned for others."

My phone goes off in my hand, a call from Cecil. He's probably wondering if I've done the chores, and if not, when I'll be back to take care of them. It's easier for him to call me from the couch than actually get up and go do them himself. Either that or he's spotted the cat again and would rather risk me being eaten than him.

"I've got to go," I say, and Hugh comes to his feet.

"I'll walk out with you."

Mrs. Hannah comes over to me, puts her hands on my shoulders, her eyes clear as she peers up into my face. "You got to let it go, young one. Some things we just aren't meant to know."

"Like five across?" I ask, and confusion floods her eyes.

"Your crossword puzzle," I explain. "A synonym for *nurse*? Second letter is *u*? It's the verb, not the noun."

"Ooohhh." Her eyes widen as realization dawns. *"Suckle."*

"Yeah," I say, "like a mom with a baby. And I don't care what you think of Annabelle Usher. She might not have been a good person, but she was a great mom."

Mrs. Hannah pulls her hands away from me as if I'm suddenly too hot to touch, the famed Usher temper igniting inside me.

"And you know what?" I add. "You're a shit nurse."

The screen door slams behind me, and I hear Hugh's heavy tread. "Tress, wait . . . Listen."

I get to the truck, lean against it, the coolness of the metal creeping through my clothing, dulling the fire. "I just want to go home, Hugh," I tell him. "I'm sick and I'm tired and somebody's got to feed the animals."

"Okay," he says, putting his hands up in surrender. "Just . . . please don't be mad at me."

"I'm not," I say, cradling my arm, feeling the swollen skin beneath the fabric.

"I wanted to tell you," he says. "So many times I almost did, but I . . ."

I think of Felicity, her gray face in the light of the single bulb. *Your dad was cheating on your mom.* Me, exploding, throwing things, denying.

"It doesn't matter," I tell Hugh. "I wouldn't have believed you."

I get into the truck, scrambling awkwardly with one good arm and hoping he doesn't notice. He comes to the open window.

"The cops are coming tomorrow. You know that, right?"

"Yeah," I say. "Questioning everybody who was in the video, trying to get a lead on where Felicity was, who she talked to."

"Right." He nods once, tightly. Eyes searching mine.

"What?" I ask. Luckily, I'm too exhausted to sound defensive.

Hugh reaches into the car, rests a hand on my shoulder.

"If you ever need anything. I'm your guy," he says.

"You already were," I tell him, and he nods.

But what I need is to have my parents returned to me. What I need is to not have Felicity Turnado's blood on my hands. I need a panther put back in his cage and for my wounds to close.

I need a thousand things, all of them impossible.

Chapter 40

Ribbit

Tuesday

"What do I smell?"

Lenore is on me the second I come in the back door, ducking low under the lintel that seems to inch downward every time I leave. This house is sinking into the ground, being swallowed whole. I adjust my stance subconsciously, knowing one side of the kitchen slants to the left.

"I asked about the smell, Usher."

She stands in front of the stove, arms crossed, demanding. Holding herself like a queen despite the crack as wide as my hand in the wall behind her. Usher blood standing upright. Usher bones in an unbending spine.

"It's nothing." I try to wave her off. "Stunt gel for the bonfire."

Her doubt fades slowly, belief in her only child restored to the extent that she can unclench her jaw. "You weren't smoking?"

"Smoking? What . . . no! I don't smoke, Mom."

"Good," she says, dropping her arms. "That'll kill you. It's what got—"

"Great-Grandpa Roderick," I fill in before she can finish, the names, dates, causes of death, and any honorable-life mentions of previous Ushers drilled into my brain.

"Yes," she agrees, but only with my recitation of facts. Her eyes are still boring, asking a question she doesn't need to vocalize.

"This bonfire . . ."

"Not for Tress." I shake my head. "I wouldn't do that to her."

Mother shrugs, the method not a concern. "Accidents happen. Fire is hard to control."

"They do and it is," I say, giving her my own dose of Usher glare. Trouble is, mine is diluted by a healthy dash of Dad's Troyer blood. It breaks against the rocks of her irises, but I'm not going to take the time to explain myself, and my voice isn't strong enough to contain my rage.

I turn my back, hear the harsh intake of breath escaping her, the surprise that I did not wait to be excused.

It's a deviation from the norm, a bright flare of rebellion, and she'd do well to mark it and pay attention. I pass the door to my father's study, the last rays of light breaking through the west window. I can just see the tuft of his hair above the chair he sits in, facing the window, staring out at Usher property that stretches down the ridge, worn-out acres holding on to old bones.

I consider stopping, letting him know. My father's resolve has weakened over the years, the desire for more dwindling into regret over actions that could not be undone. Actions that—if I'm being honest—an Usher hand had guided, and that his would have never fallen to naturally. I've taken up the mantle, and will finish the work, sparing him that final move.

I open my mouth to speak, but as happens so often in this house, I have no voice. Near my father's hand rests a bottle. I wander into the office, watch the long shadows covering his face, Usher branches moving in the wind outside, scratching at his eyes as he rests.

His mouth is open, his chest rising and falling in a soft rhythm, his eyes closed in the only release he can expect—the bottle. Mother is not wrong that there is a weakness in my blood when it comes to drinking, but I think that particular flow in my veins may have more than one source, rendering the current doubly strong.

I twist the cap from the bottle, meaning only to sniff.

But it rises to my lips, a hot brand burning my throat as it travels to my belly, releasing my voice out into the world, as it did on Friday. I sit in the dark with my comatose father, considering.

My words will be written in fire and blood; all the pinpricks of a lifetime spent nodding, bowing, fetching, submitting, doing as they willed, have congealed into a massive wound, a yawning mouth that is my own. They thought it culminated Friday night, with me naked and on display, wishes and desires, hopes and wants, shared for all to know and revel in.

Not so.

They don't know, can't see. Friday night was just their version of foreplay.

Tomorrow, I'm going to fuck them.

Chapter 41

Tress

Tuesday

My arm is a hot brand, the stitches Mrs. Hannah sewed into my skin like burning wire that holds me together. I'm shaky and weak, in body and spirit as I lie in bed, staring at the ceiling.

Hugh Broward is my brother.

It's a strange word in my mouth, one I've never had use for. The Oxy I popped as soon as I walked in the door at home doesn't help, the syllables blending and rolling as I try to speak. Try to say this new thing—*brother.*

My phone vibrates once, twice, insistently. A call is coming, and I glance at the screen, in case a client needs something, even though I'm incapable of bringing it to them at the moment. Instead, it's Ribbit's face, pressed close to mine, a selfie from last summer taken as we sat on his tailgate, our toes dangling into the Usher pond.

I answer. "Hey."

There's only silence, some muffled movements. "Hey," I yell louder, pulling the phone away from my face. "You butt-dialed me, Ribbit."

"No," his voice contradicts me, calm and cool. But not clear, not by a long shot.

"Are you drunk?" I ask.

It wouldn't be the first time. My cousin goes down hard and fast, one drink that in my blood would only set a warm glow, in his becomes a conflagration.

"Maybe don't be drunk," I tell him, glancing at my arm. "I can't exactly come over there and sober you up right now."

"Tress," Ribbit says, slurring my name. "Tress, what did you do?"

My heart plummets into my stomach. Did he talk to the woman in the BMW? And about what? The loose panther? Acres of weed? Did Ribbit talk to her about the worst thing?

Did he talk to her about Felicity?

"What do you mean?" I ask carefully, choosing each word the way you do with a drunk, hoping not to use the one that will suddenly, inexplicably, set them off.

There's a long pause while drunk Ribbit asks

himself—what does he mean?

"Friday night," he says. "Where were you?"

Well, shit. On the day I find out I have a half brother—and no further clues left on discovering what happened to my parents—my cousin decides to get a stick up his ass about me neglecting my babysitting duties at a party.

"Busy," I tell him, my mouth tight around the word.

"Doing what?" he shoots back, the consonants difficult to hit.

I'm not going to shake him this time. Not going to be able to make vague comments about weed and pills, and I sure as hell don't want to mention the basement. I'm guilty of many things, from misdemeanors right up to murder one, but is it possible I can come clean about the lesser of my sins to mask the larger one?

"Ribbit, listen to me," I say, my voice low. "The cat got out."

There's a long silence, and I wonder if he passed out. "The . . . cat?" Even those two words are a struggle.

"Yeah," I say, snapping back with a slurry of words, hoping he'll drown in the tide, concede defeat. "The panther's been loose since Friday. He was at the house, at the party. I managed to corral him into an upstairs bedroom and keep him there, but I got shut in too. So, while you were lit and swinging your wang for CNN, I was staring down teeth and claws, hoping he wouldn't go for my neck. So you know what?" I seethe, aware that righteous anger has risen along with my volume.

"What?" Ribbit asks in response, the word limp and vacant.

"You can fuck off."

"What?" Ribbit asks, incredulous. Rarely do I strike out at him. Blood is blood, after all, and most of my venom spent in his presence has been in his defense. But right now, I am just done with Ribbit Usher. I'm not my cousin's keeper, and I never have been.

"Take care of your own shit before you come after me for mine," I tell him.

I want to add that he can't drink. He's a goddamn lightweight, and he knows it. That is not my fault, and I am absolutely done with things being my fault.

But he hangs up before I get the chance.

"Whatever," I say to the blank screen.

Except, it's not blank. There's a voice mail from April Turnado. I look at it a second before tapping on it to play. Might as well make this Oxy do double duty.

"Tress?" It's April, a version of her I've never heard before. This one doesn't have a high ponytail, and her newly whitened teeth aren't on display. By the sounds of it, those teeth probably have a decent coating of liquor, and I'm betting her hair doesn't exactly have a glossy shine right now. April Turnado was trashed when she called me.

Apparently, this is what Amontillado does on Tuesday now. Drink, and call Tress Montor.

"I know I haven't always been nice to you," April says, each word slipping out like a slug she doesn't want to leave her mouth, sharing its secrets. "I know I wasn't always . . . kind."

Alone in my room, I snort-laugh. No, she has not always been kind.

"But if you know something . . . Tress, you're on the list for the cops to interview tomorrow. If you know anything about where Felicity might be—"

She wants to ask for more, maybe even beg, but her voice cracked when she said her daughter's name and after that it just became a litany of sobs. But I don't tell April to fuck off, even over voice mail. Even in my head.

Because Ribbit is responsible for his own damn problems.

But I deserve to hear this suffering. I deserve to know what I've done to April Turnado. There's more crying, followed by a deep, stuttering breath.

"I can't feel like this anymore," April confides to me, in a whisper.

Fuck. I end the message, and toss the phone away from me, out into the darkness of my room. I know where she is. I know how she feels. I've been there, rotting in the moment, aware of the endless possibilities of what may or may not have happened to my parents. I could accept their deaths in one moment, and then dial their number in the next. Absolutely certain that, this time—*this time*—one of them will answer. Felicity will never answer her mother's call, and I'm the only person who knows that.

The Oxy takes hold, anxious to pull me down into the sweet reprise of unconsciousness.

"I can't feel like this anymore," I repeat April's words. But they are entirely my own.

And I've been living in that place far longer than she has.

Chapter 42

Ribbit

Wednesday

They say a watched pot never boils, but when I get to the high school parking lot Wednesday morning, it looks like we're cooking with gas. Students swarm over everything, busy ants performing their duties in a tiny kingdom with the conviction that these things are important.

The floats for the different organizations are in formation for the parade this evening, each group eyeing the others to see if they've been outdone. And even though the art club has rendered a life-sized papier-mâché of Michelangelo's *David* (anatomically correct, and perhaps slightly exaggerated), that is not what people will be talking about tomorrow.

I'd called Tress last night meaning to get something

out of her. The truth. What happened Friday. Where the hell Felicity is. But I got drunk before I called her, which was stupid. Tress has always been stronger and faster than me, and when I'm drunk she's also smarter. She'd fended me off, and then gave me a very poignant piece of advice.

Take care of your own shit before you come after me for mine.

Good call, Tress. I will.

I park my truck near the homecoming court's float, pulling a poster tube from behind the seat. The float is hard to miss. The Astors paid for an enormous balloon arch that stretches from end to end, purple and black balloons rustling gently in the breeze. Gretchen is perched on the hood of her car, giving instructions to a group of freshman girls who are painstakingly stapling alternating black, silver, and purple strands of metallic fringe around the edge. Yards of dark purple tulle are piled in one corner, a smaller bag of light purple nearby.

"Ribbit!" Gretchen squeals as soon as she spots me. I'm her man of the hour, a place I've been once before when I found her lost little dog, William Wilson, after he bolted at a party. She'd been . . . grateful. And while being in Gretchen's good graces had only lasted a few moments (*all my texts ignored, my number blocked, my sacrifice forgotten*), those few moments had been memorable.

And now I'm back in her ever-roaming spotlight

again, whitened teeth flashing at me, ravens—carefully drawn with eyeliner so they seem to be taking flight from the corners of her eyes—crinkling as she smiles. "Anho gave everyone first period to work on homecoming stuff. Isn't that awesome? What do you think of the float?"

I suppose it probably is awesome for those who have a place here, those who belong, and those who hope to impress them by lending their hands. But I can't expect Gretchen to think of those of us who aren't on the court, don't own a jersey, or belong to a club. Those people are in mostly empty classrooms right now, playing Candy Crush on their phones and wishing they mattered.

Not me. I'm out here, holding the finishing touch for the court float. I'm out here, about to wipe that insipid smile off Gretchen Astor's school-themed face. But first I smile back, duck my head, make it clear that I feel the full weight of the honor of her presence. I grovel as befits my station, and she basks in it, as befits hers.

"It looks great!" I tell her, pretending to watch as the freshmen drape tulle over the chairs. Light purple for the underclassman attendants, dark purple for the king and queen candidates.

Royal purple.

"It's missing one thing, though," I say, tapping her on the nose with the poster tube. The sparkle in Gretchen's eyes dim, although the smile stays plastered on, years of practice keeping it in place.

"What's that?" she asks, but I don't answer, instead hoisting myself onto the float and enlisting the help of one of the freshman girls. I pop the plastic end off the cardboard tube and hand a corner to her. She follows when I motion for her to walk to the edge of the trailer, and we unroll the poster right in front of Gretchen, inches from her nose.

It's Felicity's senior banner from the cheerleading squad, "Go Ravens!" scrawled across the top, "Fly High!" along the bottom, the top of the exclamation point just grazing the inside of one thigh. She is smooth perfection in the shot, lines hinting at toned muscles, the crease at the neckline plunge allowing the imagination to ponder something softer. Her smile is innocent but alluring, her eyes charmingly bright with just the hint of provocative. It says, *I'm a good girl*, while also hinting that if someone came closer, that could change.

The girl at the other corner glances over the edge to see what she's holding. "Uh, how'd you get this?"

"Don't worry about it," I tell her.

The truth is that the windstorm that tore through Amontillado at the beginning of the school year had ripped the senior banners from the zip ties attaching them to the fence that lines the football field. But only some. I'd come in the night with a garden shears, taking the one I wanted.

"Hang it there," I say to the freshman, pointing at the head of the float where lavender letters proudly announce the *Homecomeing Court*.

"Also, you spelled *homecoming* wrong."

"What?!" Gretchen shrieks, her attention yanked from Felicity's poster to this new monstrosity. I watch as she assesses the mistake, fuming. "Janelle!" she screams as one of the girls tries to slip off the back of the float and out of sight.

"We can't put it there," another girl argues with me. "That's where this goes." She whips a plastic tablecloth off a gigantic piñata in the shape of a raven. I can only hope it's full of bird flu.

"I'll hang it from the middle of the balloon arch," I volunteer, before Gretchen can voice any objections. The girls look to Gretchen first, but she's cornered and she knows it. If she refuses to hang Felicity's poster, she's going to look like the sorest winner on record. She smiles and nods, but the ravens at the corners of her eyes seems to have lost some of their plumage, streaked away by tears of fury and quick flicks of acrylic nails.

"I thought it was the least we could do," I say, and Gretchen can only nod in silent agreement as Hugh and Brynn come up beside her, surveying the float.

"Hey, man," he says, giving me an up-nod. He's pale, his sunken eyes distracted as I hang the raven piñata. Huge looks tired, like he's only got a few leaps left in him before a lion lands on his back. Brynn pulls out her phone and snaps a pic of the empty float once the freshmen climb down, her face somber. Gretchen takes in her subjects, their flagging enthusiasm.

"Court photo!" she cries, jumping up and down. "Everybody get together!"

Brynn rolls her eyes but obediently hoists herself onto the trailer, Hugh offering a hand. He follows her up, then bellows across the parking lot for David, Cody, and Maddie. They cluster, a group of beautiful people in purple and black, the color of a bruise.

"Ribbit, can you . . . ?" Gretchen doesn't need to finish her sentence, or question that I will obey. I take her phone, back up a few steps, and encourage them to say *Go Ravens!*

Behind the camera, my smile is the biggest.

Chapter 43

Tress

Wednesday

I wake up halfway through the day, my arm a pillar of fire.

"Shit," I mutter, wiping crust from my eyes. In the bathroom mirror, my lips are dry and pockmarked, my eyes glinting with fever. I splash water on my face, but it can only help so much. Red spots burn on my cheeks, and when I press against my stitches, pus foams through. I pour hydrogen peroxide over everything, the bubbles piling high, a hiss escaping from between my lips at the sting. But it's pointless, and I know it. Mrs. Hannah was right, there's an infection in my blood, and I feel it multiplying, coursing through my body with each pulse of my heart, the beat at my chest growing weaker.

I press against the necklace, feel a tiny response.

—thwup, thwup, thwup—

I find Cecil on the couch, sorting through the mail. "The school called," he says, not glancing up. "Said you wasn't there."

"They said I'm *not* there," I correct him as he tosses a flier from the Humane Society aside.

"Look at you, knowing stuff," he says.

"It's not that hard, Cecil," I tell him, and he finally spares me a glance with his good eye, the milky one rolling away.

"You're ornery today," he observes, and I grunt in reply.

I usually won't pick a fight with him, having learned long ago that it isn't worth it. I'd either pay immediately with a slap to the head, or he'd draw it out, letting me feel safe until he pulled the rug out from under me. Once he did that literally, and I've got a scar at the edge of my temple to show for it, a chunk missing from the corner of the coffee table standing as testament to exactly how hardheaded I can be.

"You tell them I'm sick?" I ask, pulling out my phone, already assuming he had not.

"Nah," Cecil says. "I told them you were already smarter than me—or at least think you are—and that you didn't need no more schooling."

"Good grasp of irony," I say, but he only nods.

"They said the cops want to talk to you."

I freeze, and he knows that he got me with that one.

"You do something?" he asks, the milky eye somehow staring me down.

"If by *do something* you mean sell pot and pills because you told me to, yeah, I did something," I snap back.

It's his turn to go still, and he watches me in silence.

"They're talking to everybody," I finally say, backing down a little bit. "About Felicity."

"Bah," Cecil says, waving his hand in the air like the concept of a missing girl is an annoyance to him.

"You see to the animals," he says. "I've got things to deal with."

Cecil always has *things to deal with*, usually nothing related to work. It's past noon, and I'm sure Dee is going to give me a peck for every minute her breakfast was late. A hungry ostrich is not a nice thing to deal with, but an out-of-sorts zebra isn't any better. Zee has stomped on my toes more than once to get to his feed when I'm running behind, and I haven't made the mistake of wearing anything other than work boots out to the paddock in a long time.

I rest on the steps after yanking my boots on, an awkward accomplishment with just the one hand. Little white dots explode across my vision, and I lean back against the trailer, my breath coming short and shallow, sweat popping across my forehead.

I don't know what all I've got left in me. Don't know if I can get the animals fed, or even cross the yard without falling over. And if I can't do that, do the things that have pushed me through every day since fifth grade, how am I supposed to aim for something larger? I've asked questions and irritated adults, turned over rocks and found the roaches, but I am no closer to finding out what happened to my parents than I was when I woke up the morning after to an empty house and a 911 operator who needed my house number, a vital piece of information that my panicked brain could not provide.

I've heard the call. Some two-bit true-crime podcaster wanted to do a feature on my parents when I was a freshman. She'd caught me in the post office—returning stamps of all things. Cecil refused to use the stamps commemorating Sally Ride, said women had no business in space anyway, and got up to enough trouble on just the one planet. He sent me into town to get the World War I stamps (not John Lennon, because *he isn't even an American*). The woman had stopped me, asked if I was Tress Montor and if I'd be willing to talk to her about my parents.

Even though I'd had plenty of stranger-danger lessons at school (not from Cecil, he'd told me if anyone ever asked me to get in their car that I should just go ahead and hop in), I'd never had anyone ask me if I wanted to talk about my parents. Most adults were uncomfortable with it, and Cecil had told me more than once that it was bad enough I looked like my mom but I had to be a bitch about things, too.

So here was this woman I didn't know, with a nice smile and a legal pad full of notes she wanted to show me. I'd followed her out of the post office, the post-master's eyes heavy on my back, and Aunt Lenore had whisked me out of the coffee shop five minutes later, the woman left behind to face down Amontillado's finest about why she was enticing a minor.

But Lenore hadn't been able to get to me fast enough. The woman had played the 911 call for me from a file on her laptop, my voice, high and scared, the sounds of a child.

"I don't know where my parents are," I'd said.

And I still don't.

Zee brays at me from across the yard, and I raise my head. "I'm coming," I yell. Dee joins him, flapping her wings and honking. "You're still ugly," I tell her. In her cage, the painted lion's ears flick toward the sound of my voice, a ring of gold starting to show at her roots. Rue comes to the wall of her enclosure, reaches a hand through, beckoning to me.

"Give me a sec," I tell her, but I doubt my voice is

strong enough to carry. My phone goes off. I've got a text from Hugh, and one from Ribbit. They both say the same thing.

You okay?

The same words, but each of them asking about something entirely different. My cousin wants to know if I'm still on the wrong side of this fever, and Hugh wants to know if I'm okay with the fact that yesterday I discovered he is my brother.

I don't have a good answer for either of them. I could tell Ribbit I'm probably dying, let Hugh know that I'm not exactly thrilled but I'm not mad at him, either. I'm debating when a new notification catches my eye, a little red number one next to my email app.

Not exactly my email app, but one for Amontillado Animal Attractions. I'd set up our site during a preteen tear to make us bigger, better, and more profitable. I'd had college in my sights at the time, but the conservation groups spotted us before the Ivy Leagues did, and I'd nearly drowned in a flood of insults and accusations. I'd read some of them aloud to Cecil, his responses becoming more florid as the beers disappeared. Some of them were funny enough—*I'll unleash my pussy if you promise to keep yours put away*—that I actually sent them. But most had been thrown away, and I'd limited the character count in the Contact Us box to one hundred.

A few pithy barbs had come in since then, but I haven't had an email in the Amontillado Animal Attractions in-box for months.

And one popping up with a loose panther on the prowl is not reassuring.

Stomach in my boots, I click on it.

It's from a woman named Ada LaLage, and includes a link to two YouTube videos, as well as a website, along with a single line of text and a phone number.

I've been trying to get in touch with you. Time is running out.

With a shaky thumb, I click on the site link. It takes me to a sleekly designed page with a serious-looking woman—arms crossed, no hint of a smile—with the heading, *Ada LaLage: Private Investigator.*

"Shit," I say, my heart erupting into panicked beats, a trapped butterfly trying to escape. I wasn't wrong, the Turnados went and got themselves a private PI, well aware that the clock on getting Felicity back alive was ticking.

I click on the first YouTube link and am taken to a cut scene from Friday night's party, Hugh scrolling through the thousands of questions coming in from around the world as Ribbit gladly answers whatever he is asked, happy as long as everyone else is, too. In the clip, the view tightens on Hugh's feed, the questions coming so fast he can only pick one out of a thousand to answer. But there had been some repeats, one of them from the same viewer, asking over and over, insistent.

Have you ever killed anyone?

The clip grounds to a halt, zooms in on the words, pixelated and gray on a white background, fading out, just like my pulse. The screen shakes in my fevered hands, the words blurring.

"Yes," I say. "Yes, I have."

Christ, this woman is shaking me down. I click on the second YouTube link and it takes me to a private video, the woman from the site staring into the camera, her dark hair in a sharp bob.

"Tress," she says. "It's important that you listen to me."

I drop the phone. My name on her lips sends me into a panic, makes real what my fevered mind had only toyed with.

I killed Felicity Turnado, and I am caught.

Chapter 44

Rue

DarkHair, SilentCrier, FoundChild . . .
Now, SickSmell.
No, my girl. No.
In my hand, her hair, there is:
Despair. Surrender. Submit.
(CRUSHED SKULL. AN ACCIDENT. IT'S A SHAME.)
Screaming. Shaking. Spitting.
Don't sit, look up, beware
Mouthwords. Handwords. Screamwords.
Won't listen. Can't hear.
Danger, Danger, DANGER.
Take you, from me,
Like before. Empty-arms. LostChild.

(IN CASH. HARD WORKER. ALWAYS AN ALLAN.)

Girl, listen. Girl, please. Girl, hear/see my cries/words

Danger, Danger, DANGER.

No child, no.

No child.

No man will take my child.

Chapter 45

Tress

Wednesday

The email motivates me to get up and moving, like maybe if I do my chores and am a good girl it will make up for having committed murder. Or maybe I just want to make sure everybody gets fed one more time before I'm cuffed. Because if the animals have to depend on Cecil to take care of them, they better learn how to survive on hope real fast.

I learned that lesson early, and quick.

True to character, Dee gets a few pecks in and ups her game by shitting directly on my boot. "Nice," I mutter, scraping it off on the underside of the feed trough. Zee brushes up against me, leaning a little to show affection. His weight and heat are usually a welcome comfort, but not today, not with a fever and lacking the strength to push back against him. Instead, I stumble, grabbing his mane to keep my feet. Zee shoots me a concerned look, mouth grinding grain. There's a huge tick on his shoulder, inflated to the size of a grape. I dig into the pocket of my work coat, finding the lighter I keep there.

"Sorry, buddy, I should've caught that sooner," I say, touching the flame to the tick. It lets go, tumbling down Zee's chest to land on the ground, where it rolls onto its back, too engorged for its legs to find purchase.

From her cage, Rue shrieks at me, and I tuck the lighter away.

I know she's mad. I know I'm late with the feeding and ignored her beckoning to me earlier, but there's a note in her voice I've never heard before. Something between pleading and panicked. Zee stops chewing, his head up, ears back in alarm.

"It's okay," I tell him, not sharing what Mrs. Hannah had said the other night. Her opinion that more than likely things are not okay. Never have been and probably never will be. Another shriek erupts from Rue, as if to confirm that.

I leave Dee and Zee's paddock and head over to the lion, who barely acknowledges my presence. Rue goes nuts as soon as she spots me, peeling her lips back and shaking the fence. When she acts like this Cecil likes to say she's gone *apeshit*, which he never ceases to find amusing. I switch out the lion's water for fresh, but her meat from yesterday still lies on the ground, untouched, except by flies. I call out to her, and her ears twitch, but that's all I get.

"Sorry, girl," I say, my throat closing a little.

I leave the lion's pen, and Rue loses her mind. She's screeching and screaming, climbing the walls of her enclosure and throwing anything that isn't screwed down. Most of it bounces back off the fence, but some of the apples she's stashed make it through, clearing my shoulder and landing somewhere behind me.

"Calm down, Rue," I say, holding my hands out as I approach her cage. "You're going to hurt yourself."

She swings down from the tree, landing in a crouch in front of me when I'm only a few yards away, an apple in her fist. *Danger*, she signs at me, breathing heavily. *Danger, danger, danger.*

"Rue, I don't—"

She hurls the apple and it flies past me again, her aim way off, much worse than usual. Most of the time she can peg me as far away as Dee and Zee's paddock.

"You get into Cecil's beer?" I ask her, and she crouches, upper lip curled, hands flexing. Her eyes meet mine and she tries one more time.

Danger, danger, danger.

And then I hear someone behind me.

Chapter 46

Ribbit

Wednesday

Buzzards are ugly bastards, scavengers of the dead, aerial indications of something rotting below. And in Amontillado a lot of things are rotten, so collecting all the feathers to make the homecoming queen's wings didn't take that long.

Coating each one in flammable gel is a pain in the ass, though. The buckets of stunt gel—created to protect and preserve—sit empty, awaiting my new concoction. One that will be a catalyst, coaxing any flame into an inferno. The boys will believe it's the same stuff we practiced with, brought to them by someone they trust, not knowing that what they slather themselves with will meld their skin with flame, blacken their muscles, and liquefy what little fat they have on their bodies.

Controlling fire is what pushed our species above the others, keeping us warm, cooking our food, providing light so that we could devote nighttime hours to something other than pure survival, splashing our creativity on walls and immortalizing hunts, telling great stories of ourselves so that our deeds would not be forgotten.

I'm painting not with hematite or charcoal, but with a mix of antacid, vinegar, and rubbing alcohol. My hunt is about to begin, and my deeds . . .

My deeds will be remembered for a long, long time.

Chapter 47

Tress

Wednesday

I spin on my heel, Rue's scream echoing in my ears, her hands flashing through my mind, over and over, for days now.

Danger, danger, danger.

It's Odell, the guy who brought us the panther and, more recently, the lion. But I don't see his truck anywhere, and he's holding my baseball bat from the living room. The one I use to prod Cecil awake. My body reacts before my brain, every hair on my neck standing up and muscles tensing, even though my only thought is *Odell plays baseball?*

He swings high, aiming for my temple, and I instinctively roll under it, years of avoiding hooks from Cecil finally paying off, the payout for getting a drunk old man into his bed coming due. The bat rings off Rue's cage, and she shrieks again, shaking the fence, reaching through to swipe at Odell, who straightens his stance, and pulls back for the next pitch.

"What the fuck?" I say. They're the only words I have, the single string of monosyllables my brain can put together right now. Odell is swinging for the fences, aiming to clean my head right off my shoulders.

And I have no idea why.

I'm weak and weaponless, backpedaling as he advances, my hands in front of me to ward off an attack. It's instinct, and this time it's not on my side. I dodge the brunt of the swing, but he clips my bad arm, and I'm screaming to match Rue now, on my hands and knees, my arm edging past pain and into agony, then going beyond to somewhere there aren't words.

I'm down, Odell's shadow advancing, the bat raised high. I'm going to die in my own yard, skull crushed in by a man who probably tried meth for the first time and thought murder sounded good as a follow-up. Time extends, each beat of my heart drawn out for an eternity, every breath a lifetime. But some of those are terribly short, and mine will join that list if I don't . . . if I don't . . .

Do something. Feed the animals. Clean the pens. Keep your head down. Try harder. Find your parents. Make a life. Cover the wound. Hide the hurt. Grit your teeth. Grab your bootstraps. Square your shoulders. Stop moving and you die.

Stop moving and you die.

The heart pendant slips out of my neckline, swinging,

dangling, its beat thin and erratic—*thwup . . . thwup-thwup . . . thwup*—swinging across the arc of the baseball bat as it descends. I lunge for him, catching Odell in the midsection, both of us falling backward against Rue's cage. His wind leaves him in a rush, the smell of cheap cigarettes in my face just as I see two red hands emerge through the fence.

Rue shrieks, red arms welcoming him, hands closing around either side of his head, cupping his ears, her smile wide and glorious as she easily, casually snaps his neck.

It sounds like firewood, a dry, small *pop* I might hear on a walk in the woods, last year's debris under my feet. But this is cartilage and sinew, bone and blood, and a gurgle follows it, Odell attempting speech as Rue finds her own voice, beating her chest and screeching at the sky, her dominance on display.

I'm collapsed against Odell's chest, his heart stuttering out of existence as I backpedal on all fours, away from Rue. Rue, my beautiful girl who throws apples and flicks off Cecil. Rue who damn well knows plenty of sign language but prefers the swear words. Rue, who just killed a man and is a terror to behold.

It's easy to forget that our animals are wild, that any connection I have with them is built on me bringing food and water, but also closing cage doors behind me, sliding locks into place. The cat reminded me, when he opened my arm, that he is a wild thing, a force of nature who was not created to be loved or petted, but to hunt and kill. Rue shows me now, the depth of her rage, the primal forces in her blood, when she tears Odell's arm from the socket, and pulls it through the fence.

"Jesus, Rue . . . stop." I struggle to my feet, but she's already got a grip on his other arm. It separates at the shoulder, skin tearing like fabric, meat pulling from bone.

Blood pools, rolling toward me as I crawl, heading for the trailer, cradling my arm against me, the world a fireworks display in black and white as I quiver, barely holding on to consciousness.

"Cecil!" I call, dragging myself up each step, the heart pendant dinging off each one as I go, a series of tiny *pings* to counterpoint the *crunch* of Rue tearing off Odell's head.

"Cecil!" I yell again, hauling myself forward on one elbow, pushing the screen door open. I grab the edge of the doorframe with my good hand and haul myself to my feet, just as another triumphant call comes from Rue, reverberating through the living room.

Cecil pulls an afghan from his face, his one eye taking me in as I stumble forward.

"Jesus, kid," he says. "Why can't you just fucking die?"

Chapter 48

Rue

No danger, only fire belly
Red hands. Safe girl.
No mouthwords, only screams.
Mine.
His.
No handwords, only handwork
Tear.
Rip.
No mouthwords, only cries.
I am bigger, faster, stronger.
Meaner
You made me
Empty-arms, full-now.
No man can have my child.

Chapter 49

Ribbit

Wednesday

The lineup for the parade curls around the parking lot, a snake whose tail doesn't end until reaching the football fence, the littlest kids' sports teams and clubs tacked onto the back. The parents on those floats are trying to keep them from eating the candy they're supposed to throw to the crowd. Parents on the high school floats are double-checking plunging necklines and making sure nobody's T-shirts spell out anything objectionable.

On the court float, Gretchen's mother is checking her daughter's hemline from both a standing and seated position and cautioning her to sit with her knees together and to the side. Brynn's mother is leaning against her, cheeks pressed together while posing for Dad and his camera. David and Cody are posing, too, but it's off camera and that's a good thing because Brynn's dad would murder them right there if he saw what they were mimicking with their fingers spread between their mouths, long tongues flickering obscenely.

Or maybe he wouldn't know what it meant.

Huge stands off to the side, phone pressed to his ear, hand covering the other one, eyebrows drawn together.

"Huuuuugh," Gretchen calls. "Group pic!"

He frowns and waves her away, dialing again.

She rolls her eyes and draws the obedient to her. They lean together, smiling, exuberant, Felicity overshadows them, her perfection drawing the eye. The police cruiser flashes its lights, and the first few vehicles take off for their tour of Amontillado (*left turn, two blocks, right turn, one stoplight, two blocks*), and then return to the school grounds for the bonfire and king and queen announcement.

I won't get to see everyone waving or hear the marching band. I'm left behind, as usual. But this time, that's fine. This time, I have more important things to do.

Meg Cofflero, head of student council, is waiting for me when I drive up to the bonfire, eyeing the steps with some trepidation.

"You're sure these are sturdy?" she asks.

"Yep," I tell her, offering a hand up. "You can try it yourself, if you want."

"No, thanks," she says. "I wouldn't mind seeing Gretchen fall on her ass, anyway."

I clap my hands over my ears, pretending surprise. "No spoilers!"

"Well, I don't technically know she won," Meg admits, tapping an envelope attached to her clipboard. "Febrezio counted the votes. But I mean, c'mon . . . she won."

"Right," I say, nodding in agreement as I pull the garment bag from my truck. "The wings take a few minutes to attach. Should I just go ahead and put them on Gretchen, save some time?"

"Yeah, I think so. Maybe pull her aside once they get back? I don't think it'll hurt anybody's feelings. Maddie is just happy to be on the court, and Brynn is too classy to care," Meg says, her finger running down a checklist.

"So, you're taking the guys in here?" she asks, indicating the door built into the back of the bonfire.

"Yep." I pull down the tailgate of my truck. "There's a little bit of prep, so I'll get them started once they get back. Queen is announced first, right?"

She glances at her clipboard. "Yeah, I'll announce queen and she'll *ascend*"—she rolls her eyes—"then the king announcement. And they're going to come out of there, like, actually on fire?" Her voice goes up in disbelief, teeth gnawing on her pen anxiously.

"It's stunt gel," I tell her, pulling the buckets from

the back of the truck. And it is. Or, that's what the buckets say it is. The actual gel is lying in a drainage ditch, having been replaced by my own home brew, one that's meant as a catalyst, one made not to protect but to destroy.

"And Febrezio is totally okay with this?" Meg asks, in the cautious tone of a lifelong rule follower. I know that tone, have adopted it myself often, in order to cajole, convince, manipulate.

"Everything is going to be fine," I say soothingly. Meg shades her eyes as the setting sun flashes off the windshields of the first vehicles returning to the school. A black balloon is separated from a float, and it drifts out over the building, rising higher, out of sight.

"Everything is going to be fine," I say again, unzipping the wings from their bag. And that's not a lie.

Everything is going to be fucking awesome.

Chapter 50

Tress

Wednesday

"What?" I stare at Cecil, hands clutching the doorframe, my arm belting an opera of pain in every key, the heart pendant resting against my chest, pulsing weakly—
thwup . . . thwuup . . . thwup.

"You just won't fucking die," he repeats, shaking his head as if being alive is a great personal failing of mine. He sighs, grabs his ball cap from the coffee table, and pulls it down low over his brow as he gets to his feet.

"Cecil . . . ," I try again, licking my lips, willing the world to be a better, calmer, more rational place. "Odell just tried—"

"To kill you. Yeah, I know," he says, coming toward me, the ever-present cloud of alcohol fumes moving with him. "But you get what you pay for, and Odell wasn't worth two shits. Thought it might actually come through this time, with money being involved, and all."

"This time?" I repeat stupidly, disbelief crowding my mind, not making room for anything else.

"Yeah," he says, crossing over to the sink, and splashing water on his face. He looks back up at me, rivers coursing out of his eyebrows to drip onto the floor, rolling west. This place never has been plumb. My eyes follow their course, trying to make sense of words and patterns, the fact that Cecil wants me dead and Rue just dismembered Odell.

Against my shirt, the heart picks up speed.

thwupthwupthwupthwup

"Listen, kid," Cecil says, one eye boring into me. "This is gonna happen. But I'll give you a choice. How do you wanna go out? We gotta make it look like an accident. I figured a beat-in head wouldn't be too hard to explain around here."

My hand goes to my arm and the swelling there, the heat of fevered flesh. I think of the infection coursing through my veins, the bacteria replicating by the hour, a scale not tilted in my favor.

"Why does it have to look like an accident?" I ask, backing out of the trailer and down the steps, Cecil following close behind. I keep my gaze tight on Cecil's one good eye, which flicks back and forth across the yard, taking in the carnage.

"Jesus," he says. "Fucking animals."

My hand strays to my pocket, fingers brushing my phone just as Cecil's eye comes back to me. "You call the cops, what happens to your girl over there? The orangutangy?"

Cecil kicks Odell's head and it rolls, openmouthed and gaping, toward me. I jump out of the way, but Cecil is still advancing, driving me backward.

"Why's it gotta look like an accident?" He repeats my question back to me. "I thought you were supposed to be smart."

The spreading numbness of disbelief that dropped like a shroud the moment Odell took a swing at me is being edged out by something else. Something hot. Something that's sent me on more than one rampage and eventually got somebody killed.

But not the person who deserved it.

"I am smart, asshole," I say. "Smart enough to know how to hit you where it hurts."

I come at him, and he instinctively shields his crotch, losing a few precious seconds as I veer toward the edge of the house, grabbing the gasoline can that rests there, next to the Weedwacker. I dodge Cecil as he grabs at me, his fingers brushing the edge of my sleeve as I head toward the back acre, gas can banging against my leg.

"Tress!" he calls after me, confidence gone, panic edging his voice. "Wait! Don't!"

But I'm not stopping, and I won't wait. Because hitting Cecil Allan where it hurts has jack shit to do with his balls and everything to do with his money. And that's all laid out in the back acre, neatly planted rows of hand-pruned marijuana plants that are about to get lit in a way he never intended.

"TRESS!"

He's barreling down the path behind me, and I hear another screech from Rue as I dive under a tree branch, the river to the left and a meadow of ragweed higher than my head to the right. The gas can is heavy in my good hand, my bad arm pulsing like the tick I'd pulled off Zee, engorged and flailing.

"*TRESS! STOP!*"

Cecil is panicked, his voice reaching a feminine pitch as he chases me, an old man out of breath and losing a race he thought was rigged in his favor. He aims to see me dead. I don't know why, but I do know I'm going to hold on a little bit longer, just to piss him off. I slow down at the fence, flicking off the power to the electric wire running across the top, tossing over the gas can, and just clearing the stile as Cecil grabs for my ankle, throwing me off. I land hard on the other side, an elbow going into my gut. All my breath leaves me, foul and rancid, the breath of a sick person. A dying person.

Cecil climbs the fence, his breath coming in deep, heavy gulps as I scramble to my feet, grab the gas can, and dive in among the green stalks of marijuana, allowed to grow high and heavy here on the back acre, our cash crop as tall as the trailer, the thick reek of its musk cut through by the sharp tang of gasoline as I toss the can around, back and forth, leaving a long, wet trail behind me.

"Listen to me, Tress. Listen!" Cecil is still on the trail, hands on his knees, words failing him as he gasps for breath. I circle around and break out onto the path, toss the empty gas can at him. It bounces off his shoulder, and he winces. I pull out my lighter, flicking the flame into existence.

He draws in a breath, straightens his spine. Like maybe he just remembered he's an Allan. Not just *Cecil*, or *Grandpa*, though I never called him that much.

"Tress," he says very quietly, very patiently, in a voice I've never heard. It's the voice of a man who read to his children at night, and maybe even told his wife he loved her. It's a voice that hasn't been used much, so it wobbles, every word a question.

"Tress," he repeats, spotting my hesitation. "You don't know, you don't understand."

I don't. It's true. But I've spent my whole life since fifth grade not knowing and not understanding, and I am done with that.

"I don't need to," I say, and toss my lighter into the field.

Cecil screams, as unintelligible as Rue, and dives in

among the plants and the flames, his flannel catching. A trail leaps from his shoulder to his hair, white strands bursting into bright light, his hands beating, crushing, moving. But there are too many fires. Too many blazes that have come together, meeting in the shape of a human form.

He stops, seeming to sense the uselessness, then turns to me, his form still in the dying sunlight though his body dances with flame.

"Run," he says.

And then the world explodes.

Chapter 51

Ribbit

Wednesday

The homecoming court float peels away from the others, heading toward the bonfire as the crowd on foot begins to circle the pyre, everyone gathering close to the purple and black tape I ran around it. *For safety*, I'd told Febrezio. *For crowd control*, I'd said to Meg. *For decoration*, I'd explained to Gretchen. Really, it's an imaginary line that the sheep won't cross. A barrier made of crepe paper that keeps everyone in their places . . . or at least, far enough away to not be able to help immediately when the shit hits the fan.

Cody leaps off the float, showing off his calf muscles that will be roasted meat in approximately five minutes. David reaches up to help Gretchen down, easing his hand up the small of her back and underneath her shirt as she slides down. Hugh does the same for Brynn, minus the molestation.

"Guys, you wanna head on in?" I say, nodding toward the door. They go, and I pull Gretchen aside, whispering low and confidential. "Meg says we should go ahead and get the wings on you, save some time."

"Sure!" She lights up, but it's only half the wattage she'll be showing off soon. I take her hand, and we duck under the lintel, into the shelter of the bonfire.

The growing crowd outside is a dull thrum here, the smell of old pine boughs diluting the acrid scent of something deeper, wet bags full of flammable gel I stashed all along the walls. I move quickly, popping the tops off the buckets. The smell is overpowering, a reek that they can't *not* notice, so different from the retardant I'd shown them. But they are gods, and gods don't worry about what mortals can do to them.

"Here you go!" I say. "You guys better get moving. The parade took longer than it was supposed to, and the fire department wants all this cleared away by dark."

David dives elbow-deep into the first bucket, coming up covered. He strips off his football jersey, muscles neatly outlined. "Dude, get my back?" he asks Cody, like they're putting on sunscreen. Like it's a day at the beach. But I guess every day is a day at the beach when you might be homecoming king and you have abs like that.

Every day but today.

The crowd has grown, their rumble rising as I unzip the garment bag and pull out Gretchen's wings. She jumps up and down, squealing. I spin my finger at her and she obediently turns around, stretching her arms to either side, crucifixion style. I latch the first leather band around her upper arm, cinching the one near her elbow tightly enough to get a wince out of her.

"Sorry," I say, moving to the other arm.

"S'okay," Gretchen says, her nose wrinkling. "What is that sm—"

"Whew, Brynn really overdid it with that body spray, am I right?" I ask, rolling my eyes.

"Oh. My. God. Whatever," Gretchen says, appeased. "How amazing do I look right now?" She spreads her wings out, a dark angel ready to take her throne.

"Perfect," I tell her.

"Guys?" she asks, spinning for the king candidates. They're all stripped down and greased up. Pigs to the slaughter who say pig things in response.

"All right," I say, giving everyone a thumbs-up. I open the door, and Gretchen follows me, holding her wings close around her to fit through the frame. We emerge into the dying light, a crowd gathered close, an expectant congregation, the show about to go on.

"Welcome everyone to this year's homecoming parade

and bonfire!" Meg chirps into her megaphone, and the crowd applauds. Hot cocoa spills out of overly enthusiastic hands, burning fingers that people slip into their mouths to cool. *Scalding*, I correct myself. When it's liquid it's a scald. *Burning* is something entirely different.

Meg thumbs off her megaphone and consults her clipboard for a moment, eyes slipping over the announcements I printed out for her.

"C'mon," I mutter under my breath.

Beside me, Gretchen asks, "Huh?"

Meg flips the megaphone back on, eyes following my instructions as she reads, announcing the freshman, sophomore, and junior attendants first. They stand on the safe side of the line, waving as Meg recites who their parents are, their accomplishments, hobbies, group memberships, team affiliations. All the things that should amount to something. All the lily pads they will hop-frog on their path to success. Once the applause for the underclassmen has settled down, Meg refers back to her notes, her mouth voicing my words.

"Tonight is a special night, a time to look back on all that has happened, while at the same time celebrating the present, and preparing for the future. Tonight, we honor the homecoming court in the way they deserve. To make this evening special, we have incorporated some effects into the show, including some pyrotechnics."

I'm watching Febrezio, who turns to her husband, a single world clearly readable on her lips. "What?"

At the same time, one of the firemen shares a glance with the chief, who is already frowning, making his way to the front, a bear suddenly worried for his forest. Meg's head is down as she reads, unaware of the small ripple forming in the crowd.

"Tonight, we ensure that this year's homecoming will be forever remembered. And now, to announce your homecoming queen . . ."

Meg tucks the megaphone under her arm, fumbling with the envelope just as the fire chief grabs Febrezio's elbow, his words as easily readable as hers had been: "What the fuck?"

"Ready?" I call into the recess of the bonfire. The king candidates nod back at me, Cody giving me a double thumbs-up and a smile that shows off the gap between his front teeth.

"Ready?" I ask Gretchen, whose head is high, one hand held out to me to assist her as she *ascends*, as Meg had put it.

"Your homecoming queen for this year is . . ."

Gretchen takes my hand, the feathers brushing my palm as she climbs the first step.

"Brynn Whitaker!"

No. No. No.

Meg announces the homecoming queen with a smile on her face, but confusion is in her words as she glances at me, unsure what to do. Beside me, Gretchen quivers with fury, every feather trembling. I glance over at Brynn, who is equally shocked but begins threading her way over to me.

To claim her wings.

"Fuck this. I'm going," Gretchen says, and begins climbing the stairs.

"Wait," Meg says, her mouth still to the megaphone as Febrezio and the fire chief pull her aside, the guidance counselor scanning the small crowd behind the bonfire. Her eyes light on mine, and she marches toward me just as Hugh sticks his head out of the door opening.

"What's going on?" he asks.

And then the world explodes.

Chapter 52

Tress

Wednesday

I'm thrown wide and high, warm hands lifting me above a furnace, Cecil a dancing scarecrow within it, his last steps coming to an end as I begin my descent. A pillar of fire burns from the back acre, swirling with all the might of hell, belching fire and brimstone, a dense black cloud piling into the sky.

I land hard on the other side of the bank, my breath leaving me in a sigh as my lungs collapse, everything inside of them forced out. There's a moment where I consider abandoning things as they are—lungs flat, heart stunned, eyes closed. A wave of heat passes over me and my lips blister, eyebrows and lashes burnt to an ash that is blown away on the breeze.

"What the fuck?" I ask no one, but as quickly as it flared, the explosion is over. Suddenly, Cecil's panicked yells for me to *stop*, begging me to *listen*, make some sense. And in the end, when it was too late—he told me to run. He knew there was a gas pocket down here. And I just blew the back acre all to hell.

Also, Cecil.

I lift my head and take inventory.

A broken rib sticks out of my chest, a questioning bone discovering something new. My hand twitches, searching for something to grab, a job to do, a function to fulfill. From the front acre I hear Rue shrieking, and Zee's panicked brays. Debris falls around me, tiny fires taking root in my clothing and my hair. Against my chest the heart beats, insistent.

thwupthwupthwupthwup

Inside, my own lies still, unsure how to answer.

Why can't you just fucking die?

I make the choice, gasp for breath, pull it in, hot and sulfuric. I sit up, holding my good hand to my extruding rib, trying to keep what should be on the inside to stay there. An insistent high-pitched ring reverberates in one ear, the other oddly silent. I raise my hand to it, and my fingers come away bloody. I toddle to my feet, unsure as a baby, lost and confused. I know nothing.

Nothing except that I am not dead.

Not yet.

Chapter 53

Ribbit

Wednesday

Febrezio goes down before she makes it to me, the quaking ground sending her sprawling. Meg falls back on her ass, the megaphone rolling. I grab it as all heads turn toward the ball of fire on the horizon, shaky legs giving out as parents and siblings, Girl Scout troops and Kiwanis members go tumbling. Gretchen teeters on the edge of the first step, wings spread wide. I put a hand on her back, steady her, and whisper into her ear.

"Go."

"Your homecoming queen, Gretchen Astor!" I yell into the megaphone, prompting the well-trained to applaud. Most do, although a mutter of concern has begun at the edges of the crowd, people pointing where a wall of white smoke can be seen blowing in from the west.

"Go Ravens!" I yell.

A scattered response of "Fly high!" answers me as I flick my lighter.

Chapter 54

Tress

Wednesday

I am not dead. I know because I am in pain . . . but not nearly as much as I should be.

With a compound fractured rib, a ruptured eardrum, first-degree burns littering my skin, and a deep infection in my blood, the very act of breathing should be unbearable. But it's exactly that—breathing—that makes it possible for me to keep going. The entire back acre smolders, a haze of burning marijuana filling the air. I follow the river toward the trailer, stumbling along the way, unable to gauge how far my feet are from the ground, how big or small every pebble is, whether I am climbing over tree roots or floating above them.

My mind is detached, separate from my body as I cross over the river, the ash that floats in it sticking to my jeans. I slip on the bank, landing hard on one knee. I lean back against a tree, eyes closed, forcing myself to think. Cecil is dead. Rue is screaming. There's a dismembered body up by the trailer, a towering inferno in the back. Our crop is on fire and everyone within five miles is going to be high as shit as soon as the breeze changes.

Which actually is kind of funny.

I start giggling, which is not good. I can't be laughing when I call 911.

I pull my phone out to see a couple of missed calls from Hugh. From my brother. There's a voice mail, too, but I skip over it, opting instead to read the series of texts he sent a little while ago.

> Hey weird favor to ask—can you go check in on Grandma?
>
> I'm getting ready to get on this stupid float. She's not answering the phone.
>
> She has seizures so I'm a little worried. Probably nothing but if you'd check.
>
> Sorry bet you didn't think family duties would kick in this soon, am I right?
>
> Okay seriously though don't freak out if she did have a seizure. She'll come back around. But it can be scary. Shallow breathing. Very little color.
>
> There's been a few times I thought she was dead.

The heart at my chest picks up a beat, an explosion of rapid fire *thwupthwupthwupthwup, thwupthwupthwupthwup, thwupthwupthwupthwup* demanding to be acknowledged. My brain—confused, concussed, weary—sorts and shifts, showing me Hugh in his car, outside his house, one arm resting on the wheel, Felicity's name on his lips.

She has seizures . . . did you know?

His grandmother, remembering my mother, hating me.

There's been a few times I thought she was dead.

"Oh fuck," I say, my hand closing around the heart at my chest. It pulses as I squeeze, delirious with discovery. *Thwupthwupthwupthwup thwupthwupthwupthwup thwupthwupthwupthwup.* "Oh fuck, oh fuck, oh fuck."

Half of my heart beats in my chest, the other half in my hand.

Felicity's heart, matching mine, deep in the darkness.

The darkness where I buried her alive.

Chapter 55

Rue

Feet are wrong, ground like water
FunnySmoke, laughter calls
fire belly
outside now
Heated anger, spent.
The man will not have my girl.
Danger, danger, danger gone
In the air, rippling shadow.
BlackSmoothShine
returns

Chapter 56

Tress

Wednesday

Rue's cage is battered but intact, her shrieks ceasing when she sees me, her bloodied palms beating at the fence, what's left of Odell slumped to the side. Dee and Zee's barn is on fire, the two of them huddling together in the low corner of their pasture, out of harm's way. The electricity poles are blown sideways, wires snapping, which means the croc can get out, if she wants—which she will. The lion's cage is tilted away from the blast, her unmoving body still in the center. The trailer has been lifted from the foundation and dropped again, a child's dollhouse that has been shaken.

Our belongings are scattered everywhere, and small fires burn in heaps as more debris falls, catching wherever it can. White smoke rolls, the heavy scent of

a good high chasing it, and amid it all, watching me,
sitting erect, tail curled around his feet—
   Sits the panther.

Chapter 57

Ribbit

Wednesday

I toss the lighter, the small orange flame that holds only a promise turning into an inferno that fulfills my wishes. There's a *whoosh* as the bonfire catches, the flames giving a brief kiss to Gretchen's wings.

Which is all it takes.

She goes up in an instant, wings beating ineffectively, fanning the flames as she tries to escape the fate I cinched her into only moments before. She topples and rolls down the front of the bonfire a screaming mass that ignites pockets of flame as she goes, the wet masses I stashed among its dry bones.

Everyone panics as the wall of white smoke envelops the crowd, joined by the licking flames of the fire. Three figures streak from the inside of the bonfire, burning so brightly they each leave a tail behind them as the crowd parts to avoid their thrashing. A firefighter makes a dive for one of them, intending to smother the flames, but only manages to grab his ankle, the skin sliding off the bone like roasted meat. The runner sprints on with no discernable goal, collapsing on the fifty-yard line as his muscles contract to the point of no return, pulling his burning body into the fetal position.

Probably Cody, I think. *He never was good at rushing.*

Which, I mean . . . that's funny.

I start to laugh, the smoke filling my nose with something familiar as my brain slows, taking in everything, dismantling it all, examining in fine detail.

Shit. I'm high. How the hell am I high?

Gretchen is a blackened heap at the foot of the bonfire, her feathers long turned to ash, the metal frame of her wings bent and broken. A royal raven, forever grounded. Brynn pushes her way to my truck, fishing the fire extinguisher from the back and running after one of the boys—David by his size. He goes down, rolling in the grass as people scream, knocking each other over to avoid his fiery touch. Brynn yells at everyone to stand back, turns the extinguisher toward David, pulls the pin, and squeezes the trigger.

Nothing happens.

Because I emptied it last night.

Brynn turns the nozzle toward herself, looking at it dumbly as her fogged brain tries to keep up. The breeze changes and I lose her in the smoke, knocking against a small child who is sobbing, eyes red-rimmed, crying for his mother.

You might be better off without one, I almost tell him. And that's funny, too.

I'm laughing as the crowd screams, panicked parents searching for their children, flustered people fumbling with their phones with hands suddenly odd and awkward. The fire crew is struggling with the hose but can't quite seem to manage it. Everyone is high as hell and incapable as shit. This could not be going better.

Until Hugh Broward hits me like a ton of bricks.

Chapter 58

Tress

Wednesday

My knuckles are wrapped around the steering wheel, blood smeared across the back of one hand. The whine in my ear is a constant, the thrum of nothing in the other an odd counterbalance. My bad arm rests across my lap, useless, nearly numb fingers covering the hole in my side where my rib wants to pop back through.

In the passenger seat, the cat sits, staring ahead.

"You're not really here, are you?" I ask him, and one ear swivels toward me, then flicks forward again.

"I'm high," I tell him, which elicits no response.

"I'm dying," I say, and he doesn't care.

The turnoff for the Allan house comes quickly, and I slide past it, the truck's tires spinning in gravel. It takes real concentration to shift into reverse, inch backward, pull forward, repeat it again, and again, forever, until I'm turned around. Until I'm headed down the grassy drive, branches scraping the sides of the truck, twilight falling as I enter the woods, my headlights bouncing off the machinery surrounding the final resting place of the Allan house, where I buried Felicity Turnado.

"I'm here," I say, stumbling out of the truck, heading for the backhoe, the cat forgotten.

"I'm coming, Felicity," I say.

In my hand, the heart jumps.

Chapter 59

Ribbit

Wednesday

Huge sends me sprawling, the tiny hairs on my arms igniting at his touch. I try to crawl, choking, through the smoke, but his fiery fingers grasp me and I'm pulled backward, screaming, clutching the ground as chunks of grass and mud pull away from the earth under my hands. He rolls me, and I'm flat on my back, his grip closing around my throat.

Hugh has never been more of a god than right now, streaming fire, hate burning in his eyes, powerful hands squeezing the life out of me. His legs are like pillars of rock on either side of my waist as I smack at them.

A stream of water hits him with enough force to knock half his skin off his face; it dangles from his forehead, dripping, stretching dangerously near my mouth, an oily mixture of burning gel, sweat, water, and blood splattering onto me. It's an old game from when we were children, except it was spit coming from his mouth then, not blood. We've graduated to something more sinister, and even though I'm still the one on the ground, I have the upper hand.

Always I have been the victim, always the brunt of the joke, always taking it in stride. I was the helper. The dependable one. The good guy.

(*You're a good boy, Usher. Just do this one thing for Mother. Make it as it should be.*)

But still, and always—Honest Usher. True Loser.

I am a good boy who has always done the right thing, and now I get to be both. I get to be the good guy—and the winner.

Hugh's jaw works, attempting speech, steam rising from his ruined skin as the firefighter blasts him again, knocking his body away from mine. I roll away, hands going to my throat where Hugh's hands had been. Hot blisters rest there now, pulsing under my touch. I gain my feet, wander away as a crew of medics huddle around Hugh, who has gone into convulsions.

"You son of a bitch!" It's a high, crazed cry, but I turn toward it anyway, years of making myself amenable, willing to help, forces me to smile even when I see it's Brynn Whitaker coming at me full tilt, the empty fire extinguisher raised above her head.

Chapter 60

Tress

Wednesday

I can say a lot of nasty things about Cecil, but I can't say he never taught me anything.

I'm familiar enough with hot-wiring (because Cecil was always losing his keys) and comfortable enough to try anything once. When we put an addition on Dee and Zee's barn we'd discovered serious boulders (*Goddamn iceberg took a shit right here*, he'd said) that only a backhoe was going to take care of. As always, Cecil knew a guy who could get us one overnight—driven right off a construction site, I'm sure—but it got to our place too late in the day to expect Cecil to be sober. Which was approximately three in the afternoon.

He'd looked at me and said, "Kid, I'm too drunk to manage this thing. So I'll tell you the trick with big machinery—you learn by doing, and I guarantee you won't make the same mistake twice."

"Why's that?" I'd asked, thirteen and gangly, wrists skinnier than the door pull.

He'd spat in the dirt and adjusted his cap, shading his eyes from the midday sun and an early hangover. "Because the first mistake will kill you."

So I figured out how to run a backhoe by looking at nonspecific stick-figure drawings that served as a user manual on the dash, and summoning up a shit ton of bullheadedness.

That last quality is still with me as I swing the bucket back and forth, the teeth eating through the soft earth that was moved only a few days ago. Pieces of the Allan house fall with the dirt, my new pile rising as I dump brick, chair backs, table legs, the pendulum of the grandfather clock, old beer cans and shiny ones that were full just this past Friday, popped open in expectation of losing another weekend, pushing the days past, getting on with life in Amontillado, Ohio.

The Christmas lights Ribbit had strung for the party hang from the teeth of the backhoe, catching the first rays of moonlight. It's a harvest moon and just cresting the tips of the trees, large and brightly white. It illuminates everything in the dull twilight, enough for me to see the wall of brick below, dark and dirtied with the soot of time, except for one section, where the mortar is light enough to catch the gleam of the moon. I snag a crowbar from the toolbox on the floor, clutching it to my chest with my good arm as I pop the cab door.

I stand at the rim of the hole for a moment, take a deep breath.

And I descend.

Chapter 61

Ribbit

Wednesday

I did not get this far to have Brynn Whitaker take me down.

She swings the extinguisher, and I duck under it, the force of her own blow sending her reeling as it fails to connect. She skids to the ground, her homecoming dress tearing. I feint to the left as she regains her balance, wide-eyed and enraged. She doesn't fall for it, instead backing up a step, raising her weapon to her shoulder and holding it like she's about to ram me. And in an honest fight, Brynn Whitaker kicks my ass ten times out of ten.

But the world isn't an honest place, and Brynn is wearing high heels.

When she lunges at me, one foot sticks, the spike

sinking into the wet ground as the runoff from the fire hose swamps her. She goes down on one knee and loses the extinguisher, mouth twisting into a grimace as she kicks free of her shoes. I scoop up the extinguisher and toss it into the murk, the smoke now mixing with steam, hot droplets in the air and the smell of roasting flesh.

"Brynn." I put my hands out. "It was an accident. I don't know what happened." A smile strains to find its place, and a blister breaks on one cheek as the skin stretches too far, warm liquid running down my neck. She backpedals on all fours away from me, tripped up in her dress.

"You sick, sick shit," she says, wheezing in the smoke. "I'll kill you."

"You don't want to do that," I say, shaking my head at her as I advance.

"Give me one good reason," she spits, eyes narrowing as I lean down to whisper in her ear.

"Because I'm going to get Felicity now," I tell her. "I'm going to save her." The world falls away, our snow globe of smoke obliterating everything except the two of us.

"What did you do?" she asks, breathless, her eyes running with tears, her fists balled at her side.

"Nothing," I explain, watching her face, curious if my words will take hold, if my logic flows for another person. "This is simply how things work. She is my fate, and we are bound. The world has allotted all of us certain things. And I get Felicity."

Brynn shakes her head. "Hugh was right. You're a fucking psycho. And I . . ." She's crying now, tears running down her face as her lips pull into a sneer. "I *defended* you!"

I smile, a flap of lip sticking to my teeth, unable to pull away, burned skin bonding to enamel. "That was smart," I tell her. "I'll remember that."

And with that, I'm gone in the smoke.

Chapter 62

Tress

Wednesday

I ease down the embankment, the world suddenly still, each rolling pebble catching my eye, every painful inch lighting up my brain. I get to the bottom and sway, my body no longer reliable. The crowbar drags across the stone floor of the basement, the only sound to cut through the whine in my one good ear. I stumble forward into the bricks, a section giving out under my weight, a rotten spot in a peach that your finger breaks through. The mortar is still wet, my work of a night never drying before it was packed with wet earth.

I drop the crowbar and it rattles to the floor, and the beat of the heart against my skin stutters in surprise and alarm.

Thwup-thwupthwupthwup-thwup

I clasp it, holding it close in fevered fingers, pressing the other fist against a brick. The wall gives way under my knuckles, and I reach inward up to my shoulder.

"Felicity," I whisper. "I'm here."

The heart in my hand pauses, then pushes forward, racing in my palm as on the other side of the wall, cold fingers close around mine.

Chapter 63

Tress

Wednesday

"Tress?"

The voice is dry, cracked, hopeless. Her eyes reflecting dead moonlight once I've pulled down more of the wall. It's crumbled around my feet, wet mortar and bricks with nail marks in them, bloodied trails in dark lines. Jesus Christ, she tried to scratch her way out.

"I'm here," I say. "I'm here, and I'm . . ."

I'm what? So fucking sorry? I could say it, and it would be true, but those are only words, and they can't convey the pit inside me, an empty hole where guilt expands like the universe, never-ending, always present, a demon in my gut that has found a home for a lifetime.

Felicity is slow, unblinking, her pink-and-purple jester's costume streaked in every liquid a human has, the bells on her cap eerily silent because she lacks the energy to move.

"I'm getting you out," I tell her, even though I know I can't.

I've got one good arm, Felicity has no strength, and blood slicks the back of my throat. That rib went more places than just outside my body. I think it nicked a lung on the journey.

I fumble for my phone, shaking fingers having to redial 911 multiple times before getting it right. I close my eyes, unsure what to say.

I have found Felicity Turnado.

I did not kill Felicity Turnado.

Felicity Turnado is alive.

Please, just someone. Help.

I have done everything by myself and I cannot do this one last thing alone.

I say this aloud, my words breaking into sobs, blood from my mouth splattering my phone as a robotic voice informs me that all circuits are busy.

Chapter 64

Ribbit

Wednesday

I respectfully pull my truck to the side as a sheriff's cruiser from the next county over goes flying past, lights blazing, siren screaming. I make it only a half mile up the road before yielding again, this time to a string of emergency vehicles: ambulances, fire trucks, and EMS. I watch in the rearview mirror as some peel off at the intersection, half heading into town and the school, the others climbing the ridge, toward the explosion that had knocked Febrezio to her knees.

I laugh a little into my fist at the thought, but nothing about that particular situation is funny, no matter how high I still am. The only thing that could blow like that is a natural gas pocket, and the one behind Cecil's property is a well-kept secret, an invisible, endless cache of money that necessity dictates must go into the right hands—Usher hands. It's burning, announcing its existence to all of Amontillado, including the one person who can never know the value of that land. The rightful owner—Tress Montor.

Mother will not be happy.

On the passenger seat, my phone vibrates with a text from Tress.

Found Felicity. At Allan house. I can't move her. Need help.

My mouth curls into a smile as I start my truck, the universe aligning in my favor, blessing my path. Brynn hadn't wanted to hear that Felicity is fated to be mine, refused to understand that Hugh and Gretchen were predestined to burn. But my conviction is only reinforced by the fact that all is falling into place.

I will save Felicity.

I will kill Tress.

And both of these things have just been handed to me, tied in a bow.

Maybe Mother will be happy, after all.

Chapter 65

Tress

Wednesday

I've got Felicity draped halfway over my shoulder, am dragging her out of the coal chute when headlights sweep the ground above us. One of my knees collapses, and I go down hard on the other one, Felicity's weight pulling us both over. She grunts when I land on top of her, every bone in her body prominent and pressed against me. I roll to the side, afraid of breaking her, worried that I already have.

"Tress?" Ribbit's voice from above, cautious, calling.

"Down here," I yell, blood bubbling with my words. "We're down here."

My cousin comes to the edge of the pit, moonlight shining off a bald patch on his scalp, one side of his face a ruined mass of blisters, his molars on display where part of his cheek has melted away entirely.

Chapter 66

Tress and Ribbit

Wednesday

"What the hell happened to you?"

Chapter 67

Ribbit

Wednesday

"There was an accident at the school," I say. "It's bad."

I should ask Tress if she is okay, but there are reasons not to. First of all, she clearly is not, and politely inquiring won't fix that. Second, the closer she is to death now, the easier it will be to nudge her along the rest of the way.

But first . . .

First, comes Felicity.

Chapter 68

Tress

Wednesday

There's a soft moan at my feet as Ribbit starts to slide down into the pit, a river of loose dirt and pebbles preceeding him. I lift Felicity, and she slumps against me, her head lolling onto my shoulder. Her eyelashes flutter against my neck as she pulls in a deep breath.

"Ribbit," she says, the high concussive hum that hovers in my one good ear almost drowning her out.

"He's here, yeah," I tell her. "He's going to help us. I can't get you out of here by myself. He'll have to carry you."

She shudders, her whole body spasming against mine. There's a whimper in my ear, her lips barely moving.

"Ribbit," Felicity says again. "Mom and Dad."

"It's okay," I tell her. "I'll get you back to them. It's

going to be okay. Everything is . . . everything is fine."

It's not. It's really not. Felicity is raving, and my cousin looks like someone set him on fire, and things are broken inside of me that maybe no one can fix. But I just need this one thing. I just need Felicity Turnado to be alive. I need to not have killed her.

Ribbit reaches us, pulls Felicity into his grasp. She moans, clutching at me, her hair hanging in long, stinking loops as he hoists her across his shoulders.

"Hand me that," he says tightly, pointing at the crowbar. I grab it, and he climbs a few feet, leaning against it as a crutch. Felicity lifts her head, eyes finding mine, desolation in her gaze. The heart against my skin is silent, a simple piece of copper, green and useless, the bond between us broken as he carries her away.

She holds my gaze, dry lips peeling back from her teeth as she tries, one last time, to speak to me.

"Ribbit," she says, in low tones of exhaustion, easily chased away by the stones sliding out from under my cousin's feet, the broken workings of my ear.

"Ribbit, Ribbit," she says again, and then her head drops, and they disappear over the rim.

Chapter 69

Ribbit

Wednesday

I lay Felicity down on the ground, pulling her ruined clothing closer around her. The night is cool, and she's not wearing much. The crowbar falls from my grip, bouncing off rock. I lean over her, ignoring the smell, her sunken eyes, hollowed-out cheeks. All these things can be seen, too. All these things can be fixed. All these things can be remedied, and Felicity Turnado will be restored, and grateful.

Grateful to the man who saved her—again.

It would be pleasant to wallow in the thought, the many ways I will be rewarded.

But first . . .

Chapter 70

Tress

Wednesday

I'm halfway up the slope when I look up to see Ribbit standing above me, a fieldstone raised over his head.

"What?" I ask, bewildered. An answer is supplied, an image from another time, my cousin leaning over a well as I call from the bottom and his response.

Are you dead?

Cecil's voice, frustrated.

Why can't you just fucking die?

Felicity, her breathless voice finding my broken ears.

Ribbit, Ribbit.

But no, not quite. She wasn't saying his name again and again, like a child's nursery rhyme finding the chorus, unable to stop, a needle stuck in a record groove. Felicity was desperate to speak, imploring me to hear.

Ribbit did it.

Chapter 71

Tress

Wednesday

Pain is nothing compared to betrayal.

"You son of a bitch," I seethe, blood in my teeth, fire in my gut. "You lying sack of shit."

My cousin sighs, the boulder wavering above his head as his arms begin to shake. "Do you really want those to be your last words? I'm sorry, Tress. I really am. I like you, but this is the way it has to be. So, try again. Say something that matters."

I raise my head, and spit.

"Momma's boy."

Chapter 72

Tress

Wednesday

His upper lip flickers, an exposed muscle in his cheek pulling the strings as anger swells inside of him.

"I'll try to make it quick," he says. "But no promises."

He heaves the rock, and I dodge to the right . . . just as Felicity whacks the side of his knee with the crowbar.

There's a crunching sound as bones become splinters, a wet pop as ligaments snap, and a high-pitched scream of agony as Ribbit goes down at the rim of the pit, the stone flipping end over end as it passes me, crashing into the pile of bricks at the bottom.

"Why would you do that?!" Ribbit yells, crawling toward Felicity, who is backpedaling, her bare feet pushing at loose dirt, her broken fingernails and scabbed hands working frantically, an animal that knows only to get

away. I pull myself over the edge, grab Ribbit's ankle, and yank him backward. He twists, his punches wild as I gain my feet and deliver a kick to his midsection. His breath leaves him, and he pulls into the fetal position, one hand on his gut, the other hovering to his ruined knee.

I limp forward, snag the crowbar, and go to where Felicity has collapsed a few feet away. I go down next to her, hands on her face, pulling her hair away, scrambling for a pulse in her neck. Her fingers go to mine, offer a light squeeze of reassurance.

A ruined pile of a human being slouches toward us, hand outstretched.

"Felicity," he says.

Chapter 73

Ribbit

Wednesday

It was always you only you forever I love you need you please love me I'm so sorry I'll be good I'll make it okay I'll make Mother happy I'll make you happy we'll be happy little Ushers house full cornerstone solid swim in the pond don't say what's on the bottom secrets and skeletons and we won't have them only us we can do this I've worked so hard I did everything right I deserve you I did what I was supposed to now please, please love me.

Chapter 74

Tress

Wednesday

One hand reaches, her name repeated, his eyes begging. Her hands close around mine, panicked, clenching, as a shadow emerges from the trees.

The cat strolls smoothly, paws pressing against earth, shoulder blades slicing the air. A predator, hunting prey. A pause, and his eyes flick from mine to Felicity's, assessing. Behind me, she shudders. I squeeze, letting her know. It is not us he wants.

The cat finds my cousin, touches noses, judges his worth. Ribbit moans as the cat hums a low growl, a tuning fork that has hit a false note, a warning as he scents, draws back, haunches gathering for the kill; pink gums pull away from gleaming teeth, a life in his jaws, a death in his claws, my cousin's pure disbelief as the cat leaps, his lips forming his last words.

But I'm a good guy.

And then there are no more words, and he has no more lips.

Chapter 75

Tress

Wednesday

"Jesus Christ," Felicity says, her eyes on the under-growth where the cat has disappeared, pulling Ribbit's body after him. "Jesus Christ."

"We're going to need more help than that," I tell her. "Can you walk?"

She shakes her head. "Can you?"

"Not far, and not for long," I say. "I tried 911, but it was busy."

"Jesus Christ," Felicity says again as I scroll through my contacts, getting nothing but dead air. All of Amontil-lado is relying on a single cell tower while two fires burn, twin spires of smoke gray against the black sky. Most of my family is dead and my friends are unreachable.

Which leaves me to rely on enemies.

So I shoot a text to Ada LaLage, private investigator.

Chapter 76

Tress

Wednesday

Ada LaLage shows up in swirl of shiny metal, new tires spinning as the dust settles around her BMW. A heavy flashlight switches on as her car door slams behind her, then the crunch of gravel as she approaches. I lean against Felicity, whose head is heavy on my shoulder.

"It's okay," I tell her. "Somebody's here to help."

"Who?" she asks, even though I already explained twice before. Felicity's consciousness has been spotty, her fingers—threaded through mine—twitching as she opts in and back out of reality.

"She's a PI," I tell her again. "I think your parents hired her."

Felicity licks her lips. "Then you better let me do the talking."

"Tress?" Ada LaLage calls out, high beam sweeping the area. "Tress Montor?"

"Over here," Felicity says, and the light swings over to us. We cover our eyes, and I'm surprised when my fingers come away dusted with the ash of what remains of my eyebrows.

"Girls?" Ada comes closer, tilting the light away. "Is everyone all right?"

I open my mouth to tell her no. Felicity has a broken ankle, probably a concussion, needs her seizure meds, and is severely dehydrated and bordering on starvation. And all these things are my fault.

Instead, Felicity says, "I'm Felicity Turnado. Kermit Usher kidnapped me and held me against my will."

There's so much conviction in her voice I almost believe it. But it's not true, and I can't walk away from this unsullied. I raise my head to argue, to tell the truth and accept my punishment. But then my eyes meet Felicity's. They are hard and cold, accustomed to making the rules, and having them followed. I can't help but smile a little before I pass out.

Felicity Turnado will have it her way, as always.

Chapter 77

Tress

Wednesday

I still have a lot of explaining to do.

I wake up in the hospital with Ada LaLage at my bedside, flipping through an old copy of *People* magazine. If the felt-tip pen in her hand and the state of the cover are any indication, she's been drawing very precise mustaches on everyone as she waited for me to come around. I slip my eyes closed again as she glances up, aware that questions are coming, and I don't have all the answers.

In the hall I can hear voices and pick out April Turnado's among them. She's irate, but much like her daughter she conveys this by speaking in a high, clipped tone rather than yelling. She's telling a police officer she wants to see the person who did this to her daughter prosecuted to the fullest extent of the law. I hear a page turn under LaLage's fingers, but I think she's listening, just as I am.

April's sharp step approaches my room, and I crack an eye open to see her gliding past the open door, head high, fingers closed into fists. I feel sorry for the orderly who tries to tell Felicity's mom that she's not ready for visitors right now. There's a sharp crash, a yelp, and then a cavalcade of empty plastic bottles and little paper cups with colorful medication go rolling past my door as April apparently overturns a hospital cart.

I feel Ada's gaze on me and quickly close my eye, but seconds later she clears her throat. When I don't respond she walks over to my bedside, her breath tickling my neck.

"Tress, I know you're awake. I'm going to count to five, and then I'm going to sit on your bad arm. One . . . two . . ."

I open my eyes. "You're an asshole."

"And you owe me for my new set of tires," LaLage says. "You can certainly afford it."

She does sit on my bed but avoids my arm. It's swathed in bandages, an IV tube snaking out from underneath.

"What are they giving me?" I ask.

"Some serious antibiotics," she says, blowing a strand of short black hair out of her eyes. "You're lucky to still have an arm. Your ribs are another story. You broke at least two and are slated for surgery in the morning."

I shake my head. "We don't have insurance, and I can't pay for any of that. Or your tires," I add.

"Actually, you can," Ada says, crossing her arms. "You really don't know anything, do you?"

"Fuck off," I growl, a sudden wave of pain traveling up my side as I try to roll away from her. "Go find someone else without a serious medical condition to insult."

"Can't." Ada shrugs nonchalantly. "I'm being paid to make sure you stay alive, and you damn near cost me a contract by being supremely bullheaded and attempting to die in three or four different ways. Infection, immolation, explosion, and also being anywhere near your cousin counts as a near miss."

I close my eyes, no longer faking. I'm exhausted.

"He's dead," I say.

"It was always going to be him or you," LaLage says, with zero sympathy.

I remember the well, the circle of sunshine above, Ribbit's outline staring down at me. The time he pushed me away from the bank of the Usher pond, half playing, half not, as I grew increasingly tired. The river's current tugging at my ankles and then my thighs, my cousin taunting me to go farther.

But never killing me. Not quite.

I swallow, barely able to manage. My throat is swollen, blistered on the inside from inhaling the burning air of our back acre. My eyes fly open.

"Rue!" I say, pulling back on my covers. I make a move to rise, but the pain sets me back again, my body no longer following orders.

"And stay there," LaLage says briskly, eyes pinning me. "I'm not shitting you when I say keeping you alive is part of my job description. I think in good health is a part of that, and my client won't be very happy if I'm all, *Well, technically she still has a heartbeat.*"

A heartbeat. My hand goes to my chest and I find the necklace there, but it's only a charm now, dead and cold in my hand.

"Your mother's?" LaLage asks, watching my fist clench around the heart.

"How do you know that?" I ask. "And who the hell is your client that they're so interested in me?"

Ada LaLage looks at me coolly, judging my reaction when she says, "Heather Broward."

"Heather . . . ?" I remember slanted purple letters in scented pen, a slash of bright scarlet across the page. "What does she have to do with me?"

LaLage pretends to check a watch she's not wearing. "How much time have you got? Oh, never mind, you're a captive audience."

I flinch at the word *captive*, and she catches it, eyes narrowing.

"Look, I'm not an idiot, okay? But I'm also not police.

I'm a private detective, and I was hired by Heather Broward to ensure your safety—that's my job. Do I believe your cousin kidnapped Felicity? No, I don't. He was on camera for a long time that night, and that's a solid alibi. Could he have done it before he got drunk? Sure, he could have. And if anyone on the Amontillado police force is smart enough to ask that question, I'll give you ten grand. All I care about is my job, and that's centered on you. Everything else is peripheral."

"How do you feel about loose panthers?" I ask her.

"Judging by what April Turnado was wearing, I'd say this town has a higher population of cougars," she says.

I choke-laugh, and she holds up a water pitcher with a questioning gaze. I nod, and LaLage pours me a cup, handing it over carefully. A little sloshes onto my dressing gown, leaving a dark oval behind. She goes to the bathroom to grab a towel, which gives me a second to think.

Ada LaLage might not be overly curious about a roaming cat, but then again, she doesn't live here. She doesn't have to care about what killed my cousin, or whatever pieces of Odell they found up at the trailer once the fire crews arrived. Or an acre of marijuana, up in smoke. LaLage comes out of the bathroom, hands me the towel, her face suddenly serious. "How are you feeling?"

"I'm . . . okay," I tell her. "Whatever drugs are in this IV are doing the trick."

"I mean mentally and emotionally, how are you feeling?" Her gaze is intent on mine, and my heart picks up a beat, with none left to answer it.

"I know Cecil is dead," I say, my voice weak and tired, willing that to be all.

She shakes her head, her voice softening. "Also Gretchen Astor, David Evans, Cody Billings, and Hugh Broward."

The last name is a brick to my chest, a sob that pulls in on the inhale but won't let go. My hand convulses, crushing my paper cup and sending cold water across my midsection. When I exhale it's a wounded sound, a dying animal searching for a place to rest one last time.

"How?" I ask, the word scratching past my swollen throat.

For the first time, LaLage hesitates, her fingers resting on my arm. "Tress, I don't think—"

"*How?*" I ask again, teeth clenching.

"There was an accident at the homecoming bonfire," she says carefully.

I remember Ribbit's burned face, the blisters on his neck, Felicity's words.

Ribbit did it.

And then I just cry.

Because I just found my brother, only to lose him.

Because life is not fair.

Chapter 78

Tress

Wednesday

The police come, Ada LaLage blocking entry to my room, somehow expanding her tiny frame to fill the doorway and threatening all of them with lawsuits if they tried to talk to a minor without permission from her parents—and good luck finding *them*, because they haven't managed that in the past seven years. I'm still crying tears of shock but wipe them away when LaLage returns to the chair next to my bed, color high in her cheeks from turning away the police.

"I know this is a lot all at once, Tress, but I can only keep them at bay for so long. Your lawyer should be here soon, and I need to talk you through some things first."

"My lawyer? I don't have a lawyer."

"Yes, actually you do. I hired her. She's the best, and

you can afford her." I open my mouth to protest, but she holds up a finger in response. "Just let me talk."

I nod my agreement, and she goes on.

"Heather Broward hired me a few weeks ago to look in on you and determine what—if anything—you knew about your parents and their disappearance. She suspected there was a countdown on your life with your eighteenth birthday—and the seven-year anniversary of their disappearance—both coming soon. Do you understand why?"

"Because they can be declared legally dead after seven years," I say, a fact I've known since fifth grade.

"Leaving you to inherit," she adds, and I almost choke-laugh again.

"Inherit what?"

LaLage doesn't flinch. "One of the largest untouched natural gas pockets in the state."

I stare at her, unable to interrupt because I can't speak. I'd known after the explosion, but I'd never equated the gas with money. Only fire.

"You didn't know," LaLage says, and it's a statement, not a question. "Because you weren't supposed to know. All the land was held in a trust for you, per your parents' last will and testament. With your grandfather as your legal guardian, you had no way of knowing unless someone told you."

"He always checked the mail," I say to myself. "No

matter how drunk he was, he always walked out to the road and got the mail."

LaLage nods. "Probably so you wouldn't see bank statements, and yearly account updates from the trust. Everyone told you the story of the poor little orphan girl, until you believed that was exactly what you were."

"Cecil knew," I say. "He knew about the gas pocket. He . . . he told me to run . . ." My voice tapers off, my swollen throat squeezing even more tightly. LaLage wordlessly hands me a tissue.

"He knew," she confirms. "As did your aunt Lenore, and—as I'm sure you realize by now—your cousin, Kermit."

I nod, accepting that everyone related to me had wished me dead over the years, and even taken steps to make it a fact. But the truth is that Cecil could have killed me a thousand times over, allowed for a hundred situations to cause my accidental death up on the ridge as I grew up, wild and barefoot, baiting danger with every step. But he didn't. And in the end, he'd burned while telling me to save myself.

Holy shit. I think Cecil might have actually liked me.

But then again, I always thought Ribbit did, too.

"Are you ready for the hard part?" LaLage asks.

"Jesus, there's more?" I swipe a tear from my cheek as her mouth becomes a thin line.

"A lot more." She leans back in her chair, checks her phone as it vibrates. "Your aunt Lenore is in custody right now, and I promised a certain Officer Boyd a position on the Cincinnati police force if he'd text me updates." She raises her eyes to mine. "For the record, I have absolutely no ability to deliver on that."

"What is Lenore saying?" I ask, eyes closing once again, preparing for the blow.

"Mostly what Heather already suspected. Mrs. Broward has not had a good few years since leaving Amontillado, fell in with some rough people after the marriage failed. Stuck some things up her nose, stuck other things in her arms, stuck still more—"

"I get it," I say, opening my eyes. "I've known a few users."

"Yeah, so I hear," LaLage says, and I snap my mouth shut. She may not be police, but I'm also not going to start incriminating myself before my lawyer—whoever that is—shows up.

"Anyway," Ada goes on, "Heather Broward got clean a few months ago, started wanting to make things right with the world. That's one of the steps, you know?"

I shake my head. "I said I know a few users, none of them recovered."

"It's not easy. But Heather did it, and one of her biggest motivators was you. Well," LaLage corrects herself, pointing a finger into the air, "more like your mother. They were friends."

"Best friends," I correct her, hand closing over the necklace again.

"At one point, sure. Then things got a little screwy. How much do you want me to tell you?"

"I think I know the worst of it," I say, fingers rubbing the rough edges of the heart, the rough edges pressing into my thumb pad. "They were swingers, and then my mom said no more after Hugh and I were born. But Hugh was my dad's kid, so I guess the damage was kind of done."

"And your father and Mrs. Broward continued to see one another, causing a fallout between the two women," LaLage finishes for me. "But before that happened your mother confided to Mrs. Broward about . . . well, about all kinds of things. Most important, she informed Heather that she'd snookered her sister out of the most valuable land in the state, possibly the whole country."

"She knew about the gas? But how?"

LaLage takes a deep breath, weighing her words.

"Look," I tell her, "I already know that my parents weren't perfect. So just out with it."

"They may not have been perfect, but they were simply enjoying each other's company"—she puts air quotes around that phrase—"one night when they went for a walk along the river. They enjoyed each other's company to the point of becoming dizzy and nearly passing out . . . which, I may not have to tell you, but that doesn't happen every time."

"Right, you have to really love each other first," I deadpan, and it's LaLage's turn to laugh.

"Fair enough, kid. So, their little love walk turned into quite the discovery, once they figured out it was natural gas going to their heads and not their natural urges. But that particular piece of land had already been set aside for Lenore. Your grandmother was still alive at that point and had evenly split the land between her two daughters. Lenore, being the eldest, also got the Usher ancestral home, as long as she promised not to change her surname upon getting married. Your mother was tied to no such agreement, but she knew the worth of the land by the river, and she wanted it. So she went to your grandma with a sob story about how much she loved her childhood home. If she couldn't have that she understood . . . but there were some really beautiful acres down by the river that she could see herself building on and raising a family there."

"And Grandma went for it?" I ask.

LaLage shrugs. "The way I understand it, your grandma was half out of her mind with pain, refusing to go to a hospital, insisting she die under an Usher roof and be buried on Usher land, all while ensuring that her husband—Cecil—was ejected from that same home and left penniless. Your mother's request seemed innocent enough, so she altered her will. And I'm sorry if saying so is upsetting, but the two of them sound like spiders in a web, pulling every thread to see who or what they can catch."

I ignore the jibe, knowing it's true. "And Aunt Lenore figured this all out?"

"Oh"—LaLage's eyes bulge a little—"Aunt Lenore was *pissed* at the will reading, according to Heather."

"Pissed enough to make threats?" I ask, but she shakes her head.

"Pissed enough to smile and pretend that everything was fine," LaLage says.

I know that smile. I saw it on Ribbit's face right before a panther tore it off.

"Sounds about right," I say.

"Your mom and Heather stopped talking at some point, and my client gave the other half of that necklace back to your mom as you kids got older, Hugh looking more like a Montor than a Broward every day. Mrs. Broward got scared, knowing how people in Amontillado can talk. She didn't want her son growing up with that cloud over him, and she didn't want anything more to do with Annabelle Montor, either. But she couldn't quite talk herself into going so far away that Lee Montor's dick couldn't reach— Sorry—"

LaLage breaks off, actually blushing.

"Doesn't matter," I say. "Not anymore."

"Well, anyway, they all stayed. And they all pretended like everything was fine. Lenore pretending she didn't want to kill Annabelle. Annabelle pretending her husband wasn't screwing Heather. Heather pretending her son was her husband's kid. And then things got weird."

"Then?" I ask, with eyebrows raised. Or at least, the part of my face that used to have eyebrows.

"Things started happening to Annabelle and Lee. Little things at first, black ice covering the back steps when it hadn't snowed the night before, a rabid stray dog showed up in their yard, a small fire caught in their garage but didn't get the chance to spread."

"Accidents," I say.

"Enough to make them nervous," she agrees. "And when they found your dad's brakes cut, Annabelle went to Heather, took all their old memories—the necklace, their shared journals—anything she thought would work to call on the friendship and bring the other woman around. She was worried something would happen to her, so she came clean, told Heather everything, and made her swear to look after you, if it did."

"But she didn't," I say.

"No." LaLage shakes her head. "She split town half scared out of her mind and did everything she could to forget every Montor she ever met."

"Including her own son," I add.

"I've been in this town three days," Ada says. "I would've left, too."

"So she got clean, wanted to get right with Jesus, and she hired you. You come down here and can't get near me, so instead you email me a link to—"

I break off, suddenly aware of what LaLage was trying to do. She'd specifically cut the video from Friday night at the Allan house to show me the username asking Hugh over and over to ask Ribbit if he'd ever killed someone . . . and I'd never finished watching the video she'd made where she asked me to listen to her. Instead, I assumed she was shaking me down, that the question *Have you ever killed anyone?* was aimed at me, not my cousin.

"That was you, wasn't it?" I ask her. "You wanted to see if Ribbit would confess right there on the livestream."

She nods. "It would have been inadmissible in court, but I had my own questions about how honest the former junkie Mrs. Broward was being with me. She was promising to pay me well but also insisting that she couldn't . . . just yet. I hadn't formally accepted her as a client, but I had a news alert set up for Amontillado in the meantime. I caught that livestream and knew which-ever way the wind blew in this town, it was going to blow hard. You might be aware of a little something called sexism?"

I snort. "Yeah, I'm familiar. I grew up with Cecil Allan."

"Well, he doesn't own all the real estate on it, kid," LaLage says. "Trying to make it as a woman PI hasn't been easy. And even though Heather Broward couldn't cough up the change at the moment, I wanted in on whatever was going down. So I decided to come for a visit, dig around a little. Take in the locals, you know. Get my tires slashed."

"Yeah, I'm not apologizing for that," I tell her.

"No, but you're paying for it. And for this lady right here." She gets up, nodding toward a woman in a pant-suit who has just come through the door, her blond hair pulled into a bun so tight it would give me a headache to look at if I didn't have pain meds in my IV.

"Tress, I'm Berenice Morella, your lawyer. We need to talk."

Chapter 79

Tress

Thursday

So I talk.

Kind of.

Morella lets me know what I should and should not say, and reminds me that any crimes that occurred at my home—including animal maltreatment and whole-scale production of marijuana—fall at the feet of Cecil, who is beyond the long arm of the law.

"What about murder?" I ask her, and her cool blue eyes don't even flinch.

"You're referring to the parts and pieces of an adult male that were found on your property, correct?" Morella asks, tapping an expensive pen against the side of my hospital bed, making a *ping, ping, ping* I can feel in my teeth. I came to realize over the past few hours that she only does this when she's warning me to be careful with my words.

"Yes," I say tentatively.

"I assumed that unfortunate gentleman had a run-in with your rather ill-tempered relation, since deceased," Morella says, gaze still on mine. "Is that correct?"

"Yes," I say again, mentally adding—*Sorry, Cecil. But also, you're still a dick, and I'm not hanging that on Rue.*

"What's going to happen to my animals?" I ask.

Morella glances to LaLage, who checks her phone. "Officer Boyd says with the exception of a deceased lion, all the animals seem to be all right. The Humane Society found an alpaca farmer to take the ostrich and zebra, and they've settled for the night, although apparently the ostrich took off a little bit of Boyd's ear when he got too close."

"Yeah Dee's a bitch like that," I say, my eyes slipping closed. The sky behind the hospital blinds is turning a light gray, morning creeping in after the longest night of my life. "What about Rue, and the crocodile?"

"Rue is the orangutan?" LaLage asks, and I nod. "She's still in her cage. The animal control officers didn't feel like they had proper containment for her elsewhere. A volunteer from the Humane Society has offered to see to her feeding and care, if you'll provide instruction. As for the crocodile . . ."

LaLage scrolls through her messages from Officer Boyd, our connection to the outside world in the safe little room that these women have created for me, letting no one in other than hospital staff.

"I see no mention of a crocodile." LaLage glances at Morella, her worry lines crinkling.

"Best to leave that alone," the lawyer says.

"Swim south, shithead," I say, exhaustion pulling my eyes closed once more. A nurse comes to wheel me into surgery, the fluorescent lights flashing by overhead as I count them. I don't get far as they push something else into my IV, and I slide away from the world.

I wake in a recovery room, my brain thick and slow, foggy with sleepiness and slow to process. A cheery woman with a pin on her scrubs that has a big bone with the statement *I Found This Humerus* takes me back to my room. In the hall we pass Brynn Whitaker carrying a huge balloon bouquet, her eyes puffy from crying. We lock eyes, and she nods at me, continues on down the hall, no doubt to Felicity's room, which I glanced in as we passed by. It's full of flowers and balloons, stuffed animals and real people.

When I get back to my room it's just my lawyer and a private detective. They've both changed clothes and applied fresh makeup, ready to tackle the day. Meanwhile, my midsection was open to the world just a few

hours ago, most of my family is dead, and apparently I
have no friends. Morella glances up from her laptop.

"How are you feeling?"

"Inconsequential," I tell her.

"That's not possible when you're a millionaire.
Happy birthday, by the way," LaLage says. "And your
aunt Lenore wants to see you."

"Fuck her," I say, and Morella flips her laptop shut.

"Under normal circumstances, yes, fuck her," she
agrees. "However, nothing about this situation is normal. There's a media circus outside, and Amontillado
just went wide."

LaLage hands me her phone, but I only give it a quick
look. Headlines scream at me, *Homecoming Court Catas-
trophe. Backwoods Bullies Burn. Lost Local Beauty Found. A Cat
Roams Former Coal Country. Internet Star Implodes. Family Feud
Reaches Shocking Finale. Where Exactly Is Amontillado, Ohio?*

"Good Lord," I say, handing LaLage her phone back.
"What does this have to do with Aunt Lenore?"

A muscle in Morella's jaw twitches, and her eyes flick
to LaLage before she continues.

"Whatever." Ada shrugs in response. "It's her call."

"With her son dead, your aunt Lenore has reversed
her former opinion of you," Morella says. "It seems that
the very thing that made you her target has now made
you her savior."

She doesn't have to go on. "I'm the last Usher," I

say. But I'm also the last Montor, and the last Allan as well. Three ancient family lines, condensed into one, a girl with no eyebrows or eyelashes who looks constantly surprised.

To be honest, I kind of am at this point.

"What does she want?" I ask again.

"She's asking to see you," Morella says, flipping open her laptop again. "Are you familiar with a Brynn Whitaker?"

"Yes," I say. "She's down the hall right now, visiting Felicity."

"Miss Whitaker gave a statement to the police concerning your cousin's actions before, during, and after the homecoming fire that were incriminating. He also made comments to her that support Miss Turnado's accusation that he kidnapped her and held her against her will. Whitaker's statement was enough to warrant a search of the Usher property, and all it took was a flash of the badge for Mr. Usher—"

"Troyer," I correct her. "Ribbit's dad never took Lenore's name. She wouldn't let him."

"Well then, Mr. Troyer proceeded to sell out his wife for a variety of crimes, in exchange for a lighter sentence for himself. Among those crimes was the murder of your parents."

I thought I'd felt everything, thought enough air and

light had been let inside of my body to illuminate the dark corners. But this is the first time my parents' disappearance has been called a murder, the first time I've been forced to truly recognize they are dead. And have been since the night I stared down out of my bedroom window at Felicity Turnado in the driveway, the hem of her nightgown trailing on the ground, her hand in my mother's.

"With her son dead and her husband folding on her, Lenore Usher wants to see you," Morella says.

"Why would I?" I ask, my face scrunching in pain as my surgery meds begin to wear off, the tightness in my chest constricting still further.

"Because she says she'll tell you where your parents' bodies are."

Chapter 80

Tress

Saturday

I've got five days in the hospital before they'll let me go.

Felicity comes to see me on the third day.

Her wheelchair rolls up to my door, the rims just visible as she leans forward, blond hair in a sweep over her shoulder as her eyes meet mine.

"Hey," she says, raising a hand.

"Hey." I wave back, trying not to bump the IV tree. She wheels over to my bedside, bringing a fresh scent with her. Something clean and new, probably expensive. Her mother must have brought her these things. Fresh clothes. Body spray. A hairbrush.

I reach up to my own hair. Half of it burned away in the explosion, and the other half hasn't been washed in . . . well, in a while.

"You're fine," Felicity says, following my thoughts.

"I'm a mess," I tell her. "I don't even have eyebrows, and I look like I stared into hell for five years."

It's true. There's a flash burn across most of my face, leaving me red like a white girl who fell asleep in the sun on the first day of a hot summer.

"Will it . . . go away?" she asks. Of course Felicity is worried about my looks. You can lead a dog to water, but you might have to drown it to make it understand. A spike of anger flicks through my stomach when I think of Goldie-Dog, bright tufts of hair floating in the croc-odile pond.

"Yeah," I tell her, shifting in my bed. "Doctors say I should look pretty normal soon enough."

"Good," Felicity says, cautiously reaching out to touch my hand. "How are you?"

"I don't know," I tell her, and it's true. A week ago I was an orphan with vengeance on her mind and mana-cles in her hand. Now I'm a boiled rich girl, with a debt owed to a person I tortured.

"You didn't have to do that," I tell her. "You didn't have to say Ribbit—"

Felicity shakes her head. "It's done. Leave it alone."

I fall silent, and we're quiet for a moment, the clock on the wall ticking by the seconds as her hand rests over mine, cold and motionless.

"Did that really happen?" I finally ask. "Did you feel it, too?"

Felicity's hand goes to her chest, where the other half of my heart rests. "All I had was darkness, Tress," she says. "But then I felt a heartbeat that wasn't mine, and once I even heard your voice."

"I was there," I tell her. "I heard you, too. The coal chute must not have been entirely covered when they knocked the house down."

"My doctors said the same," she nods. "Otherwise I would have suffocated."

I shudder, my face caving in as I think of pitch black, voices from above and dirt all around, a fevered heart beating against her skin, echoing the rhythm of the person who tried to kill her.

I tried to kill her, but she didn't die. Tress Montor, who never gives and doesn't quit and will have her way no matter what the cost went toe to toe with Felicity Turnado . . . and she didn't back down. She didn't give in even when the only thing she had to fight was a brick wall. Felicity Turnado sat in a puddle of her own piss and shit and vomit, with fading strength and decreasing oxygen, zero chances and even less hope.

And she didn't die.

There's still brick dust under her fingernails. I take her hand, feeling the pulse there, a beat that once rested against my chest, dangling from a necklace.

"I'm so sorry, Felicity," I say. "I'm just so fucking sorry."

She's quiet, rolls her palm over so that it's touching mine, our fingertips—both calloused now—come together.

"I am too," she says. "I didn't want to face my pain for seven years, Tress. Didn't want to think about what happened that night, so that I could just go on with my own life. I wasn't thinking about you, your pain, your loss, what your life was."

I slide my hand out from under hers. "My life wasn't all that bad," I tell her, and turn my face away, toward the window.

The truth is that I love Felicity Turnado, and our hearts might always beat as one, but they'll go in separate directions. She spent her life learning how to say the right thing, look the right way, please the eye and the ear and the people around her. I grew up pitching shit and pinching buds, learning how to land a low blow and cut a deal with someone craving their next fix.

The truth is that we aren't friends anymore, and never will be again.

"What do we do now?" I ask, turning back to her.

"We go to Hugh's funeral," she says.

Chapter 81

Tress

Saturday

Hugh, Gretchen, David, and Cody are all buried on the same day.

Morella and LaLage don't want me to go, neither does my doctor and staff of nurses, who have all been considerably kinder after my lawyer informed them of my net worth. I tell everyone to screw off and hire a private car to drive me.

I'm discovering the benefits of money.

Unfortunately, I'm also discovering the magnitude of the story. A press corps is outside the hospital, and Morella—who insisted on coming along—makes me duck down as we exit the parking lot. I cradle my arm gingerly as I do, taking shallow breaths. With my IV out I'm under orders to not stress myself. I'm sure my doctor wouldn't be happy with me right now, just as he wasn't pleased with the stitch job Mrs. Hannah had done on my arm.

"She was drunk," I'd defended her. "Also, probably a sadist."

The stitches they put in at the hospital are smaller, tighter, and cleaner. The onslaught of antibiotics has brought down the swelling, and the three slashes across my arm no longer look like they're holding back a dam of infection.

Morella lets me sit up once we're out of sight of the hospital, my arm resting in my lap, taking deeper breaths as we approach the cemetery. A line of cars begins at the gates, the one gravel road among the stones already packed. People fan out among the graves, a massive grouping around each of the four tents, senior banners hanging from each one.

No one gathers around a simple stone marked *Usher*, or the fresh hole waiting there.

I roll down my window but can't hear anything other than sobs and the occasional phrase (*gathered together . . . as they were in life . . . celebration of*). Hugh's banner shifts in the breeze, his last movements caused by the wind, not his will. I drop my head as black spots burst in my vision, and my mouth goes dry, blood pressure bottoming out as my body decides whether to fight or flee.

I've been fighting my whole life and don't have any left in me.

"Let's go," I say when Morella's cool hand rests on the back of my neck, questioning. "I want to go."

"Wait," she says quietly.

I look up to see a woman approaching the car. She's tall and would be broad if she weren't so emaciated. A cigarette hangs from her hand, trailing smoke as she raises it to her face to shield her eyes from the sun.

"Tress?" she calls. "Tress Montor?"

"That's Heather Broward," Morella tells me. "She texted LaLage earlier and asked if she could speak with you. How do you feel about it?"

I swallow hard as the groups of mourners start to break up, the reporters who line the walkways deciding who to approach. If I'm spotted, I'll be front-page fodder.

"Tress?" Heather calls again.

"Shit," I say to Morella. "Yeah, sure. But tell her to shut up and get over here already."

My lawyer walks over to Hugh's mom with one finger over her lips, escorts Mrs. Broward to the car, and then she motions to the driver to get out, then she gets behind the wheel.

"Mrs. Broward," Morella says, turning in her seat, "this is my client, Tress Montor. I understand that you wish to speak to her. She has agreed, and I will allow it, however I retain the right to end this conversation at any point. Do you understand?"

"Uh, yeah. I mean, sure," Heather Broward says, the lit cigarette in her fingers shaking. She takes a drag and lets the window down a crack, exhaling into the open air. "Nobody smokes anymore," she says. "Probably a good thing, I guess."

I just stare at her, searching for any resemblance to Hugh, something to hold on to.

She glances up at me, nervous, her eyes darting. "You look just like her. Your mom."

"I know," I tell her. "And Hugh looks like my dad."

Heather nods, takes another puff. "You know about that, huh?"

"Just a few days ago," I say, watching as she begins to pick at her hangnails, hands tearing each other apart. "You abandoned him."

Her hands clench, knuckles white against one another as the ember of her cigarette bobs. "I know what I did," she says, grit in her voice, the girl who defied my mother years ago still in there somewhere.

"Why come back?" I ask her. "You didn't have to be here."

She nods, agreeing, pulls at a stubborn strip of skin at her cuticle. It lets go, leaving a small drop of blood behind. "No, I didn't," she says. "I couldn't be there for him when he was alive, so I thought at least I could be here now."

I want to tell her she could have been here for Hugh, that it was a choice she made same as the one that brought her to his funeral. But the red tracks in her arms make me hold my tongue. The woman has her own scars, and her own darkness to deal with.

"Your mom . . . ," Heather starts, flicks some ash out the window, and tries again, her voice slightly steadier. "Your mom wasn't a very nice person."

"Neither is yours," I tell her, and she laughs, snorting two streams of smoke from her nostrils. "But did you really come here to tell me that?"

"No." She shakes her head, wiping away a stray tear with her thumb. "I . . . Look, Tress, I've done some things in my life I'm not proud of."

I know the feeling and am silent.

"But Hugh was never one of them."

"And I'm not ashamed of my parents, either," I tell her. "I know they weren't great, kind, wonderful people. But I'm starting to think nobody is."

"Why's that?" she asks.

"I might be alive because you hired Ada LaLage to keep me that way," I tell her, looking out my own window. "But you knew about the value of the Montor land,

and that your own son could stand to inherit as well. All it would take was a DNA test, and it's rags to riches for him . . . and for you, too. Was that the plan? Waltz back into his life with a corrected birth certificate and open a new checking account?"

A little smile forms on her face, and her eyes flick away from mine. In the driver's seat, Morella clears her throat. The mourners and their cars have mostly crept away, leaving the big machinery to come in and finish the ugly work of burying someone, entombing them with earth.

"Anything else you want to say to me before I never see you again?" I ask Heather Broward.

"Two things," she says, pointing her cigarette at me. "Never start smoking, kid."

"And?"

"Get the hell out of Amontillado."

Chapter 82

Tress

Sunday

Aunt Lenore looks smaller in a prison uniform.

It doesn't help that she's lost weight, the hollows of her cheeks deeper and more shadowed than before. Her hair, previously tinged silver, is now a white mane, her lips flat and lifeless against her teeth. She stands up when I enter the room, the chains that keep her tied to the table clanking like Felicity's manacles had.

"Tress," she says, a smile actually stretching across her face. I pull back and won't approach the table until she sits.

Morella is with me, as is Lenore's lawyer. Lenore and her lawyer are across from us, and give each other terse nods before we begin, Morella clicking a recording app on her phone and setting it on the table between us.

"My client is ready to sign over all her property, all lands, domiciles, ready cash, investments, and all personal belongings to your client," Lenore's lawyer—a man named Oxley—begins, speaking to Morella. "She has already divulged the location of certain items—"

"Bodies," I say, my voice harsh. "They're bodies. My parents' bodies. People your client killed. Her own sister."

Oxley clears his throat, straightens his papers, glances to Morella, who leans closer to me. "It's best to try to keep emotion out of this for now. Lenore has in good faith divulged the location of your parents' final resting place—"

"In exchange for what?" I ask. "Was there a plea deal?"

"Your aunt will be spending the rest of her life in jail," Morella says. "And your parents will be properly buried. You can't ask for more."

I can't, technically. Morella has already explained to me that while Ohio has the death penalty, it's rarely used. Aunt Lenore will be a bird in a cage, trapped but alive. Wings clipped but heart still beating. Maybe I can't ask for more, but I want to. I want her to feel guilt.

But like my mother told me, the only person I can control is myself.

But that doesn't mean I don't have power.

"Where are they?" I ask, raising my eyes to meet Lenore's.

"The pond," she says, unflinching.

"What did you do?" I ask.

Lenore looks to her lawyer, and Morella leans forward to turn off the recording device. Oxley nods to her that she can continue.

"We blocked them in on the bridge," Lenore says, remorseless eyes staring into mine. "I tried to talk some sense into her, Tress. I swear, I did. I told her I just wanted that land back, the land that was supposed to be mine, and she had cheated me out of it. All I was left with was rocky untillable acres and scrub forest. But she didn't listen, so . . ."

Lenore shrugs. "So I tried to *make* her listen. My husband had a gun on Lee, but your dad was always a romantic. He dove for the gun, and of course my husband panicked, shot Lee in the leg. Annabelle dragged the girl out of the car—I thought it was you, and what a gift *that* would have been—threw her over the side of the bridge, trying to save her. Such heroes, your parents," she says, rolling her eyes. "Such lovely, lovely people."

"And you shot her?" I ask. "You shot my mom?"

"I did, specifically, yes," Lenore says. "My husband was pretty useless at that point. Kermit had heard the first shot and run down from the house to find us on the bridge. His father was incapable of helping me any further. So, I asked Kermit to."

"You *asked*— Jesus . . ." My voice cracks, and I have to look away from her, from the dead stare and stream of cold logic that seems seamless, but only in her own mind.

"You had your eleven-year-old son kill someone?"

"Kill your father, yes," Lenore says. "Your mother I handled.

"We put the bodies in the trunk and the car in the pond. My husband was at least lucid by then, so he helped with that and I sent Kermit to walk the riverbank to see if he could find the girl. When we caught up to him she was out cold on the rocks. Kermit was standing in front of her, saying that she was his, and we couldn't have her."

"Unbelievable," I say, resting my head on my hands.

"I know," Lenore agrees, forehead wrinkled in true confusion. "My own son, defying me."

"Are we done here?" I ask Morella, lifting my head.

"No," Oxley says, snapping open his briefcase and pulling out a manila envelope. "As I said before, my client is prepared to hand over all her assets to you as her only living heir, on the condition that you change your name to Usher, pass the name to your children, restore and reside in the ancestral home, and ensure that she is buried on the property upon her death."

"Take a minute to think about it," Morella says to me.

But I don't need a minute. I don't need a single second to question the trap Aunt Lenore has made for me. Inherit unusable acreage and a cursed name, a ruined house and damnation for my children, swimming in the water their grandparents rotted in.

"Fuck you," I say to Lenore, and watch her smile fade. "Fuck you. Fuck your house. And fuck your name."

My chair scrapes against the concrete floor as I stand to leave, Lenore's shriek matching it as she dives at me across the table, straining against her chains, wild-eyed and lost, knocking Oxley aside. Morella grabs my arm and pulls me to the wall as guards stream into the room, jockeying to grab my aunt as she fights her restraints, bloodying her wrists.

"Tress!" she screams. "Listen to me! Just . . . just listen!"

I know what she wants, have seen Lenore do this to Ribbit over and over throughout the years. She'll repeat her argument, heighten her speech, make it clear that anyone who goes against her train of thought is an idiot. Ribbit told me once that his mom was like a terrier; if she got something in her teeth she'd shake it till it was dead or agreed with her, whatever came first.

She already tried to kill me. It didn't work.

And I definitely don't agree with her.

"Goodbye, Aunt Lenore," I say as she begins to rave, her shrieks echoing down the hall as I walk away from my last living relation, her high erratic laughter chasing my steps.

Chapter 83

Tress

One Month Later

I buy the Usher house at the sheriff's auction and have it bulldozed to the ground, filling in the pond. I take pictures and send them to Prisoner #1809, refusing to recognize my aunt by her name.

As for mine, I change it to Broward.

Chapter 84

Tress

Six Months Later

"Is that everything?" Ada LaLage asks as she helps me close the tailgate of my old truck, Rue peering out through the back window, one hand pressed to the glass.

"Yeah," I say, pulling up my shirt to wipe sweat from my brow. It's hot for May, and we'd all been dying to get our gowns off yesterday at graduation. Some media had shown up, anxious to cover the "Cursed Class of Amontillado" as we walked across the stage, accepting our diplomas. Felicity and Brynn had received standing ovations; Hugh, Gretchen, David, and Cody each a moment of silence. Kermit Usher was not mentioned, and no one knew quite what to do when my name was announced. Tress Broward is a new creature to them, a girl who had forsaken three powerful last names in favor of an unremarkable one.

But I'm rich as shit, so a lot of people clapped anyway.

April Turnado pushed Felicity and me together, her capped teeth flashing behind perfectly outlined lips as she told us to smile and took our picture. We did, arms around each other, but a distance between us that can't quite be gulfed, and never will be.

"You really should get a new truck," Ada says as she looks doubtfully at my ride. "Can this thing even make it to Cincy?"

"It'll make it," I say, and she tosses me a set of keys.

"That's for the apartment above my offices," she says. "I know we agreed that you'll move into campus housing when the fall semester starts, but you realize you don't have to, right?"

"I know," I tell her. LaLage will never understand that college had always felt like an impossibility to me, the chance to live in a shitty dorm room an unrealizable dream. I'll be starting my courses in criminal justice in the fall, and Ada has already offered me a job as her assistant once I've graduated. The truth is I don't ever have to work if I don't want to.

"But I just want a chance to be normal," I tell LaLage now as she leans against the truck.

"Right," she agrees. "Normal but living with an orangutan."

"Hey, you have five cats," I shoot back. "Plus, two in the office."

"Yes," she says. "The normal amount."

"Whatever," I tell her as I open the driver's door. "Follow you there?"

"Follow me there." She nods. "I'll check in my rearview to make sure your tires don't come off."

I fire up the truck and hand Rue an apple, which she turns in her hand nervously as we head toward Amontillado and the state highway. She takes a bite, then offers it to me. I wave her away, and she rolls down her window, tossing the apple out. It bounces off the monument in the town square, splattering all over the last names of the founding families.

Allan, Astor, Montor, Usher.

"Classy," I tell Rue, and she gives me what Cecil called her shit-eating grin.

We stop at the one light in town, waiting for it to turn green. Rue waves at some young kids who stare at her from the crosswalk. When none return her greeting, she flicks them off. We drive out of town, past the library and the school, past the cemetery, where the new graves have settled in, fresh grass growing over the dead. We pass the village limits, the sign welcoming residents home and urging visitors to return again soon.

And I swear as we head for the highway, I spot a panther on the side of the road, shaking the dust of Amontillado, Ohio, from his feet.

Just like me.

ACKNOWLEDGMENTS

First, thanks as always goes to my agent, Adriann Ranta Zurhellen, who hears me out even when I may not be making much sense. Secondly, to my editor, Ben Rosenthal, who makes it all make sense.

There are so many people (and animals!) in a person's life that lend a hand in the writing of a book. I was lucky enough to adopt the most wonderful of Dalmatians during the pandemic, and Gus has given me more love, cuddles, and support than any human can be expected to. Kate Karyus Quinn and Demitria Lunetta are invaluable to me as sounding boards in both my professional and personal life. They keep me sane, which is a task.

I'm often asked how I can accomplish everything I do,

between writing, traveling, speaking, and my podcast, among other things. All I can say is that it comes at the expense of my personal relationships, which is only partly a joke. The biggest thank you goes to my family, my friends, and my boyfriend, all of whom support me with understanding, kindness, and patience.